COPYRIGHT

DEDICATION

To Dizzy Miss Lizzy.
Because we saved the best for last. I love you.

GET IN THE CAR, JUPITER

CHAPTER ONE

Ezra Brandon's soul was older than his body. He wasn't always like that, though. In fact, at one point not long before what Frankie and I badged as "the change," he'd been fully entrenched in activities that would indicate his soul was *exactly* the age of that body, but circumstances being out of his control, the soul tired of parties, friends, and happiness. He adopted the cynicism of a forty-five-year-old man, threw it on like an old coat, and buttoned it up to his chin. It insulated him from the outside world so well that within a year of the adoption, he was forgotten by everyone at Endicott Academy.

But not by me. No, not by me. He was just as beautiful to me then as he'd always been.

"You're drooling again," Frankie said, startling me. My eyes popped open. I brought a hand to my lips to wipe away any evidence of her accusation but felt nothing. Frankie snorted then laughed. I threw a disparaging glance her way.

"Why you gotta be so rude?" I sang at her.

3

"'Cause. You're an idiot. You've got zombie face again, and it's so obvious people are gonna start wondering if they should intercede on your behalf. Report your Forrest Gump ass to social services or whatever."

I laughed. "I can't help it, Frankenstein. He's so on the brink."

"On the brink of what, Jupiter?" She turned Ezra's direction and drank him in. She leaned in close and whispered, "The only thing he's on the brink of is a sudden exclamation of '*What's it all mean!*' before jumping headfirst through that window."

We both looked out the second story toward the looming earth below and gulped.

I shook my head. "He is *not*," I argued.

Frankie pointed toward the front of the classroom where Ezra was sitting, his hands buried in his chin-length brown hair, knuckles white with intensity. Maybe she was right. Maybe just a little. I stared at him again.

Ezra was tall, taller than most guys I knew. Six foot two inches, one hundred seventy pounds is what his old published lacrosse stats stated. He had killer light brown hair, eyes so light green you felt like you could see right through him, and a smile so catching, I could still remember it despite the fact I, nor anyone else for that matter, hadn't seen it for almost two years.

"Life is like a box of chocolates, Jupiter."

I threw another annoyed look her direction. "Can you please let me ogle in peace, Lieutenant Dan?"

"No, jackass. The bell rang. Get your rear in gear or you'll be late again."

"Gah!"

My next class was clear across campus. I scrambled to

4

get my stuff together, decided it was as intact as it was going to get, and hauled ass up the aisle, but when I turned to complain to Frankie for the thousandth time since the beginning of our senior year that it wasn't fair to assign kids back-to-back classes that far away, I was abruptly halted by the very body I'd been ogling not thirty seconds before. We collided in spectacular fashion —papers flying, books crashing. My elbow met his gut, which made him grunt and double over, which then made his forehead punch my left boob, which made me die a million mortifying deaths within a second.

"I'm so sorry," I told Ezra as I felt my face warm to impossible temperatures. I took a second to glance toward Frankie for some sort of best friend intervention but only caught a glimpse of her signature Jupiter's-a-dweeb facepalm instead.

"It's okay," he said quietly, his voice like silk, the inflection of which swam through my head, tingling down each strand of hair all the way to the ends, and making me shiver.

I watched like an idiot as he bent to gather all my stuff for me. He stood, handing me the lot, offering a crooked smile when I stared at him like he was a betta in a bowl.

"Thanks," I wheezed, taking all that had fallen.

He shrugged, hiking his bag higher on his shoulder, tucking his own fallen papers and books between his hip and the palm of his hand. "See ya," he offered before heading out the door.

Before long, Frankie shouldered me. "Whoa," she said.

"Whoa," I agreed.

CHAPTER TWO

Obviously, I was late to my second-period class, mostly because I was duh-duh-duh'ing the whole path there, though. As always after school, I went to Frankie's because, one, Frankie's house had real food, and, two, Frankie refused to step foot onto my property any more than she had to. My parents were eccentric people. Eccentric is being kind, really. They're nutty, to be honest, but they were my little cashews, so I loved them. Frankie loved them, too, though she loved them as one admires an impressionist painting—from a safe distance.

I lived in an adobe UFO. My name is Jupiter, guys. It's not that far of a leap, is it? It was painted a bright white, because, you know, we've got to be easily seen by the mother ship, y'all. Plus, how are you going to embarrass your teenage daughters if your flying saucer house isn't the brightest white you can get it? We did live on the water, though, so as loath as I was to admit it, it was a pretty spectacular place to grow up.

"I can't believe we're graduating in three weeks," I told Frankie as she fished a gallon of Blue Bell from her freezer.

She tossed it on top of the counter. "I know," she said, her face turning a little pale.

I laughed. "What's up, buttercup?"

She flipped the lid of the ice cream then went to the cupboard to get two bowls. "Nothing, I'm just a little apprehensive about leaving home in a few months. I don't feel ready, you know, emotionally."

Frankie set the bowls down on the counter and started to dole out a few scoops in each. When she was done, she slid me mine and I caught it with my spoon.

"Frankenstein, you got this," I told her as she put the gallon away. She sat next to me, hooked her spoon into her bowl, and pulled out a heaping spoonful large enough for Tommy Jones, our high school's seven-foot basketball player who could gulp down a cheeseburger in one bite just because he could. I know because I was there. I saw it. You'd think he'd climbed Everest with the way everyone freaked.

"I don't know, Jup. I don't even know what I'm doing anymore. I can't believe people are letting me decide what I'm going to do with the rest of my life when I can barely tie my shoes in the morning. I shouldn't be trusted with that kind of decision-making. For God's sake, Jupiter! I've killed at least three goldfish a year on average since the third grade because I forget to feed them."

"First, let's address the fish fiascos for a second by acknowledging the fact that any animal you possess should be only of the four-legged persuasion as they are the only kinds capable of letting you know they're starving. What say you, counselor?" I asked.

"Agreed, your honor."

"Okay, let's proceed to problem number two. Will you

shut your pie hole?"

Frankie eyed me with feigned disdain (that rhymes) and stuffed her mouth full of ice cream, which made me fall down across the top of the counter in laughter, which in turn made Frankie lose control of herself. Ice cream went dribbling down her chin.

"Ba! You look like a vampire with a cow fetish!"

"Shut it," she said, swiping a napkin across her mouth.

I sat back down and sighed. "In all seriousness, Frank, it's not a big deal you're undecided about what your life will be. Go anyway, live a little, discover what you want, then decide."

She snorted. "Easy for you to say, brat. You already know what you want to do."

I shrugged. She was right. I knew exactly what I wanted to do. "Well, I got lucky's all. Just wait, your time will come."

I tossed my book bag onto the countertop and pulled out the pile of papers that had fallen when I'd run into Ezra that morning. I hadn't had a chance to organize them since I'd been so distracted by the whirlwind of impending finals.

"I can't believe what a friggin' idiot I was this morning with Ezra."

"I can."

"Frankie!"

"I'm sorry but you're a dinkus when you're around him."

"I know." I sighed. "It's just him, too, man. I don't get it."

"I get it," she teased, getting up from her stool. "You, like, *like* him," she sang. "Jupiter likes a boy!" She clutched her hands to her chest and opened her eyes brightly in mock idiocy. "And he's dark and broody and misunderstood." Frankie started skipping around her kitchen island. "Jupiter's a cliché! Jupiter's a cliché!"

"For the love of God, Frankie, I know, all right? I know! It's pathetically stupid."

She threw herself onto her stool and smiled at me, her chest panting from the effort of my ridicule. "What's wrong with pathetically stupid, anyway?" she asked. "Pathetically stupid is real. It's rife with adventure. It's utterly fun. And totally me. It's *us*."

"To pathetically stupid!" I yelled, lifting up a spoonful of melting ice cream.

"To pathetically stupid!" she yelled as well, clinking her spoon with mine.

I started to shuffle my pile of papers, organizing them by subject into my folders, when I came upon a piece I didn't remember putting into my folders that morning.

"Why would I put my acceptance letter to UW in here?" I asked no one.

Frankie yanked it out of my hand. "Because you like to stare at it? Because it's *so* pretty?" she answered, petting it.

"I *know* I didn't put that letter in there, though," I said, confused.

"Maybe Mercury did it."

"I don't think so."

"Maybe aliens did it!"

I snorted. "Shut up, fool."

Frankie laughed. "Well, you must have accidentally tossed it in with your homework or somethin'. Was it on your desk?"

"Yeah, but—"

"Wait a second," Frankie interrupted, her face

drawing closer to the letter. "Dear *Mr. Brandon?*" she started reading. "It is with great pleasure we offer you admission to the University of Washington…"

My heart started pounding. "Wait, *what?*"

"Holy shit!" Frankie exclaimed. "Ezra Brandon and you are going to the same school."

"Wait, *what?*" I repeated.

"No way!" Frankie said, dropping the hand that held Ezra's acceptance letter onto the countertop. "That is so weird," she said. She eyed me warily. "Did you *know?*" she asked, her brows furrowed in obvious disgust.

"No!" I insisted, meaning it. "I'm not that chick."

"You swear?"

"I swear on our tickets to Bumbershoot," I said, crossing my heart with my thumb.

"So you definitely did not know," she said thoughtfully. "*Dude,*" she said, drawing it out as if in disbelief.

"I know."

"This is so weird."

"I know."

"Well, what are you going to do about it?"

"Nothing," I said.

"I don't get it. You've liked this boy for almost two years and you're not going to do anything about the fact that you'll soon be sharing a school across the entire United States together?"

"Right. There's nothing *to* do."

"You're a dweeb, Jupiter."

"Yeah," I said, too distracted by the strange coincidence to zing her back.

"Huh," Frankie grunted after a few seconds of silence.

I looked up at her. "What?"

"I just, I have this idea."

10

Understanding dawned on me. "No. No. I know what you're thinking, and the answer is no."

"Oh come on!" she whined. "This is it! This is the answer you've been looking for."

"Absolutely not!" I practically shouted.

"Jupiter, it feels like fate!"

I laughed hysterically. "No way, Frankie. No way."

"Listen," she said, her eyes reflected a mischievous gleam, "your parents refuse to help you get to UW because they're crazy—" she began when I interrupted her.

"They're not crazy," I insisted, though she was a little bit right.

They'd told me that college was only for brainwashed, corporate lackeys who sold their souls at graduation for a job at a desk and no sun when I told them of my acceptance to the University of Washington. So I basically had to do everything by myself, obtaining grants as well as a few scholarships to pay for my classes, books, and room and board. The only thing I hadn't worked out was how I was going to get to Seattle since I didn't have a car.

"Oh, they're crazy all right, but let's get back to this scathingly brilliant idea I just had."

"Frankie, I can't. It's too much." She smiled at me deviously. "Frankie! I'd rather kiss a dissected frog than drive the length of the United States with Ezra Brandon. I'd die of embarrassment every five minutes!"

"My condolences then," she said and winked.

CHAPTER THREE

I'd returned Ezra's acceptance letter with an apology for the collision first thing that next morning. He took the letter with a shrug and tossed it into the bottom of his school bag, as if he hadn't even realized he'd lost it. He threw a "see ya" over his shoulder and headed to his first-period class.

The last three weeks of school passed by so quickly it was unsettling. By the time we were done with finals and prom, my head was spinning.

"Jupiter," I heard softly, someone shaking my shoulder.

I rolled over to see who it was. "Mercury?"

"Get up or you're gonna be late."

I took in the morning sun streaming through the round window above my bed and sat up abruptly. "What time is it?" I asked.

"Nine."

"Nine!" I exclaimed. I glanced at my phone, only to discover I'd forgotten to plug it in the night before. "Oh my God!" I said, my voice rough from disuse and anxiety. "I'm supposed to be there at ten! It takes over half an hour just to drive there, and Frankie will be here in twenty minutes!"

"Damn, and I've been up for hours," she said.

"Why didn't you wake me up?" I squealed.

I stood and ripped back the old vinyl accordion doors of my closet, yanking my robe and shower towel from their hook.

"I didn't know you weren't up yet!" she answered defensively. "I would have gotten you up if I'd known."

I sighed. "Sorry, I'm just pissed. I wanted to do my hair and take my time looking nice."

"Sorry, man."

I ran to the bathroom, peed quickly, and hopped into the shower, washing my hair and shaving my legs in less than ten minutes. When I jumped out, I flipped my hair into a towel and cinched it tight, hoping it would leach out as much water as possible while I applied my makeup. I didn't really have time for anything but simple so I swept on some mascara, eyeliner, blush, and a little lip gloss. When I ran to my room, I tossed my robe onto my bed and started to scramble through my underwear drawer.

"Where's the underwear I just bought?" I asked myself. I tossed the garments from the drawer around the room but couldn't find it. I even checked the top of my dresser but it wasn't there. "I can't believe this," I said to no one. I hit the button at the front of my phone to check the time. "Cheese and rice!" I only had seven minutes.

All my stuff was in the wash, so I was forced to wear the only pair I could find. The pair everyone has stuck in the back of their drawers. You know, the pair you never wear because it makes you feel like a beached whale and you only really own because your granny gave you a pack for Christmas and also made you open them in front of all your cousins and aunts and uncles? Yeah, that pair. I grabbed a bra and tossed it on as well. A knock sounded on my door and it opened. I looked over to see Mercury.

"You okay in here?" she asked, glancing at the mess I'd made searching for my new underwear.

"Yeah, fine," I tossed over my shoulder. Mercury took a seat at the end of my bed, eating a bowl of cereal. I glanced at the corner of my room. "Where is my dress?" I asked her.

"What?" she asked, her mouth full of homemade granola.

"My dress! My dress! It was right here!" I said, pointing at the old chair I kept in the corner of my room where I'd laid out my outfit for graduation.

"I didn't see any dress there earlier."

"*What?*"

"There wasn't a dress there when I came in this morning."

"A dress just doesn't get up and walk away, Mercury!"

We both stared at one another, eyes wide. Mercury set her bowl on my dresser as I put my robe back on.

"Mom!" I yelled, climbing down the metal winding staircase that led to Mercury's and my rooms. "Mom!"

"What?" she asked, walking into the kitchen from outside. She wiped dirt-smeared hands onto her gardening apron.

"Mom, there was a dress on the chair in my room. I set it out last night," I said evenly, hoping she didn't do what Mercury and I were both sure she probably did do.

"Oh that?" she asked, dismissing it with a hand. "It looked like something a lady of the evening would wear,

14

so I donated it to the Salvation Army."

"Hooker, Mom. You mean hooker," Mercury chimed in. Mom chided her with an irritated look.

"That was Frankie's dress!" I yelled, losing control of myself, my arms extended and palms up in exasperation.

"That explains it then," she added, humming to herself as she washed the dirt off her hands.

I fell into a kitchen chair, my hand going to my head. "Why do you always do this?" I asked her.

"Do what?" she asked, seemingly unaware of what she'd done.

Mercury sighed. "Mom, didn't you think it kind of a coincidence that Jupiter had a dress laid out on the chair she *always* lays her clothes out on, the night before graduation?"

Mom looked thoughtful for a moment. "Oh, dear," she said, realization dawning on her. "I'm so sorry, honey," she soothed, coming to my side. She leaned down. "Listen, I have this old dress I used to wear back in high school tucked into the back of my closet. It's amazing. It's all these shades of brown and the collar turns up—"

"Mom," I interrupted, "I'm not wearing that." She stood up, a hurt look on her face. My heart softened. "Mom, it's okay. Don't worry about it. I'll find something else."

Mercury and I trudged back up the stairs and she helped me fish a few pieces out of my closet that were somewhat decent enough for a graduation ceremony.

"I guess I'm going eclectic," I said, staring down at the hodgepodge worth of pieces on my bed.

"Yeah, that's what this is. *Eclectic*."

I couldn't help but laugh. "Thank God for the

graduation gown."

I threw on a bright blue floral-print pencil skirt that had hints of hot pink in it, tossed on a nude spaghetti strap camisole and a sheer pink blouse over that, and tucked both into the long band of the skirt.

"Here," Mercury said, rummaging through the hooks over my bed that held all my jewelry. She unhooked a large, chunky gold necklace and placed it around my neck. I sat at the edge of my bed and put my heels on. Mercury tore the towel off my head, her mouth screwed into disapproval.

"What?"

"You look like a drowned cat," she said.

"Oh nice! Thank you for that."

She laughed. "I'm sorry but it's true."

The doorbell rang and I stood, resigned to my fate. I teetered down the metal staircase in my heels with my graduation gown and cap in hand and answered it.

"Ready to—" Frankie began but stopped when I opened the door. "What the hell, Jupiter? What are you wearing? Why is your hair wet? What happened to all our careful planning?"

"I forgot to charge my phone last night and woke late."

"But where's the dress?"

"My mom. I owe you one dress."

Frankie nodded her head in her usual resignation when it came to my mom. "I see. Come on then," she said, walking toward her jeep.

I swept the door closed with a kiss on Mercury's cheek and a promise to see her at the ceremony later.

"Does it really look that bad?" I asked.

"The outfit's cool, like Gwen meets Marilyn, but your

hair, dude," she said, rummaging through her hobo bag. Her own long blonde hair fell across her shoulders as she dug deeper. "Where is it?" she asked absently. She pulled a brush out and tossed it onto my lap. "Clean ya'self up."

I started at the ends to get the tangles out. "What's the point anyway? It's just going to get all messed up on the drive."

"I got you." Frankie laughed. "Sorry, didn't have time to put the top up." She pulled a scarf out of her bag and handed it to me. She pulled one out for herself and tied it around her head to protect her hair.

"Thanks, but I think I'll let it dry in the wind."

"S'your funeral," she said, backing out of my driveway like it was turning to quicksand.

"Jesus, Frankie! You drive like you're on fire!"

"Didn't you know?" she asked, throwing the jeep into drive. "I *am* on fi-ya!"

She peeled out on my street, our laughter singing in the wind behind us as we headed out toward Overseas Highway.

Endicott Academy was only about twenty minutes away from my neighborhood in Key Largo, but the graduation ceremony was being held at the small convention center on Thatch Island, which had the most incredible natural beaches, a rarity near the Keys. As Frankie's jeep crested the edge of the island, I was struck with a sense of finality. The reflection shimmered off the surface of the crystal clear water and white sand beaches.

"I can't believe I'm moving to Washington," I said quietly.

Frankie peered my direction before placing her hand

on my shoulder. "It's okay, Jup. You'll be back for the summer next year before you know it."

I smiled at her. "And until then, we'll live it up."

"Yes, ma'am!"

We pulled in to Leighton Amphitheater, our car stalled behind a line of our fellow classmates. Several boys had gotten out of their cars to peruse the passengers behind them, including a very tasty-looking Jason Packard.

"Oh ma gawd, look at Jason," Frankie whispered. She leaned out of her door and cupped her hands around her mouth. "Jason Packard, get back in your vehicle! You are hindering the line's progress. I repeat, return to your vehicle!" Frankie yelled in monotone.

Jason, of course, turned around and sauntered our direction.

"That boy is too fine for his own good," Frankie said under her breath to me as she checked her lipstick and removed her headscarf, making me laugh.

"Well, hello there, Frank'n'beans. Looking good," he said, his eyes crawling the length of her legs.

"Check your hormones, meathead," she said, making Jason guffaw. Actually guffaw, which I didn't really believe could happen in real life, despite all the times I'd read books that used the insipid word. There's another word that doesn't belong in a book. Insipid. So ersatz. Okay, I'll stop now.

"You like my hormones," Jason teased, edging closer to Frank's face. She swallowed. "A lot," he continued. "I'd say you'd do anything for my hormones."

I fought a smile, biting my lip, and looked out the windshield. My mouth opened in disbelief. Ezra Brandon was two car lengths ahead of us, his '65 black GTO turned perpendicular with ours as he was following the line into the parking lot, and he was looking directly at me. Nay, he was *staring* directly at me. He'd noticed I saw him, yet he didn't look away. His penetrating stare did things to my insides, heating me up all over, and making me feel like I was tumbling over and over myself, spinning out of control. Blood rushed to my head and I felt dizzy for a moment, my heart pounding in my chest. I looked away quickly, my hands smoothing my skirt as I attempted to gain control of my breathing. His stare still laid heavily on my face and shoulders and chest. I glanced back up. He was still gazing at me, his eyes squinted almost imperceptibly but I noticed, and I wondered what he was thinking, wondered why he was taking me in, wondered what he was memorizing so acutely.

My brows furrowed, my mouth opened slightly in confusion, and in question, but he didn't answer. He had nothing to say. Instead, he shifted in his seat to face the lot again.

I breathed deeply, caught off guard by his gaze, but also because his stare felt sharp, intruding, and I wanted to know what it meant, why he did it, but mostly I needed to forget how it'd made me feel, how it seemingly altered me from the inside, raising the temperature of not just my body but also scorched my heart, because it felt as if he'd branded me with that stare, and I belonged to no one but myself.

I looked out onto the amphitheater, anxious to get inside and leave behind my strange moment with Ezra Brandon, when I caught a glimpse of myself in the side-view mirror.

"Frankie!" I gasped, startling both her and Jason.

"What?" they yelled.

My eyes began to sting. "My hair," I whined.

The wind had indeed dried my hair, but it had also twined it in that unforgiving manner wind seemed to bestow on God's most awkward creatures, namely me. You see, if Frankie had let the wind blow through her hair, she would have defined the phrase "windswept," but not me. No, not me. The wind offered me no such favor.

"I look like I stuck my finger in a light socket!" I complained, a few tears sprang free of their own volition.

"It's okay," Frankie assuaged, trying to smooth down the sides, but her face betrayed her words. Her hands lifted from my hair. "It keeps springing back up," she said, fascinated by the mechanics of my insane hair.

"Now I know why he was staring," I mentioned absently. "I look like eighties Sarah Jessica Parker!"

"Who was staring?" she asked.

"No one," I answered and sighed.

Frankie pulled into a parking spot and we hopped out of the car. There was nothing I could do. It was sort of my luck that on the last day I would see all my classmates I resembled Cousin Itt.

"I can braid it," Frankie offered, gathering all my hair that fell at my waist and twisting it around her palm.

"It's too late now. We're needed at the practice. Maybe after that but before the ceremony?"

"Sure, babe," she said.

After we parked, we all congregated at the front of the amphitheater waiting for the principal to call us up in sections according to the first letter of our last names.

"You're lucky you're in the C's," Frankie observed. "Such a pain in the ass that my last name is Zajkowski. Now I'm going to have to stand in these horrendous heels for half an hour while they get everyone situated."

"Sorry, Frankenstein," I said, bumping my hip with hers.

"It's okay," she answered, smiling, and bumping me back.

Good ol' Frankie. She was never bummed for long.

"Okay, B's and C's!" the principal called out.

"Bye, buttercup."

"Bye, jelly bean."

"Yo, Jupiter, what's up with your hair, man?" Jose Vasquez commented.

I shot him a dirty look. "Oh yeah? Well… What's… What's up with your face, Vasquez?"

"You got that?" he teased.

He and a few other boys started snickering, painting my face red. *Kill me now.*

"Mister Brandon?" I heard the principal call out.

"Here," Ezra answered quietly.

"Take a seat here, son."

Ezra did as he was told and sat. He glanced around him and his gaze fell on me, an emotion flitted across his face, but it was gone before I could decipher it. He looked away and then my stomach clenched. *Uh-oh. Uh-oh.* My last name was Corey. *Okay, so it was Brandon and then Carrington. Wait, Molly Carrington moved away last year.*

Oh.
Shit.

"Miss Corey?" the principal asked.

My hand self-consciously went to my hair. I kept pulling the length through my hands over and over. "Yes, sir," I croaked, before clearing my throat. "Yes, sir," I said clearly.

"Sex with Ezra, please."

My head whipped up. "*What?*" I asked, appalled.

"*Next to Ezra, please.*"

I giggled nervously, earning me a strange look from Principal Harris. "Yes, sir."

I started walking toward the seat next to Ezra's but made the mistake of looking over at Frankie. My face flashed a million shades of red as she opened her mouth, her tongue sticking out at the corner, her brows close, her nose scrunched, all in an annoying attempt to tease me. I waved at her to stop, but it only spurred her on more as she started to spank the air in front of her like an imbecile. *I'm going to kill you, Frank.* I peered over at Ezra but his head was down, his hair falling forward over his face.

I sat down next to him, wrapping my arms around myself and shoving my knees away from him as far as I could get them in an attempt to make myself smaller. My hands went to my blonde, frizzy hair and I started to attempt to smooth it down over and over again, running my fingers throughout in a futile attempt to tame it.

Ezra's head lifted abruptly and a small smile tugged at the corner of his mouth, but he refused to look at me, facing the front of the amphitheater instead. *Yes, kill me now.*

CHAPTER FOUR

After the practice session, Frankie and I sat at the steps leading to the amphitheater's stage while she intricately plaited my hair into a Dutch braid, but she pulled at the loops of the braid to give it fullness and a deconstructed feel. She wrapped the braid at the side of my nape and stabbed two chopsticks we found in her glove compartment into it to keep it from falling. When she was done, we went to the bathroom to relieve ourselves and for me to examine her handiwork.

"Damn, Smalls, you did good," I complimented her, examining my braid-hawk in the bathroom mirror as we washed our hands.

"Thanks, Wendy Peffercorn. You look scorching."

I dipped my shoulder in feigned sexiness. "Thank you, baby."

We stepped back and examined ourselves. Bittersweet emotion filled me.

"This day is going to radically change the way we're used to living."

Frankie sighed. "I know."

She held her hand out to me and I took it, squeezing it

briefly, before dropping it as we headed toward the parking lot to meet our awaiting classmates. We all watched in anxious anticipation as our friends and family filed in to take their seats, waiting to join us in celebration. At noon, they lined us up as we'd practiced and we proceeded to our awaiting chairs serenaded by the incredibly cheesy, yet incredibly emotional, "Pomp and Circumstance."

Ezra Brandon walked ahead of me, his intriguing scent of oakmoss, sandalwood, and other spices I couldn't name, assailed me. I closed my eyes and took a deep breath, memorizing that smell, knowing even though we were going to the same school I'd probably never see him again. As he walked, his right shoulder dipped slightly from the small limp he'd developed after "the change."

Junior year was the best of Ezra Brandon's life. Everyone knew it. Captain of the lacrosse team, homecoming prince, and dating Jessica West, head cheerleader at Endicott. It was nauseatingly cliché. He was the most popular guy of our class and had been that way all his life. He had a myriad of friends but wasn't a snob by any means. He hung out with everyone. He was a social bridge of sorts, comfortable and accepted in every social group.

But this all changed when he totaled his truck over Christmas break our junior year. Ezra woke from a three-day coma to discover he'd shattered both his legs. Lucky to have even survived, he spent a grueling year rebuilding and working through physical therapy. The hard, painful work made Ezra bitter, and he sank into himself almost immediately.

He wasn't thankful for being alive because it meant

he'd never be able to compete again. In losing his ability to play, he'd lost his identity. Jessica broke up with him because he'd stopped calling her, or so she said. Friends abandoned him because he refused to answer his door or talk to them in class. It was a turning point for Ezra. He'd had previous outspoken plans to attend Syracuse in the fall after his senior year on a lacrosse scholarship, but those dreams were replaced with three hours a day in a therapy pool. He was forced to rethink his life, and his new plans made him bitter and angry and very alone.

But I knew him. He was callused, yes, but I knew deep down he was still the same guy we'd all grown up with.

He was *Ezra.*

We sat down in our graduation gowns and caps. I smiled to myself. *If I look as ridiculous as I feel right now, I must look like an idiot.* I kept smiling, though. I didn't care. I was beginning adulthood. It was scary and it was unknown, but it was the beginning of it all and that was a thrilling prospect. The sky was the limit for me and I relished the possibilities.

"What's so funny?" a deep, silky voice asked, startling me.

I stole a glimpse of Ezra from the corner of my eye. "Me?" I asked.

He laughed quietly, shocking me. "Yeah, you."

"Nothing," I lied.

"Sure," he replied, not believing me.

He turned his body more toward me and smiled, shaking his head a little.

I swallowed hard. *Ezra Brandon thought I was amusing?* My heart raced in my chest.

He leaned in. "I liked it better before," he said softly, bewildering me.

"Huh?"

"Your hair. I liked it better before."

I gulped, afraid to reply for fear he'd vanish into thin air.

After a few moments, I said, "I looked like a rejected cast member from *Hairspray*."

He laughed, genuinely laughed, shocking me further. I stared at him like he was a wild animal about to spook.

"More like Penny Lane from *Almost Famous*," he commented. I almost went catatonic.

What a friggin' compliment. Suddenly I was hyperaware of myself. I self-consciously patted my gown down as if it needed smoothing since it was made of fabric not much stiffer than the linoleum in my mother's kitchen. I straightened my cap and checked the tassel.

"You're always fidgeting," he said, my hand freezing on the tassel.

I brought it to my lap and turned toward him. "I do? I don't mean to."

"Nervous?" he asked.

Sweating like a pig, I thought. If Ezra hadn't been next to me, I probably would have been flapping my arms like a chicken to improve ventilation. "A little," I lied again.

We stared at one another, stuck in a sort of mesmerized state, and a million thoughts raced through my mind. *What are you doing? Are you talking to me because it's the last day and you're feeling nostalgic? Is it because of our shared collision? The fact I returned your letter? Why, you unbelievably hunky bastard?*

"Brandon!" Justin said from behind us, like he'd been trying to get his attention for a while. "You're up, dude," he explained when we both turned toward him.

"Sorry," Ezra rushed out as he stood.

We both sprinted to join the rest of the line from our row. As we edged up the amphitheater stairs Frankie had done my hair on, I felt a little nauseated. I hated it when people stared at me, and this was an entire amphitheater getting ready to watch my clumsy ass flit across the stage. *Stop it, Jupiter. Stop. You'll psych yourself out.*

"Ezra Julian Brandon," Principal Harris announced. A corner in the back of the amphitheater burst into applause. *His family*, I thought. He took the diploma that wasn't really his diploma since they always use decoys, shook the principal's hand, and walked across the stage flawlessly.

See? Not so bad. Now, just duplicate that, Jupiter.

"Jupiter Willow Corey."

I took careful steps, wincing a little at my ridiculous name. I made it halfway across, shook the principal's hand, and took my fake diploma.

Hooey! I got this. I got this. This stage is my biatch! I was confident. *Too* confident. I turned to wink at Frankie. She started to smile but then her eyes blew wide and I knew it was over. I knew I was in for it. I turned in time to see a large electrical wire catch the tip of my heel. I pitched forward, closing my eyes and bracing myself to toss forward on my face, but instead of the concrete stage, I was met by warm arms. I looked up to see Ezra's face and blushed in equal parts mortification and relief. He set me right then helped me down the steps as the audience burst into applause. I could feel the burn of hundreds of eyes, and it brought the embarrassment up a notch.

"You okay?" he asked, his eyes imploring mine.

"Yeah. Thank you so much for catching me," I whispered.

"No problem," he said, the corner of his mouth ticking up charmingly.

He released the arm he'd been holding and I looked down at the white imprints his fingers had left, watching them fade as the color returned to my skin. All evidence of his touch vanished save for the feverish current that had taken residence in my belly when he'd rescued me on stage and had yet to leave.

His brows creased. "Your middle name is Willow?"

My face heated once more. "Uh, yeah," I answered.

He nodded, an inscrutable look on his face.

I thought it was an odd question, but I didn't get a chance to ask him why he wanted to know because he turned without another word and went back to his seat. I followed suit, feeling a little dizzy by the strangeness of the day.

Ezra didn't say anything the rest of the ceremony, not because he was avoiding me, at least I didn't think that was why. Instead, he seemed distracted by his own thoughts, retreating into himself in that usual way Ezra did, which curiously relieved a bit of anxiety I'd felt. He'd been acting so unpredictably it'd thrown me off.

It was quite incredible, that day. I'll remember the smells of the youth surrounding me, i.e. the cologne baths, the smiles, and the unbridled potential. The valedictorian gave a rousing speech encouraging us all with the same eternal optimism that each and every one of us possessed, if for no other reason than because we were, each of us, packed full with dreams. Those dreams were bursting at the seams, ready to unfold, to uncurl in glory in the what-ifs. The sky was the literal limit.

We all rose at the end. Ezra turned toward me, a small lopsided smile upon his lips. "Congratulations," he whispered.

"Congratulations," I told him, my heart pounding with his soothing inflection.

Then we tossed our caps into the air with the rest of our class. I closed my eyes for a moment as they rained back down to the earth, a sea of onyx seeking their owners. I opened them again to see Ezra's and my caps tumbling through the air, spinning and carefree, briefly tangling with one another before wresting free from each other, and falling with finality in the row ahead of us.

I leaned forward to retrieve mine but Ezra stopped me with a hand on my forearm. He bent at the waist and scooped them both up, glancing down at them, then handed one over to me.

"Here you are," he said, looking down at me.

He was at least a foot taller than I was, and I strained to peer into his face. My hands gripped the edges of my cap as I held it against my stomach.

"Well, I guess this is goodbye," he said.

"I guess so," I practically whispered with a wobbly smile.

To me it *was* goodbye. Even though I knew we were both going to the same schools, I also knew the likelihood of running into him there was pretty slim.

"Goodbye, Jupiter Willow Corey," he said with finality, pitching toward me, his voice going deeper at my name.

"Goodbye, Ezra Julian Brandon."

He turned away, his cap in hand, and headed straight toward the parking lot in the direction of his car, not bothering to say goodbye to any of the kids we'd grown up with our entire lives. I watched until he was no longer visible.

"He's a strange cat," Frankie said beside me.

I gasped at her unexpected presence. "Jesus, Mary, and Joseph!" I said in my best Irish accent, which was terrible.

"Come on, doofus," she said, dragging me by the arm toward the parking lot.

"What are you doing?" I asked. "Aren't we going to stop and say goodbye to everyone?"

"What are you talking about? We'll see everyone tonight at the bonfire."

"Yeah, but everyone's in their caps and gowns now. It's different."

"Stop being stupid, Jupiter. We have to catch Ezra before he drives off."

I stopped in my tracks but my arm went with Frankie. I winced at the pain and pulled my wrist away, using my other hand to rub away the sting.

"I'm not doing that," I said, meaning it.

"That's okay, you don't have to. I will," she said, continuing her pursuit of Ezra.

"Stop! Are you trying to embarrass me, you brat?"

She laughed at that. "I'm always trying to embarrass you, idiot."

"Yeah, but this will mortify me, even worse than my almost crash and burn on stage just now."

She laughed again. "That was epic. Really epic, actually. But the crash and burn isn't what made it epic," she said, rounding a huge SUV. "What made it epic was the palpable freaking tension between you and that boy right there," she said, pointing at Ezra as he got into his GTO. "You don't have enough brass to ask him for the ride, but I do."

"Please, Frankie. Seriously, Frankie. Don't. You'll seriously embarrass me."

She slowed but didn't stop. "Then you better get your behind over there and start asking before I do."

I caught up with her, a little out of breath, and stared at her as we drew closer to Ezra's GTO.

"Don't make me do this, yo."

She smiled. "Dude, bite the bullet."

"I can't," I whined.

"You can," she mocked.

"I don't want to."

Frankie stopped and pointed her finger toward Ezra's car. "Do it or God as my witness, I will do it for you, and you won't like how I'll do it."

I crossed my arms, my lips pursed, feeling pissed. Ezra started to back out of his space and Frankie made a move like she was going to go after him.

I jumped in surprise. "Fine! Fine!" I huffed, and she stopped where she stood.

"You're the meanest person I've ever met, Frankie Zajkowski!" I called out.

"You'll thank me later, idiot! Now go!"

I reluctantly ran toward Ezra's car and came upon him just as he'd cleared his space. He'd started to hit the gas to drive forward but stopped when he saw me running toward him, a look of pure confusion crossed his face and stayed there.

"Ezra," I said, out of breath from the brisk walk but also from the nerves.

"What are you doing here?" he asked over his rolled-down window.

"Sorry, but, uh, I wanted to ask for a favor."

"*Okay?*" he asked, puzzle apparent in his tone, making

31

me exceedingly anxious.

I took a deep breath and ordered myself to act cool. "It's kind of a big favor, but, well, as it turns out, we're both going to the University of Washington," I began.

Ezra looked baffled. "Why didn't you say something before?" he asked.

"Well, 'cause, well, I didn't think we'd actually see one another or anything. It didn't even cross my mind that you'd, ya know, care that I was going to the same school or whatever."

"Why wouldn't I care?" he asked, surprising me.

"Uh," I stuttered, "I don't know." I shook my head to gain control of myself. "Anyway, uh, well, I have no way to get to school. My parents aren't exactly thrilled that I'm leaving or whatever. So basically, I need a ride."

"Oh," he said, obviously astonished at my request.

"Listen, it's okay if you're, like, not comfortable or anything." I laughed nervously. "I mean, I get it. Honestly. It's a huge favor, so don't worry about saying no, 'cause it's a lot to ask."

He studied me with an inexplicable look I would have given anything to decipher. I'd rested a hand on his door but let it drop when he didn't answer immediately. I looked down at my shoes so I didn't have to look at him any longer. My neck felt hot and I contemplated turning tail. I took a deep breath to compose myself and met his gaze.

"Okay, so I guess——" I began, but he interrupted, my head whipping up.

"You can ride with me," he said. "My cousin Kai was coming down from Chicago to help me with the drive. You okay with that?"

"Uh, sure," I said, almost in disbelief he'd agreed to

let me tag along.

"I promised my mom that I'd spend a few days in Chicago to break the drive up, but also to see my aunt and uncle. Are you cool with that, too?"

"Yeah, no problem."

He leaned over and picked up his phone. "What's your number?" he asked, my adrenaline kicking into high gear.

"Three-zero-five. Five-five-five. Seven, four, nine, three." *I just gave Ezra Brandon my number.* He punched in the numbers as I'd rattled them off then looked up at me, another unreadable look on his face. "I'll text you the day before we leave to get your address."

"Okay," I said, numb with the coursing blood running through my hyperaware body.

Ezra put his black GTO into drive. "Oh, and Jupiter?" he asked, the vibrations from the engine thrumming through my stomach, heart, and head.

"Yes, Ezra?"

"Travel light," he said with a smile that could only be interpreted as mischievous. "It'll be a tight fit." He looked ahead then pressed the gas.

"Well, well, well," Frankie said at my right, slinging an arm around my shoulder, "I do believe we have ourselves a solution to your previous problem."

I took a deep, shaky breath. "Yeah, I have a ride now," I commented.

Frankie laughed. "That wasn't the problem I was referring to."

CHAPTER FIVE

Three months later…

What's your address?

The text sat on my screen. It'd scared the shit out of me when I'd first received it. The strangest feelings of anticipation, fear, nausea, elation, and anxiety flipped through my body like a folding Rolodex. I didn't really like it. It felt stupid. Liking Ezra from afar was one thing, but my reaction to him when he was real, tangible to me, knowing we'd be spending weeks in close confinement was another, and it made it feel too real. I had to abandon the fantasy and embrace the reality, and I wasn't sure I was prepared for that.

I'd spent the summer working at a retirement home, giving yoga camps to all the residents there. I'd earned enough to pitch in for gas for the cross-country trip as well as purchase a few things for my dorm when we finally got to UW. The rest I had plans to save for those unpredictable things that life threw at you and since I'd know no one in Seattle, save for Ezra, I wanted a contingency plan, a cushion of sorts.

34

I opened a checking account at a bank I knew was also in Seattle, which felt so foreign, such an adult thing to do. Basically, butterflies had taken up permanent residence in my stomach.

I glanced down at the text and those butterflies fluttered and flew, reaching into my throat.

I don't think you even need my address, I texted back.

why, was his simple reply.

because everyone knows my house they just don't know who lives in it, I wrote.

lol okay hit me with it

Ezra writing "lol" felt odd to me. It added a human element to him I'd never really lent to him before.

promise not to laugh? I texted.

scout's honor, he wrote.

I took a deep breath. **I live in the UFO house**

There was a pause. I assumed he was laughing, and that did something funny to my insides. It hurt he could be laughing at me, at my family's home, unusual as it truly was.

seriously? he texted. **I love that house. always wanted to know who lived there**

His answer took me by surprise. **well it's me haha I live in that house**

and I guess I did always know who lived there, he texted.

yeah

Just reminding you that my cousin is coming to help with the drive

ok cool

Name's Kai. We'll be staying with his family in Chicago for a few days

that's cool with me
B there at 7am K?
7 got it, I replied.

I set my phone on my desk then threw myself over the side of the bed. My hands went to my face.

"Oh my God!" I screamed, but it was muffled by my hands.

"Oh my God, what?" Frankie asked, prancing into my room with a bowl of granola. Frankie was always eating.

She set her bowl on my desk then threw the suitcase I'd been packing onto the floor and laid next to me.

"Ezra Brandon will be here at seven a.m. tomorrow morning."

"Yeah, baby," she teased.

I laughed. "Shut up."

"No, you shut up."

"No, *you* shut up."

"Why don't you both shut up?" Mercury said, leaning against the jamb of my bedroom door.

She walked into the room, grabbed a few pieces of my mom's homemade granola from Frankie's bowl, and sat at the desk.

I stood up, grabbed my suitcase, and laid it back on the bed. I started gathering all my stuff and carefully grouping what I would actually need and what I wanted in two separate piles. I piled everything I needed in my small suitcase and gauged what else I could fit.

"What are you doing?" Mercury asked.

"Trying to decide what I should leave and what I should take."

"Just get another suitcase," Frankie said, swinging a dangling leg back and forth.

"This is the only suitcase I'm bringing," I said.

Frankie sat up and Mercury looked at me like I was crazy.

"Why?" they asked in unison.

"Because there's three of us traveling in Ezra's GTO and I want to take up the least amount of room possible."

"You can't be serious?" Frankie observed before adding, "And who is this third person?" She was annoyed I hadn't told her.

I laughed. "Ezra's cousin Kai. He's from Chicago. He came down to help with the drive. We're going to be spending a few days at his parents' house to break the trip up, too."

Frankie looked at me as if I'd sprouted another head. "Why in the hell wouldn't you tell me there was a third person going with you?"

"Because it's not relevant?"

Mercury shook her head at me.

"It is *too* relevant, dinkus!" Frankie burst out.

"Okay, well, maybe I didn't say anything because I know you."

"What are you trying to say?"

"I'm trying to say that you are a voodoo priestess or something and can make weird things happen, and I didn't want you to meddle."

Frankie fell over laughing before sitting back up. "I would have too," she said. "I would have made sure this Kai guy wouldn't be there."

"*See?*"

"Still should have told me," Frankie complained.

"If she had told you, she'd have been more miserable than she is now," Mercury chimed in.

"You think she's miserable about sharing close

quarters with Ezra Brandon?" Frankie asked, leaning toward Mercury.

Mercury, in all her innocence, replied emphatically, "Yes! She probably wouldn't have even gone if you hadn't stuck your big nose into things."

Frankie had the decency to appear sorry. "Mercury," she said softly, "Jupiter would have made it there one way or another."

Mercury started tearing up, so I went over to her and kissed the top of her head before hugging her shoulders. "No worries, Mercury. It'll all be okay."

"No, it won't," she cried. "You're going across the country!"

Mercury's pain made me tear up as well. "I'll call you," I told her. "Often."

"You lie," she said, pulling her legs up and sniffling into her knees.

"I'm serious, Mercury. I'll call, like, every day. You'll be so sick of me. Promise."

She looked up at me with Precious Moment eyes. "Promise?"

"Double promise," I said.

She took a deep breath and composed herself before getting up and heading toward the door. "Every day," she insisted one more time as she whipped back around.

"Every single day, Mercury."

Mercury left my room and before long, I heard her door shut.

"Poor kid," Frankie admitted quietly. "I don't blame her. I'd be beside myself too at the possibility of being here all alone here for the next four years with those two nutters downstairs with their homemade granola and astronomy readers."

I smiled. "You are an idiot, Frankenstein."

"I know," she acquiesced.

I narrowed my frivolities and shoved them into my case, shut the lid, and zipped it closed.

"There," I said. "Done."

"Wait," Frankie said. "I have a parting gift for you."

She bolted out of my room before I could even acknowledge her. I could hear her leave the front door open for a moment before returning and shoving it closed. She climbed the winding staircase and reemerged in my bedroom carrying a large box.

"Oh, Frankie," I said, my eyes tearing up. "You didn't have to do this."

"Please," she said, shoving the box into my hands with an ungraceful push and avoiding eye contact.

"What did you do?" I asked, reading her body language.

"It's nothing, okay? My parents got me a new one and I asked if I could give this one to you and they said yes, so just take it already and shut up."

I bit my lip to keep from smiling and set the box on my bed before prying the lid open. I gasped. "Frank!" I exclaimed. "I can't take this!" I insisted, staring down at the laptop she'd only gotten eight months before.

"You can and you will, you annoying minx."

"This is practically brand new!"

"So what? My parents got me a new one for when I start college in the fall and this would have been wasted on my brother since he has his own gaming station and all that."

Big fat tears fell down my face, landing on top of the smooth silver metal surface of the computer she'd handed me.

"You're such a liar," I told her.

Her mouth gaped open as she tried to fight her knowing smile.

"Listen, I wasn't about to let you go to your first class with a freaking notepad and pen like a first grader. We have a reputation to uphold."

I threw my arms around her before pulling back, a watery smile plastered across my face. "No one knows you in Seattle, Franks."

"Yeah, yeah," she said, straightening her clothes. She looked at her feet, avoiding my eyes. "Well, anyway. Uh, let's go get some ice cream or something." She turned around and headed for the door.

"Are you crying?" I teased.

"No," she lied.

"You're crying!"

"I am *not*, idiot, now come on."

"Fine, let's go," I said, grabbing my purse, heading down the staircase, and following her outside. When our feet hit sand, I threw my arm around her neck as we walked to her car. "Thank you, doofus. Love you."

"Love you too, dumb ass," she said, squeezing me around the waist.

We hopped into her jeep and peeled out onto my street toward the strip near our houses with little shops. Frank turned BØRNS on and we sang at the top of our lungs the entire way, reveling in our last day together.

CHAPTER SIX

I woke up at five a.m. the morning Ezra was to come, my stomach in incredible knots. I'd laid out my clothes. I hadn't put much thought into them other than I just wanted to be comfortable for the first of many long days driving across the United States.

I still could not believe I was moving to Seattle. The average summer temperature in the Keys was a balmy ninety degrees. In the winter? Our lowest low last year, the temperature everyone broke jackets out for? Sixty-five degrees Fahrenheit. Seattle's average winter temperature is thirty-six degrees, and their winters start early from what I'd read online.

I grabbed my phone and searched Seattle's current temperature.

"Sixty-one degrees," I whispered. The hand holding my phone dropped to my side.

I'd packed jeans and T-shirts in my bag because they were the warmest I could find in my wardrobe full of cutoff shorts and tanks. I didn't even own a long-sleeved shirt, let alone a coat. I had a pretty sweater jacket, but that was mostly for looks, not functionality.

"What am I doing?" I asked no one. "How am I going to survive up there? I don't even have the clothes I need, not to mention I'll be all alone." I sat down at the edge of my bed, dejected, my outlook feeling bleak.

My phone dinged, alerting me to a text. I brought the screen up to my face.

get your ass up and stop feeling sorry for yourself whatever problem you've invented is bull and you will overcome it

A few seconds pause then…

You are woman! Hear you roar!

I laughed at Frankie's texts, tears streaming down my face at how grateful I was to her, and amazed at how well she knew me.

thanks Helen Reddy

welcome now shut up i actually need some sleep

I tossed my phone aside and stood up a renewed person. Frank was right. Anything life threw at me, I could bat it out of the freaking ballpark. I hopped in the shower, shaved my legs, and put my underwear and bra on while I dried my hair. I flipped my head over to dry the bottom half, but when I flipped back up, I caught a glimpse of myself in the mirror. I studied myself. Shoulders too narrow, hips too wide, boobs too small, hair too curly, eyes too big. I was too *everything*, and wondered why I couldn't have been a little more proportional, more like Frankie.

I took another good, long look at myself. "Who the hell cares!" I said to no one and smiling just because I freaking could.

I slipped on a pair of light jean cutoffs, folded the hems up once, and threw on my burgundy halter crop top, strapped my mom's vintage seventies lace-up boots that came to mid-calf, and walked purposefully to my vanity and sat down with equal gumption. "I can do this, damn it!"

I took my time doing my makeup because Ezra Brandon was going to be picking me up in a short half hour and I wanted to feel powerful. Makeup was a release for me. It allowed me to feel like I could paint myself up to be anyone I wanted to be: sharp, witty, fun, outgoing... anything I wanted to be. Let me correct myself—makeup gave me the *freedom* to be the things I already felt, and that morning I wanted to be the lead in my own story, and my face was going to reflect the same.

When I was done, I grabbed my most precious belonging, my e-reader, and tucked it into my hobo bag. My e-reader was contraband in my parents' house. I had to charge it at Frankie's every few days. It's not that my mom and dad were opposed to reading, but they felt books should be enjoyed in a tangible way. I wasn't knocking it. In fact, I had a reverent respect for books in print. They are things to be cherished. But! Here's my caveat: paperbacks and hardbacks are expensive and at the rate that I devoured them, my habit couldn't be supported on the income they got from our organic home farm.

Whenever I had a birthday or if Christmas was coming up or something, I always requested gift cards from friends and family. They supported my addiction. *Just one more book, dude. I promise I'm good for the money. Just spot me this one time, man.* At least three times a week I would hear someone coming near my room and I'd have to shove the thing under my covers. #Lame

When I was done getting ready, I sat back in my vanity

chair and really took in my room, really memorized it. I closed my eyes and breathed deeply. My eyes began to sting with sadness so I stood quickly and shook my head to free myself of the fear, of the nerves, of the sadness.

"Ready for your adventure?" Mom asked from my doorway.

I faced her. "Yes. No. Both."

Mom walked through the room, scaling the mess on the floor, the ever-present clutter that was Jupiter Corey's life.

"You don't plan on tidying up before you leave?" she asked.

I tossed my makeup bag into my weathered leather suitcase and closed the lid. "Where would the sense in that be?" I asked. "When I return for summer everything will be exactly where I remembered it to be."

"So you won't be coming home for Thanksgiving then?" she asked, defeated, and slumped on the bed next to my suitcase.

"I will if I can catch a ride, Mama."

She nodded her head. "Try for me?"

"I'll try my hardest."

"Be careful while you're up there?" she asked.

"Of course."

"I've heard it can get cool there," she remarked.

"Yeah, it can get cold," I said, smiling at her.

"What will you do for a winter coat, Jupiter?"

"I'll figure it out, Mama. Don't worry about me."

Mom stood up. "Give me a second. I remembered something."

I waited patiently for her. Knowing my mother, whatever she remembered could mean absolutely anything.

44

I eventually heard her climbing the winding staircase and she emerged from the hall shortly after. In her hands was a light tan suede coat that would fall to the knees when on, and it was lined with thick, furry wool. My eyes bugged wide.

"Where did that come from?" I asked her.

"I don't throw anything away. You know that."

"Yeah, but was it yours?"

"Yeah, back in '76 we had an unexpected cold front and your grandfather bought it for me."

"This is really beautiful, Mama."

"Thank you," she said quietly. Her eyes met mine. "Would you like to use it?"

I stared on her. "I would love to use it."

"Then you should take it," she said, reaching for my case.

I reached over and unzipped my bag. She carefully folded it and laid it on top of my belongings. We both shut the lid, carefully zipping it, though it was bursting at the seams.

"Why such a small case?" she asked.

"Because Ezra's bringing his cousin along to share with the driving and I didn't want to be a burden."

"I see," she said, then began to weep in her hands. The guilt speared my guts.

"Oh, please don't cry, Mama," I begged her. I wrapped my arms around her and hugged her as tightly as I could without hurting her.

"It's okay, Jupiter," she said, patting my hands. "I just wish you would see the foolishness in this idea. I just wish you would see reason."

I let go of her. "I don't expect you to like the idea of me going to school," I said softly, "and across the country at that, but I do wish you wouldn't worry about me. I promise I'm not doing anything that will ruin my life. I promise."

She nodded her head. "I'll accept your leaving, but please don't expect me not to worry for you. I'm your mama, Jupiter, I will always worry. Even when I'm dead I will worry for you. You are mine to worry for."

"Worry then," I said, and she smiled at me.

An audible "We come in peace" sang throughout the house. I rolled my eyes. The doorbell. My heart leapt into my throat.

"That must be your ride."

I swallowed. "Must be," I said, my throat going dryer than I'd ever felt it.

When I came down the winding staircase, my dad was waiting for me at the door.

"Jupiter," he said solemnly.

"Daddy," I said, dropping my case and hugging him around the waist. He hesitated a moment before wrapping his arms around me tightly.

"Be a good girl, Jupiter," he spoke into my hair.

I let go of him and looked into his eyes. "I will, Dad. I'll make you proud."

"I have no doubt of that, but also, please don't hesitate to come home to us?"

"I won't," I answered.

I took three steps across our minuscule kitchen and opened the door. The doorway was filled with Ezra Brandon's shoulders, chest, and height. I swung the door wider and indicated he could come in. He had to duck under the half-moon frame to get inside. I'd never realized how big Ezra Brandon really was until he stood his full height underneath the roof of my tiny house.

I swallowed. "Hi, Ezra," I said as calmly as possible.

"Hey, Jupiter." He looked at my mom and sister before settling on my father. He reached his hand out. "Mister Corey? I'm Ezra Brandon."

My dad took his hand and shook it. "Nice to meet you," he said.

He shook my mom's and Mercury's hands as well, introducing himself and learning their names. Mercury's eyes shot wide when he took her hand, then turned dreamy. I rolled my own eyes and hid my smirk. This guy was kryptonite to the Corey girls, it seemed.

The room turned quiet.

"Well," I said, drawing it out in the silence. "I guess we should go?" I asked him.

I bent to grab my suitcase but Ezra surprised me by grabbing it first. "I got it," he said softly.

"Thanks," I whispered and opened the door for him.

My family followed us down the deck stairs but stopped at the base of them, watching us.

"Live long and prosper!" my dad joked. My face warmed to an impossible heat. My palm met my forehead.

I followed Ezra to his dead sexy GTO, the engine rumbling. An equally imposing guy with black hair sat in the passenger seat and when he saw us, he opened the door and unfolded himself from the car.

"That's your cousin?" I asked.

Ezra narrowed his eyes at me, looking for something, gauging me for some reason. "Yeah, that's Kai."

"Hey," his cousin's deep voice greeted. "I'm Kai," he said with a sweet smile and open eyes. He reached his hand out to me and I took it.

"Nice to meet you," I told him. "I'm Jupiter."

Kai looked up at my UFO home then back at me. "It fits," he teased, making me laugh.

Ezra's eyes narrowed once more at us before making his way to the trunk of his car. Kai waved at my family before opening the door and pushed the backseat forward. I started to get in, but he stopped me with a warm hand on my shoulder.

"What are you doing?" he asked me.

"Getting in?"

"Uh, no, Ezra would kick my ass if I let a girl sit in the back."

"Oh, okay. Well, thanks," I said, but stopped. "Maybe we can take turns?" I asked

"Sounds like a plan," he said, a charming smile spread across beautiful teeth.

Kai jumped in the back and pulled the seat back so I could climb in. I sat down, but before I could shut the door, Kai reached over me and yanked it closed.

"Thanks," I said, smiling at him.

"Don't mention it."

Ezra slammed the trunk closed, walked to the driver's side, and opened the door. "Surprised you didn't sit up front, Kai," he said, sitting down and putting the car in drive.

Kai laughed and leaned against the backseat, sprawling muscular arms out on top of the bench. He looked strikingly similar to Ezra, just darker features. Black hair, hazel eyes.

"You *and* my mom would kill me if I had."

"True," Ezra said, his face stoic.

I pressed my hands against the glass of the passenger-side window and stared after my sad-looking family, fighting back my own tears. Mercury blew a kiss my way and I caught it, pocketing it for later. *I love you*, I mouthed, and they waved before heading back inside.

I laid flat against my seat, trying to compose myself. A single tear left my eye, but I wiped it away discreetly. I looked on Ezra then but if he'd noticed, his face didn't betray he had. I took a deep breath and let the moment pass. We drove over Overseas and I felt it, that feeling of excitement, of joy, of fear, and anxiety. It was such a heady, strange feeling, but I cherished it all the same. I was in charge of my own skin and mind. I was deciding my own fate. And I liked it.

I lifted my left leg onto the sticky black leather of my flat bucket seat and leaned my side into its back, resting my chin on a fist. "So Chicago?" I asked Kai.

"Yup, born and raised there."

I looked between him and Ezra. "So whose parent is the sibling of whose parent?"

Ezra glanced at me, his eyes lingering a little longer than necessary, sending a silent thrill through my gut. "My dad and his dad," he explained.

I kept my eyes on Ezra's until he broke away toward the road. "That's pretty nice that you'd come down here to help Ezra with the drive," I observed.

"I know, I'm a saint," he said, a devilish smirk on his face. I laughed, convinced of the opposite. I was ready to tell him as much, but Ezra turned toward me briefly, studying me before looking in his rearview mirror, catching Kai's attention. Kai coughed into his hand to avoid laughing then leaned forward. "So what's it like living in a UFO?" he asked, changing the subject.

"I couldn't even tell you if it was strange or not, because I've never known any differently."

"Is it small on the inside?"

"Kind of," I admitted, a little embarrassed. "It's basically a simple two-story house except all the walls are oblong."

"That's kind of cool, actually," Kai said with a genuine smile, bolstering me.

"Thanks," I said, smiling back.

My phone beeped. I turned in my seat again, gathered my hobo bag at my feet, and fished it out. It was a text from Frankie.

how goes it? she asked.

it goes

come on gimme something to work with

no way jose, I texted.

have you kissed him yet

Jesus, Mary, & Joseph, Frankie! No!

did he carry your bag to your car for you

of course dinkus

that settles it then, she said.

what in the world does that settle, I asked.

She didn't respond, which made me nervous, because it was Frankie and she was crazy. I locked the phone and let it fall in my lap. I waited but no answer came so I tucked the phone back into my purse.

"Who was that?" Kai asked right next to my ear, startling me.

"Oh, my best friend."

"Is she hot?" he asked.

I smiled. "Totally."

"That's rad. What's her name?"

I studied Kai. "What does it matter? She lives so far away from you."

"Kai is a girl aficionado," Ezra chimed in, surprising me. I was still stunned every time I heard him speak.

Ezra and I shared a look and I smiled timidly, but instead of smiling back, he whipped his gaze back toward the road, confusing me.

I turned toward Kai. "Is that so?"

"I-lok-em-alawt," he said, his eyes glued to the ceiling.

"You're a dork," I teased.

He was ready with an infectious laugh again. "I know."

"So, tell me, what's up with your cousin over here?" I asked point-blank. Ezra's whole body tensed. I didn't think there was any sense beating around the bush. We were going to be driving for days on end together and I wasn't about to tiptoe around him just because he was so obviously tortured.

Kai's eyes blew wide. "You don't pull any punches, huh?"

Ezra white knuckled the steering wheel, and I bit my lip wondering if I'd made a bad move.

"Ezra got his heart broken right along with his legs in the accident."

"Kai!" Ezra shouted, swinging his head toward him. He looked incensed.

"Hey, hey," I soothed. "I'm sorry. I didn't mean anything by it, really. I was just curious. Please, let's change the subject," I offered, angry at myself.

Kai fell into his seat and the car got really quiet, thanks to my big, fat mouth. After twenty minutes, I tested the waters again.

"How old are you, Kai?" I asked softly, turning around in my seat again.

"Nineteen," he answered.

"Go to school?"

"I'll be starting my sophomore year at the University

51

of Chicago."

"That's cool." I paused. I threw my head toward Ezra. "Did he tell you how I roped him into giving me a ride?"

Kai fell back into his seat again, his arms spread across the top of the bench. I was discovering that was his favorite way to sit.

"Nuh-uh. Enlighten me, why don't ya?"

"I'm a klutz," I began, making him laugh. "Anyway, I was late for my class because I'd been dawdling, daydreaming, really," I said. Ezra swallowed. "I started to run and collided with Ezra."

"Really?" Kai asked, glancing at his cousin.

"It was epic," I told him. "Papers strewn everywhere, people screaming, children crying, paramedics puking in the corner."

Kai laughed. I bit my bottom lip, glanced Ezra's way, and noticed a small smirk. I internally sighed in relief that he didn't appear to be mad at me.

"And?" Kai asked, eyeing me with genuine interest, like he'd only just really seen me.

"Well, Ezra bent to help me scoop up all our papers, but his acceptance letter got mixed in with my lot."

I bit my lip again, mentally chiding myself to stop the annoying habit I'd picked up every time I looked at Ezra Brandon.

"But how did that land you in that seat?" Kai asked, pointing.

"Well, I was going through my papers, trying to organize them, when I noticed the letter. I was confused. I'd left mine at home and didn't know how it'd gotten into my satchel in the first place." I looked at Ezra once more. "That's when I figured out it was actually *Ezra's* letter, not mine, and came up with the devious plan to trick him into taking me with him," I joshed.

"Huh," Kai said, confusing me.

"What?" I asked.

"Small world is all," Kai practically whispered, eyeing his cousin with scrutiny. Ezra watched me and I smiled nervously at him. "You know who you kinda look like?" Kai asked.

"Penny Lane?" I asked, not realizing how stupid that was until the muscles in Ezra's shoulders constricted. He sat up, his back ramrod straight, and my cheeks heated to an impossible warmth.

"That's *right*," Kai said, sounding astonished. He looked at his cousin again but smiled this time.

Ezra narrowed his eyes at Kai through the rearview. The leather on the steering wheel whined from the pressure of his grip.

"Oh, well, Ezra mentioned it once to me," I told him, trying to prevent whatever it was that was going on. The tension in the car was almost palpable.

"Is that so?" Kai asked.

"Mmmhmm," I answered.

"Why isn't your seatbelt on?" Ezra asked. I was stunned at his almost desperate tone.

"Huh?" I asked.

"Your seatbelt, Jupiter."

I glanced down at myself. "Sorry, I didn't even realize. Guess I was distracted."

Ezra threw a small glance at his cousin. "Please put it on?" he asked me politely, but there was a warning undertone there, whether it was for me or his cousin, I didn't know.

I slid the belt across my body with a *click*, the sound deafening throughout the car.

"Should we play a game?" Kai asked.

"No," Ezra said.

"Yes," I said at the same time.

I laughed a little. "Come on, Ezra," I prodded.

He glanced at me. "Fine then. What game?"

I turned toward Kai. "What game?"

"Dance or Die!" he said.

"No, I'm not doing that," Ezra said.

Kai laughed. "He's a spoilsport."

"What's Dance or Die?" I asked.

"Okay, it's when the driver yells 'Dance or Die!' and yanks his hands from the steering wheel. He can't put them back until everyone in the car is dancing in their seats."

My eyes bugged. "Kai, you so *crazy!*"

He laughed. "Come on! You too?"

"Yeah, me too! I will never play that, Kai," I said, laughing a little.

"You're no fun, guys. Sometimes it's fun to drink the Kool-Aid every now and again. You know, taste the forbidden fruit." He wagged his brows at Ezra and Ezra threw an arm into the backseat, hoping to connect with his cousin, but he barely missed him when Kai slid out of the way, laughing.

"You two," I said. "I can tell this is going to be one wild ride."

Kai winked at me. "To borrow your word from earlier, it's going to be *epic.*"

CHAPTER SEVEN

I'd drifted off, my head resting against the window. I hadn't a clue how long I'd been out, but when I finally became aware, Kai and Ezra were arguing.

"Shh! You're gonna wake her, dumb ass," Ezra said.

"You're transparent, dude," Kai said quietly.

"I don't know what you're talking about, Kai."

Kai snickered under his breath. "You know *exactly* what I'm talking about. Best be honest with yourself before you do something to ruin it."

"Whatever," Ezra answered.

I wasn't supposed to hear this, but I didn't want to embarrass Ezra so I shifted my body a little to let them think I was just coming to. They stopped talking so I sat up, stretching my arms above my body then rubbing the goosebumps on my legs.

"Cold," I said, my voice scratchy from sleep.

"Here," Ezra said, reaching behind my seat and pulling up a reversible sherpa throw, the plush side a dark purple velvet.

I took it from him and ran my hands over it. "This is *incredible*," I said, bringing the velvet to my face and running the fabric over my skin. I removed my lace-up boots, kicked them to the car floorboards, and unfolded the throw, covering myself in the luxurious feel. I giddily snuggled in with a sigh.

My face grew warm when I noticed both boys staring at me as if I'd grown two heads. "I-uh, I like the feel of fabrics and textures." I cleared my throat. "Thanks for the blanket."

Ezra shifted in his seat as if he was uncomfortable that I'd thanked him, which I found strange. "No problem," he said.

I laid my head on the back of my seat and caught Kai from the corner of my eye forming a finger gun and pointing it to his temple, pulling the imaginary trigger, all the while smiling at Ezra, but Ezra didn't react save for the slightest tick in his jaw. I wished I'd known what was going on between them.

"What time is it?" I asked, yawning.

Ezra's definitive smirk made an appearance and I made a mental note to memorize it. I couldn't believe I was riding in a car with this guy. I'd grown up with Ezra, yeah, but although Ezra had been cool with every clique at Endicott, he was still untouchable. He touched others, but no one could really reach him the same way.

At his peak, Ezra was phenomenal. His lacrosse was on point, earning him a scholarship. He was intelligent, as evidenced by a stellar GPA, but Ezra wasn't just smart, he was also *wise*. Common sense was a theme in so many of his answers during open forums in class. His girlfriend, Jessica West, was the ideal—her tall statuesque figure, brilliant almost coppery brown eyes, and hair to match. Ezra loved her, anyone who watched them for even ten minutes could have figured that out. He looked at her with a devotion I would have killed for. At times he didn't seem real.

"It's eleven in the morning," Kai remarked, staring down at his phone, texting someone. I nodded my thank you, drinking in the qualities that made up Ezra Brandon.

I pulled down the vanity mirror above me and checked myself quickly. No, I could never compare to Jessica West. We were different types of pretty. She was classically so, while I was defined by something entirely different. I pushed the mirror back into place and laid my head down once more.

Ezra ran a hand up and down his upper thigh, cringing at the obvious pain there, but continuing nonetheless.

"Does it hurt?" I asked him.

He peered over at me. "Yes," he said succinctly.

"I'm sorry," I told him and meant it.

Over that Christmas break, he had broken both legs in the accident and, as you know, he changed. He had grueling physical therapy for weeks while coming to school in a wheelchair. All of us thought his change in attitude and personality would adjust as he improved, but it did nothing of the sort. He'd grown dangerously introverted, in an unhealthy way. It wasn't unkind, just unavailable. Eventually no one tried to get his attention or his friendship anymore. Eventually people forgot about Ezra Brandon. Eventually everyone did. Except for me.

"Pull over," Kai said, "you need to stretch your legs, walk a little."

Ezra didn't respond but found the nearest exit and pulled into a gas station. He pulled next to a pump and turned off the engine. I hopped out of the car and let Kai out. All three of us stretched. We'd been driving for four hours without stopping.

Ezra went to the pump and started to fill his tank as Kai stalked off inside the store. I walked over to Ezra and leaned against the back of the GTO.

"What does it take to fill this thing?" I asked.

"Why?" he asked defensively.

"'Cause I'm kicking in some cash, yo."

"Uh, no, you're not."

I stood up. "What?" I asked, outraged. "Why not?"

"Because I don't take money from girls."

"What in the heck are you talking about? I asked *you* if I could hitch a ride, remember?"

"Exactly. I was going this direction anyway," he said, his smirk making yet another appearance.

"Uh, Ezra, that's cool as crap that you're offering, but I would feel like absolute crud if you didn't let me cover my half."

Ezra rested his backside on the fender of the car, his right hand clenched on the pump handle, his left grabbed at his right shoulder, the muscles straining under the cuff of his T-shirt, and turned his head toward me. His eyes grazed me from my boots, crawled up my legs, cutoffs, and halter, before stopping on my face. The action made my skin heat to an unnatural warmth, my toes curl in my boots, and my stomach churn with butterflies.

"No," he said.

I shook my head. "Is it because you think I'm poor?" I asked. He laughed, incensing me. "Listen, I got a job explicitly over the summer to help with my share, dude. Let me do this."

"Uh, no. Not happening, Jupiter Corey," he said. His using my name like that felt strange to me for some reason, a little intimate. Stupid, but it did.

"That's insulting," I told him, stomping over to the passenger side. I got in and swung the door closed.

Ezra shoved the pump handle into the pump, replaced the cap, and got in beside me. "It's not," he insisted, starting the engine.

My blood boiled. "It is, Ezra! I'm not a damn charity case!"

"I wasn't saying you were," he insisted, peeling out of the gas station.

"Then let me pitch in!"

"I can't, okay? I just can't."

"You are infuriating!" I said, as we entered the on-ramp to the highway.

"Listen, I would feel like shit taking money from *any* girl, okay?" he said, checking his blind spot as we got on the highway. "It hurts my pride, all right? Just stop arguing with me, damn it!"

I huffed in my seat, crossing my arms over my chest, peeved he was acting so chauvinistic. I turned to get Kai's opinion, but he wasn't there. I idiotically searched the floor behind my seat as if a six-foot guy could have hidden there.

"Kai! We forgot Kai!"

Ezra whipped his head toward the back bench. "Shit!" he said, cutting across two lanes to exit and turn around.

"Jeez Louise, Ezra!" I yelled, my hand grasping the dash and the back of his seat to brace myself. "You're crazy!"

He looked me dead in the eyes as he shifted gear. "You've no idea."

I rolled my eyes at him just as his phone rang. He answered it. "Yeah, sorry, dude. I'll be right there." He hung up and dropped it in the space between our seats.

I clenched my teeth, feeling pretty angry at Ezra for the display he just pulled. It wasn't that I couldn't appreciate a guy wouldn't feel right taking money from a girl, but it put me in a precarious situation. I would feel awkward around him forever now knowing I hitched a ride like a parasite on a hippo's back.

"Stop," he said as we approached the light to turn left toward the gas station we'd left poor Kai at.

"Stop what?"

"Stop doing the girl thing."

I huffed. "What in the world does that mean, Ezra Brandon?"

"The girl thing. That girl thing. The thing you do when you feel like you've been slighted or whatever when it's just something I don't want to do, okay?"

My heart softened toward him. "Fine," I acquiesced, "on one condition?"

"Depends on what it is."

"Ezra!"

"Spit it out, Jupiter."

I huffed. I was doing that a lot with Ezra, I noticed. "Let me pick up a meal once in a while?"

"No," he said emphatically.

"Ezra Brandon, you're starting to piss me off."

Ezra laughed, really laughed. It was such a far-off memory, that gorgeous laugh, that it startled me, arrested me, took me a moment to gain my senses.

"I don't care, Jupiter. This is my car. I do what I want."

"Ezra flipping Brandon!" I yelled, as we pulled into

the gas station.

Kai stood at the station's entrance, his arms wide in a classic what-the-hell-dude pose. Ezra came to a halt right in front of him and I jumped out, pulling the seat back forward for him to get in.

"I'm so sorry, Kai," I said.

He looked at me like I was insane.

"Ezra," Kai said, acknowledging him as if nothing had happened.

Ezra turned around toward his cousin. "Sorry, dude."

Kai laughed. "Don't worry about it. You were distracted."

Ezra narrowed his eyes at his cousin when I bent down to look between them. They were staring at one another hard. I'd missed something.

"What's going on?" I asked them, drawing it out in confusion.

Kai began to open his mouth, but Ezra interrupted him.

"Get in the car, Jupiter."

CHAPTER EIGHT

I tumbled back into my seat and shut the door before we ambled our way back toward the highway.

"Two hours until Orlando," Ezra said after a very silent ten miles.

"Is that where we're stopping?" Kai asked.

"Yeah, for the night." My brows furrowed in confusion and Ezra noticed, his neck turning crimson. "I can't drive for more than six hours at a time," he explained. "My legs won't let me go any farther."

Understanding dawned on me and I chastised myself for not putting two and two together earlier. I thought it was a little strange he wanted to leave so early for school, but I assumed it was because he wanted to be extra prepared for classes, moved in, and comfortable. It never occurred to me he was limited because of his injuries.

"Oh, that's cool," I said, desperate to distract him from something that obviously embarrassed him.

We'd had one of Kai's playlists going and when it had cycled through twice, I asked if I could play one of mine. Both nodded, so I took the cable from Kai's phone and put it into mine, rummaging through my extensive sets of playlists until I landed on my favorite. I'd named it Ezra, not that I would have told him that or anything, but it had all my favorite songs on it so I named it after my favorite person, aside from Frankie and Mercury. If I was being blunt, it was a collection of the sexiest songs I had ever heard.

When the first song began to play, Ezra looked over at me and without realizing he'd done it, I think, licked his bottom lip. Electric waves rushed through me when he did this. "I love this song," he told me.

"Do you?" I asked.

"I do," he answered.

"But do you really?" Kai asked, jumping in between us.

I giggled. "Shut up, Kai."

"We don't know each other well enough for you to tell me to shut up yet."

My brows furrowed in apology. "I'm sorry, Kai. I was just playing."

"I know. I'm just teasing, baby." He laughed. Ezra's arm muscles contracted. I noticed because I was watching him. Because I couldn't help but watch him. "That was just my way of opening up a dialogue, Miss Jupiter. So, tell me, what's your last name."

"Corey," Ezra answered for me with a slight smirk.

"Is that funny?" I asked him.

"No, not funny."

"Why the smirk then?"

"I didn't smirk."

"Yes, you did."

"I did not."

"Oh my God!" Kai interjected.

I bit my lip to keep from laughing, but Ezra

swallowed. Nerves, I suspected. What he had to be nervous about, I wasn't sure, though.

"So," Kai continued, "how old are you?"

"Eighteen."

"When's your birthday?"

"July tenth," Ezra answered again.

I was a little startled he knew when my birthday was. "How did—?"

"My birthday is the fifth. In second grade I had a birthday on a Sunday and yours was on a Friday. They gave us parties together, remember?"

I didn't. Shockingly. "That's crazy you remember that."

"Is it, though?" Kai asked with possible sarcasm, confusing me.

My phone rang. I dug through my bag to get at it, but before I could answer, Kai ripped it from my hands.

"Kai!"

He answered and put the phone to his ear. "Jupiter's phone," he greeted. His eyes lit up. "She's a little indisposed at the moment." Pause. "I'm Ezra's cousin Kai. Who's speaking?" Pause. "Oh, the hot one!" *Frankie.* Kai laughed heartily at whatever Frank said. "No, not yet," he said, looking at me with a smile. Another pause, lengthy this time. Kai laughed. "I see." He looked at Ezra. "Oh, *really?*"

I'd had enough so I took off my seatbelt and reached back. Kai reared back, laughing. "Gimme!" I shouted, our arms tangled. "Give it to me!" I insisted, pulling his arms apart and plucking the phone out of his hands.

I sat in my seat once more and brought the phone to my face. "Frankie," I said.

"Well, hello there, angel. How are you today?"

"Idday ouday ustjay mbarrasseay emay!"

"I might have," she answered.

"Frankie, really?"

"No, dinkus, I did not say anything embarrassing. Scout's honor."

"You are not a Scout."

"Okay, I promise on my new All Fired Up MAC lipstick."

I sighed in relief. "Okay, what's up, buttercup?"

"Just checking in. Have you kissed him yet?"

"Frank, I gotta go."

"Just ring me when you do!"

"Shut up, Frankie."

She laughed. "Love you too!" she said before hanging up.

I stuffed my phone back in my purse.

"So," I sang.

"So, where were we?" Kai asked. "Any siblings?"

"A sister," I answered.

"Is she hot?" he asked.

"Ew, Kai, no."

"Ezra you met her. Is she hot?"

My eyes blew wide.

"I don't remember," Ezra answered.

Liar.

"You lie," Kai accused, voicing my thought.

Ezra stared into me when he answered Kai. "I didn't really notice her," he said, making my stomach churn.

Huh.

"So, Jupiter, let's flip the script here, find out what you know about Ezra."

"Uh, no," I said, my face betraying my nerves.

Kai ignored me. "You already know how old he is, but

let's see what else you know. I'll start with a few easy ones."

"You don't have to do this," Ezra practically whispered.

"It's okay," I said.

"Let's start off with something simple. What's his last name?" Kai asked.

"Brandon," I answered.

Ezra smiled and I nearly keeled over.

"How many siblings does he have?" Kai asked.

"Ezra has two older brothers."

"Correct," Kai said, "but do you know their names?"

"Finn and," I said, pausing, trying to remember him, "Holden!"

Finn was only two years older so I attended Endicott for a year with him before he left, but Holden was four years older so I never knew him personally.

"Correctomundo," Kai responded. "Now," he said, "what is Ezra's middle name?"

I was stumped. "I can't remember," I told him.

"Julian," Ezra's deep voice offered, sending cool shivers down my skin. I looked over at Ezra. "And your middle name is Willow," he told me.

All the air in my lungs rushed out at once. "That's right," I told him.

We stared at one another for a long moment before he turned his attention back to the road.

"So, uh," Kai began, unsure of himself for once, which I could tell was uncommon for him. "Jupiter," he said gaining control again, "did you and Ezra hang out a lot?" he asked.

I turned toward Kai, both my hands on the back of my seat, and said, "Never."

"Oh," Kai said, obviously surprised at how well Ezra knew me since we hadn't ever really hung out. I was just as surprised, let me tell you.

Ezra didn't comment. Instead, he stared straight ahead, apparently done with participating.

We arrived in Winter Park at a quarter to two in the afternoon, pulling into a condo timeshare Ezra and Kai's grandparents owned there. Ezra grabbed my bag first and all three of us walked up the short path to the condo's aluminum door. When he swung it open, we were greeted with the smell of cinnamon and vanilla.

"Smells amazing in here," I said, making Kai laughed. "What?"

"My grandma's obsessed with potpourri," he explained. "It actually drives Ezra and me crazy."

"This is your room," Ezra said, gesturing to a door to the right of a small living area that connected with the kitchen. The open room ran the length of the condo to an open porch that butted against a golf course. There were two rooms with a Jack and Jill bathroom in between. Ezra set my bag inside the comfortable room then bounded back out to the GTO to get his own.

I stood within the frame of my bedroom door, leaning against the doorjamb as Kai fell onto a wicker couch with a bright tropical pattern on the cushions. He sighed.

"Want to go swimming?" he asked. "There is a wicked resort pool here."

"Sure," I said, grateful I threw in my suit at the last minute.

Ezra walked in. "We're going swimming," Kai told him.

"Cool," he said, taking his bag into his room.

Kai made a funny face at me and I laughed. "Are you

going to come, dumb ass?" Kai yelled at Ezra through his door.

"Think I'll just rest," Ezra yelled back.

Kai shook his head in exasperation. "Suit up," he said to me. "Be right back."

I shut my door then dug through my case to find my C-3PO swimsuit. Two-pieces were impractical where I lived since we were always boating, etc., so I settled for a novelty one-piece instead, and it rocked my socks. I threw my hair into a haphazard topknot, tossed my black swim tunic over my head, and slipped on my gold flip-flops. I looked at myself in the mirror. *Missing something.* Bright red lipstick and I was good to go.

I opened my door and sat on the wicker sofa where Kai had been earlier. I heard hushed voices arguing back and forth and decided to give them some room. I slipped out the front door and made my way to the main clubhouse on the property, hoping to catch a few signs directing me to the pool.

I slid my phone out of my pocket and dialed my sister.

"Hello?" she answered.

"Mercury, it's me," I said.

"You called me," she said, her voice barely a whisper.

"I told you I'd call every day and I meant it, even if I just saw you this morning. I promised."

She took a breath. "Thank you," she said, her voice more buoyant.

"How are you holding up?"

"I'm fine now," she said, "but it's only been a few hours."

I giggled. "Will you tell Mom and Dad I arrived in Orlando?"

"Sure," she said. "Love you, Jup."

"Love you too," I said, smiling as I hung up.

I tucked my phone into my tunic pocket. "Who was that?" a deep voice asked, startling me.

My hands flew to my throat as I took in the hulking figure beside me.

"Ezra," I breathed. His smirk showed itself. "It was my sister, Mercury. I told her I would call her every day. She was pretty broken up that I was leaving."

"She must love you a lot then."

"I hope so. I think so." I glanced his direction. "Decided to come, did you?"

He laughed and I thought I'd never get used to it. "Yeah, Kai can be pretty *convincing*."

It was my turn to laugh. "He's a bully," I corrected, "but he's a well-meaning, sweet bully."

"Is there such a thing?" Ezra asked.

"I think so. There are people who want so badly to do the right thing, they'll stop at nothing to do it."

"That's Kai," Ezra observed.

I checked out Ezra's board shorts but my eyes traveled lower to his calves, and that's when I saw the scars from the many pins he'd had in his legs. I winced, remembering how many he'd had. He'd sat in that miserable wheelchair for weeks as they healed, only to endure painful, from what I'd heard, physical therapy.

My knees went a little weak at the memory.

"You looked so miserable back then," I told him when he'd caught me looking, his gaze following mine.

Ezra swallowed but didn't respond. We walked in silence until we reached the gate.

"Kai was right; it's a wicked pool."

"Over here!" Kai yelled, motioning us over to where he sat near a group of girls, already working that suave, and making me giggle.

"How did he beat us here?" I asked.

"Took the shortcut, I guess."

"Ah," I commented, then turned toward Ezra. "Why didn't you?"

"Wanted to make sure you got here okay."

I nodded and bit my lip to keep from smiling.

"He is shameless," I said, nodding toward a flirtatious Kai.

"He is a Lothario," Ezra added.

We closed the distance between us and Kai.

"Ezra, Jupiter, these are some new friends of mine," Kai said when we drew near. "This is Kate, Sophia, and Lane."

"Hey," Ezra said with a nod, taking up a pool chaise between Kai and the girl named Kate.

"Hello," I said with a smile, setting my stuff on the chaise to Kai's far right.

I sat down.

"Are you here for Disney?" the girl Kai introduced as Lane asked.

"Nah, just passing through. Ezra and I are cousins and this is our grandma's timeshare," Kai explained.

"On vacation?" Ezra asked her.

"Yeah, we wanted a little girls' getaway," Kate answered for Lane. "We're going out tonight if you all want to join us?"

"Maybe, yeah," Ezra answered, surprising me.

I glanced around to see where the pool towels were but couldn't find any.

"Are you looking for the towels?" the girl named Kate asked me.

I smiled at her. "Yes, point me in the right direction?"

I asked.

"Here," she said, standing up. "I'll take you myself."

When she stood, I finally noticed she was wearing an extremely small string bikini. I nearly cringed knowing I'd have to take off my coverup in front of Ezra, knowing he'd probably be comparing me to her. As we walked toward the pool towels, I could feel their eyes on us, and my face heated in embarrassment.

"You from around here?" Kate asked.

"No, Ezra and I are from Key West and Kai's from Chicago. Ezra and I are going to the same school in Seattle, and Kai is helping us with the drive."

"Oh, that's cool of him," she asked, looking over her shoulder.

"So, uh, are you and Ezra, like, together?" she asked.

"Nuh-uh," I answered. I looked over at him wishing otherwise, though.

"Cool," she said, her voice seeping in excitement, despite her attempt at squashing it down. "Here you go," she said when we arrived at the cart. I pulled a few towels off before we set back toward the group.

Kate left me in her dust, making a beeline for Ezra's side. I felt my stomach ache. I threw Ezra a towel, which he thanked me for, and then did the same for Kai. The girl named Lane had moved to the end of his chaise and had begun talking to him about her major. She was a university student in New York visiting her grandparents for the summer. I laid my towel out on my lounger and sat.

Moment of truth, fraidy cat. I pulled my tunic over my head then sat back. *There, not so bad,* I thought.

"Whoa!" Kai said, startling me.

"What?" I asked, bringing my hands to my chest to

.

check if the scissor sisters had escaped their hatch. They hadn't.

"That suit!" Kai said, pointing at me.

"What about it?" I asked, my face getting hot.

"Ezra!" Kai said, waving him over. "Ezra, come look at Jupiter's suit."

"No, no, that's okay," I said, bringing my tunic up to cover myself.

Soon all three girls and Ezra stood trying to get a peek at it. My hand went to my face. *I am going to kill Kai Brandon. Kill him dead.* I removed my hand and gave Kai a death glare.

"Uh, never mind," he squeaked. *Oh yeah, that helped.*

"What is it?" Kate asked.

I intensified my look and Kai started to pray under his breath. I stood up and let the tunic drop, forced to own the moment.

"It's C-3PO," I told them, running my hands down the design. "You know, 'Don't call me a mindless philosopher, you overweight glob of grease.'"

I looked up and took a deep breath, but it caught when I met Ezra's eyes. They burned at me, filled, and sparkled while looking at me. At me.

"Do you like it?" I breathed.

Ezra swallowed, the line of his throat moving up and down slowly. "It's, uh," he said, clearing it, "it's cool, Jupiter."

"Thanks," I said.

I turned toward the pool because I needed to hide my big, gigantic, geeky Star Wars grin, and jumped in. Soon bodies started piling in beside me, so I stood. Ezra, Kai, and the girls had jumped in as well.

"You mad at me?" Kai asked.

"Nah," I told him, thinking of Ezra's facial expression.

CHAPTER NINE

We decided not to go out with the girls from the pool after all and instead watched *Star Wars* at Grandma Brandon's timeshare. The next day we all three piled into the GTO after a decent night's rest. Kai sat in the back again.

"You can have shotgun," I'd told Kai.

"No, I don't believe I could," Kai had cryptically told me.

We barreled down Interstate 75 after stopping for gas, which Ezra again refused to let me help pay for, which irked me, but he refused to argue, so I was forced to give him the silent treatment, but when I give the silent treatment, it only lasts five minutes because I don't have the willpower.

I turned to talk to Kai, but he was asleep with his mouth open. I took a picture for future extortion purposes.

"That was evil," Ezra said quietly, but his smirk was present, so I didn't think he actually thought it was all that evil.

"Not evil. No. It's, uh, a bargaining chip of sorts."

"Ah, blackmail fodder."

"Precisely."

We were quiet for a moment.

"How are your legs?" I asked.

He shifted. "Fine," he said.

"You don't have to be afraid to talk about it," I told him.

"What if I don't want to talk about it?" he asked.

"Well, then I won't force you."

We rode for five minutes in silence.

"They only hurt when I've been sitting for long periods of time," he said, shocking me a little. I checked my excitement.

"Well, that's only natural," I told him.

"I, uh, I hate taking medicine for them because I'm afraid I'll get addicted, so I just work through the pain instead."

I shifted my body toward him. "That sucks, Ezra."

He looked at me briefly before looking back onto the road. "It's not that bad, really. I just have to make sure I move them so they don't get stiff is all." He was deflecting, but I wasn't about to call him on it. Pride was a big thing for Ezra Brandon. I was discovering this.

It's why I hadn't offered to drive. He'd insisted on doing all the driving, as if giving up the reins meant he was less of a man or something.

"What happened that day?" I asked him.

I counted the breaths he took and with each one, he exhaled his thoughts. I could see them floating in the air around him, those worried, anxious thoughts. He didn't like to admit a weakness. He loathed it. I could tell. I could see him working up the nerve to tell me when we both heard a grating, scratching noise from behind us.

We turned just in time to see Kai sparking a lighter to light up a joint.

"What the hell, Kai!" Ezra yelled.

"Kai, are you insane?" I shouted, echoing Ezra's outrage.

Ezra pulled over on the shoulder in the middle of nowhere. There wasn't a car or town to be seen for miles. We both jumped out. Ezra met my side, reached in through my window, grabbed the joint from Kai's mouth, and flicked it into the field next to the GTO.

"What the hell, Kai?" he roared. "I told you, you weren't allowed to do this shit on our road trip! I told you you had to quit if you wanted to come, and you promised!"

"Chill, man," Kai said, placing the palms of his hands on Ezra's shoulders, but Ezra shrugged them off.

"No, I can't afford to get caught with this shit in my car, Kai!"

"Damn, dude, fine. Sorry. I won't light up another in your car again," he said, attempting to appease Ezra.

"Damn right you won't," Ezra said, marching to the trunk of his GTO and opening it with his keys. He pulled out Kai's bag and started to toss out all his belongings onto the gravel below.

Kai's hands went to his head. "You've lost it, dude! That's all my stuff, man!"

"Ezra, let's talk about this," I said as calmly as I could.

"Don't worry," he told me. "I'm just going through it to find whatever else he might be hiding in here so I can toss it as well."

"Aw, man, that's harsh," Kai said, folding his arms like a little kid and kicking at the gravel.

I rolled my eyes. "Bad, Kai," I mocked, shaking my

finger at him. "This is very bad, Kai!"

Kai fought a smile. "Oh, shut up, Jupiter."

"Ha! Should have respected your cousin, man."

"I didn't think he was serious."

Ezra stopped searching his bags for a moment to stare at him.

"Ooh, boy, you better run," I teased.

"Where is it?" Ezra asked, gesturing toward Kai's luggage.

"There," Kai grumbled, pointing at a pocket on the outside of his case.

Ezra dug his hands inside the outside pocket and pulled out a bag of *Cannabis sativa*. He dumped it into the grass, surprising me, and Kai groaned.

"Don't worry, Kai. In just a few weeks, you should have a full plant here soon," I teased.

Ezra looked up at me as if I'd lost my head.

I shrugged my shoulders. "*What?*"

"You're not helping," he told me.

I bit my lip to keep from laughing.

"I can't even believe this," Kai moaned. "I'm not gonna be able to smoke again until Chicago!"

"Kai." Ezra sighed in exasperation and made a move to put Kai's stuff back but stopped. He looked up, his face serious. He sniffed. "You smell that?" he asked.

Both of us stopped, raised our noses in the air, because, you know, those few inches make all the difference in the world.

"What *is* that?" I asked, smelling something smoky and sweet.

"The field," Ezra said eerily quietly with a raised finger.

Kai and I turned toward the ten feet worth of grass

between the road and the long stretches of pine trees lining the highway.

"It's on fire!" Kai said, panicking.

"The joint," I whispered, catching Ezra's eyes.

All three of us ran toward the building fire.

"Think that blanket in the car could smother it?" I asked Ezra.

"Let's see how bad it is first," he panted as we rushed toward the smoke. "Maybe it will be a simple fix."

Kai reached it first. "It's not that bad!" he screamed toward us, and instant alleviation flooded through me until he reared his foot back.

"No!" Ezra and I shouted, but it was too late.

Kai *kicked* the fire. Kicked it. Like an asshole.

Ezra and I were forced to watch red burning embers fly through the air and hit dry grass in a ten-foot radius. Kai realized his mistake too late.

"Oh shit!" he yelled as if in slow motion.

"You're supposed to stomp it, dumb ass!" Ezra hollered.

Frantically, we ran from burning fire to burning fire, wildly trying to tame the spreading flames, but as soon as we were done with one, we'd turn only to find another. Soon, the patches engulfed got bigger and bigger, but Ezra refused to give up. He repeatedly stomped and pounded, striding across the fire's boundary edges. Kai and I kept pace with him. I was inhaling smoke, making me choke and cough, but I kept going.

"Get that moving blanket in the trunk of the GTO!" Ezra yelled at me over the roar of the fire.

I nodded and ran as fast I could, my legs weak from the effort of stomping. I reached the back of the car and rummaged around until I found the blanket then ran back. Ezra spread the blanket over a big patch of flames, hoping to cut off its oxygen enough that we could stamp it out.

To my utter relief, we were able to put the fire out more quickly than it could spread, and we dragged that blanket all over the embankment, smothering flames and preventing them from licking at the trees that lined the road. That would have proved disastrous, to say the least, because we'd be screwed with no orange juice as they would have likely driven up and out.

Ezra put out the last burning ember, and we all three collapsed to the burnt grass in severe exhaustion, but free from our fear of the forest catching.

I gulped in air at a dangerous rate.

"Slow down, Jupiter," Ezra whispered, winded.

I tried to slow my breaths. I inhaled through my nose and out my mouth, but they both burned from the new cool air.

"It's the smoke," he said, sitting up. "You'll be okay," he said, grabbing my hands.

I batted them away. "Just let me die," I whined, swallowing air in faster than Frankie inhaled popcorn on free refill night at The Galaxy.

Ezra laughed and yanked me up anyway. "Not a chance in hell," he said.

He made me stand against the side of the car as he reached into a cooler in the trunk for a water and cracked the lid open. He thrust it in my face.

"Drink," he ordered, still heaving.

I took it from him but was unable to drink because I was wheezing so hard. I gulped before bringing my shaking hands up to my lips and swallowing water. It felt so unbelievably good sliding down my chafed throat. I watched as Ezra took a swig of water, swished it around his mouth then spit, so I copied him. We both drank until we were no longer panting.

Ezra took a bottle of water over to Kai, who still laid in the grass.

"I'm quitting the ganja. Today," he wheezed.

"Let's go," Ezra said, leading me to my side of the car.

He opened the door for me so I sat. I tried to lift my legs, but they ached with fatigue. Ezra noticed and bent, though I know it was probably painful for him, and lifted them into the car for me. His hands scorched the backs of my knees. I practically hissed at the electric currents they caused as they ran up and down the length before settling in my stomach.

"Thank you," I whispered, unable to make eye contact.

Please don't let him notice my reaction to him, I thought.

Ezra closed my door for me before swinging around the front of the GTO. I watched him, covered in black soot from head to toe, and a side-splitting guffaw left my lips. I looked down at myself and discovered I looked the same. Kai popped up in my side-view mirror for a brief moment then headed for Ezra's side of the car. Ezra opened the door for him and Kai plopped into the backseat, dead tired, and covered in black soot and grit.

Ezra got in and closed his door. The three of us looked ridiculous.

"'Ello govna!" I exclaimed with the goofiest smile I could muster. "Chim chimney! Chim, chim, cher-oo!"

The car quieted a moment before both of them laughed. When things stilled down again, Ezra started the engine and pulled back out onto the highway.

"We're freaking covered." Ezra sighed.

"You have a nice laugh," I told him.

Ezra smiled at me, actually smiled, and I inwardly swooned.

"Thanks," he said.

"What should we do now?" I asked, gesturing my hands down my smoking body. *Tsst!* Yeah, I did that.

"Well," Ezra sighed again, "I'm thirsty as hell, and hungry, and I just want to sit down and eat."

"Agreed," I said. "What do you think, idiot?" I asked Kai, turning around.

"I could eat," he answered, his voice muffled by the seat, and shrugged.

Ezra pulled into a little aluminum bedazzled roadside diner a few miles down from where the fire had been. We all three got out and started walking the gravel path toward the entrance. Ezra opened the door for me and once we'd all piled inside, the din of the diner, busy with passing truckers and families on last-minute summer road trips hushed, turning to stare at us. A woman sitting at the register, fitting every diner-waitress stereotype known to man with her beehive, button nose, scalloped apron, and smacking gum, gawked at us.

"Your finest table!" I announced, making Ezra choke.

"This way," she said, tossing an arm at a booth in the middle of the diner.

I slid into the booth first, my heart lurching when Ezra chose to sit next to me. Kai sat, spreading out his arms in his usual manner, and the waitress slapped plastic menus down for us.

"Can I get ya anythin' to drink?" she drawled.

"Water," we all croaked at once.

She eyed us like we were three people sitting in a diner in the middle of the most rural county in Georgia mysteriously covered in black soot... *Wait a minute.*

"Be right back," she told us, smacking her gum again.

I looked around the diner and out the glass window onto the highway before noticing the tables had those old-fashioned mini jukeboxes on them. "Got a dime?" I asked Ezra.

"Sure," he said, reaching into his pocket and tossing it my direction.

I caught it and put it into the little slot, winding the little metal knob until it clicked and you could hear the clink of the dime tumbling throughout the little machine.

"B-four," I whispered, clicking the buttons.

We waited but it didn't work.

"Aw, man," I fussed. "Too bad."

"You owe me a dime. Or a song," Ezra teased.

"No way, José. Who carries a dime around with them?"

"Uh, *I* do," he answered, acting offended.

I ignored him. "I do have a lovely singing voice, though."

"Really?" Ezra asked, leaning back in the booth.

"Yeah, people have told me I have a similar sound to Charo. I sing a mean Cuchi Cuchi Coo, if you're interested."

Ezra's face broke into an ear-splitting grin. "There's that smile again," I observed.

He shook his head, burying his chin in his chest as if he was embarrassed, and my heart grew two sizes at how charming that was. *I could eat him up.*

My hands flew to the table, searching. "Why are there never any spoons when you need them?"

"What are you talkin—" he began, but stopped when the waitress laid three glasses of water down as well as a full pitcher.

"Somethin' told me you'd be needin' it, darlins," she said and winked. She'd gotten over the initial shock, it seemed. "Be right back to take your orders."

We perused our menus. "Wonder if I could get this gravy on the side," I said to no one.

Someone turned up the television.

"We interrupt your regularly scheduled programming to bring you this breaking news—" a woman drawled.

"I don't think I want anything this heavy, though." I sighed, remarking upon the greasy chicken fried steak.

"—of a grass fire off Interstate 75 in Crisp County that has spiraled out of control—"

"But then again, who knows when we'll be stopping again and I don't want to be hungry later."

"—encroaching on the forested area and heading south toward —"

I slammed my menu down. "I don't care! I'm getting the chicken fried steak," I declared.

"Dance, Dance, Dance" by The Beach Boys flared through the diner's speakers.

I gasped, sitting up. "My song!"

Ezra whipped me from my seat so fast my next sentence blurred in the wind.

"What's everyone staring at?" I asked the stunned diners.

He threw me over his shoulder, his warm hand splayed against my backside, and my cheeks turned beet red. I could feel it.

"Ezra!"

With the diner patrons hot on our heels, he pushed the door open with his free hand, and followed Kai out to the GTO with me bouncing over his shoulder.

"The keys!" Kai yelled at Ezra.

I felt more than saw him toss them at Kai. A moment later the unmistakable rumble of the engine sounded and I was shoved into the backseat of the GTO. Ezra fell on top of me as Kai tore out of the parking lot, gravel kicking up behind our tires, the passenger-side door swinging as the car fishtailed onto the on-ramp.

Ezra pushed up, leaning over the back of the front seat and pulled the door closed.

"What was that?" I asked.

"The fire," Ezra wheezed.

"What fire?" I asked.

Ezra and Kai both gave me a deadpan stare.

I cleared my throat. "Oh, uh, *that* fire."

"We should have stayed longer to make sure," Ezra huffed.

It got quiet before Kai whispered, "We're fugitives."

Ezra settled in next to me, looked over, and rolled his eyes.

"Turn on the radio," Ezra said.

We both sat up and leaned against the front seats as Kai flipped through station after station to get any kind of news about the fire, but we couldn't find any. Apparently it wasn't news enough for the bigger stations.

"What should we do?" Kai gulped, visibly nervous.

"I don't know, Cheech. Maybe you should consult Chong?" Ezra asked.

I looked at Ezra, my mouth agape. "Who is *this*?" I asked him.

His signature smirk appeared and I almost fell over. *I want your babies! Or, well, maybe not your babies. Um, eventually your babies, like, in ten years or something. Maybe we could just adopt a rescue dog or something first! You know, feel things out! I* screamed. Well, in my head I screamed, because, as you know, doing so out loud would have been highly inappropriate. That, and since I had almost two weeks left with Ezra, things would have been awkward if I had, and awkward Jupiter was an overall bad look on me.

"It never would have happened if you hadn't thrown it into the grass, dude."

"*Dude*, it never would have happened if you'd never lit up in the first place!"

They began shouting back and forth, hurling insults.

"Boys! Stop!" I chimed in, and they both looked at me. "Oh, I'm sorry, I didn't actually think you'd stop. Continue."

"Kai, drive through this godforsaken county, find a motel, and we'll hole up for a few hours, check the news," Ezra ordered.

"Yeah," I said, puckering my lips. "Runnin' from the law. Shufflin' the pigs. Dodgin' the 5-0. Giv'n the bacon the ol' slip!"

"Jupiter," Ezra said, sounding exasperated. He ran a hand down his face. I swear I saw him fight a slight smile, though. I wouldn't bet my life on it or anything. Maybe Frankie's. There's a possibility I'd bet Frankie's.

"Got it, sarge," I said, saluting him.

We drove in silence for almost two hours, desperate to get as far away as possible from our crime scene. A state trooper passed by us, and we all threw on our best Martha Stewart postures. I plastered what I thought was a very genuine smile, but Ezra told me I looked like one of those dog memes where someone has Photoshopped human teeth on them, which I thought was very rude.

Kai turned into an ancient motel called Huckleberry Inn. It had one of those signs from the 1950s, that at the time, probably seemed cheery and sweet, but now looked like the panning entrance shot of a film where cheerleaders yield chainsaws while chanting, "Gimme a D! Gimme an E! Gimme an A! Gimme a D! What's that spell? You! That's what it spells!" Then they move at a snail's pace to come hack at you, but for some reason you've forgotten you have legs, so you sit there screaming with your hands up.

"I don't know about this," Ezra said warily.

"Yes. Yes, it will do just fine," I told him.

"You want to sleep here?" Ezra asked, obviously bewildered.

"Sleep? Oh no. No, I meant murdered. This will be the perfect place to be murdered."

"Kai, turn around. Keep driving."

"This is just as good a place as any, Ezra. We need to shower, clean the car out, and all that. We can't keep going because we run the risk of running into police."

Ezra sighed. "Fine then. I'll get us a room."

"Wait," I said. "Pull over to the side of the building. You need to change your sooty clothing and maybe run some water over your face."

Ezra nodded. "Good idea."

Kai pulled around and we all got out, meeting at the back of the GTO. I leaned in for the cooler and started to yank out a water bottle but stopped when I noticed a water hose stuck to the side near a pool pump.

"There's a water hose," I said, pointing it out.

"Oh cool," Ezra said, yanking his T-shirt over his head in the way boys took off their shirts that made girls drool.

I wiped at my mouth. Ezra was built. Brick by brick, that boy was stacked. *Someone call a docta, I'm feelin' faint!* I felt my mouth fall open and was powerless to close it. He strode over to the hose like the director of an Abercrombie shoot was nearby. I almost keeled over.

"Careful," Kai whispered in my ear, startling me.

It was the motivation I needed. I cleared my throat. *Act cool.* "I wasn't looking!" I shouted at him. #Facepalm

His smile was wide when he winked. "Jupiter, your Great Red Spot is showing."

I covered my face, mortified.

"Kai, please don't say anything to him."

"Oh, I'm going to say something."

"Kai!" I yelled, clutching his shirt and bringing him in close, eye to eye. "Hell hath no fury, Kai," I gritted.

Kai paled and swallowed. "Okay, okay!" He backed away, straightening his clothing, and put some distance between us. He looked off into the parking lot behind me. "I think... Yeah, I think I saw my life just flash before my eyes." I held up two fingers at my eyes then jabbed them toward him. "Gah! I promise. I promise. Just please go back to the old Jupiter." I smiled prettily at him and he looked horrified. "That isn't... That's just not normal," he muttered to himself. He walked off toward the courtyard at the back of the motel.

I turned my attention back to Ezra and sighed in ecstasy. He was bent over to keep the water from dousing his jeans and shoes. It ran over his hair, face, and neck as he scrubbed the black soot away. Oh my gato. He was so flipping beautiful. When he was done, he turned off the water and stood; rivulets of water sliced down his chest and abdomen. I bit my bottom lip, because that was what Ezra Brandon did. He made me bite my lip like some sex-crazed lunatic in one of those period romance dramas.

He walked toward me, the water cutting over his shoulders. He smirked at me, and my hands covered my eyes.

"Too much," I told the air in front of me. "It's just too much for one girl to endure."

When he reached me, he pulled my hands down. "Are you okay?" he asked, looking concerned.

"Yes," I squeaked, averting my eyes. "Here you go," I said, noticing a housekeeping cart a few rooms down. I ran toward it and picked up a towel, bringing it back to him.

"Gee, thanks," he told me, drying off his hair, face, and neck.

Gee? Gee! *Don't say adorable things like* gee, *Ezra, or I won't be held responsible for the utterly psychotic reaction I would inevitably have, which would probably involve me licking the water sliding down your neck right now.* My tongue darted, and I knew I had to get out of there. I sprinted toward the GTO and approached his bag.

"You need a shirt," I squawked, channeling the Mad Hatter.

I could feel the heat from Ezra's body at my side. I lifted the lid to his case to get him a T-shirt, but he slammed the case shut, shocking me.

"I was just going to get you a T-shirt," I told him.

He leaned over me. "I've got it," he breathed silkily.

"Oh, okay." I shivered.

Ezra kept my gaze, reached in quickly, retrieved a tee, and let the lid fall before zipping it closed. Never breaking our stare, he pulled on the T-shirt. There was a strange intimacy to the act, and I felt my throat go dry. *Okay, now I really do need that water shifting down his neck. Don't get distracted; he's hiding something.*

I smiled at him and he smiled back.

"What's in the bag, Ezra?" I asked. I could see my question surprised him.

"I have a dead body in there."

"Cool. Let me see it."

"Uh, well, I'm not really comfortable showing you my dead bodies so…"

"What's in the bag, Ezra?"

"An extensive collection of celebrity hair."

"That's disgusting. What's in the bag, Ezra?"

"My Pokémon memorabilia. It's a little embarrassing."

"Just a little?" I smiled, reaching for the lid.

Ezra startled, reaching for my hand. "*Jupiter*," he sang.

"*Ezra*," I sang back, landing on the zipper.

He started to laugh. "Jupiter, don't," he told me when I began unzipping the case.

His hand stopped mine, and there was a zap of electricity between us, warming me up from the inside. It swam up my arm, coiled in my belly, and took up a happy residence there. I began to inch the zipper back.

"You know, I like this playful Ezra," I told him, slowly making progress with the zipper.

He didn't stop me but he kept his hand on mine, sending a thrill up and down my spine.

"I've always been playful," he said.

"You were playful before the accident but not after."

It was the wrong thing to say. He yanked his hand back, taking mine with it, and slammed the trunk closed, locking it with his keys. I didn't know how to keep a good thing going. It was as if we were made of this colorful ink, but my words came down in a downpour, washing all our wonderful, bright paint down at our feet, never to be brought back to life in that moment.

Color me Cecilia Giménez.*

*Cecilia Giménez is that cracked-out old Spanish woman in her eighties who attempted to "restore" a priceless nineteenth-century fresco of Jesus and royally messed up. #SMDH

"I'll get us a room," he said, turning and walking toward the motel office.

I sighed, strolling the direction I'd seen Kai walk, and followed the line of the building toward the back courtyard with its ancient but well-kept pool and retro aluminum umbrellas under tables lining the pool itself.

The place literally hadn't made a single update since 1956, it seemed. A tall, elderly man with horn-rimmed glasses walked by, a towel draped over his arm.

"Buddy Holly? Is that you?"

He stopped. "Huh?"

"Nothing."

I walked around the pool and courtyard area but didn't find Kai anywhere. I circled the entire building looking for him, but he never came into view. I skirted past the front, back to the GTO, and found Ezra there.

"Get the room?" I asked.

"Yes," he said, dangling an actual key in front of me.

"Good God, that's a key. To an actual lock."

"Quite the detective."

"Hey! I— well— you—" I stuttered.

"Good one," he zinged.

I huffed and crossed my arms. "You're a punk. And an ass. You're a punk ass."

"Come on," he said, opening the trunk and yanking bags out of the back. He looked around me. "Where's Kai?"

"How should I know?"

Ezra took his phone out and texted presumably Kai. "Room four thirteen," he said, throwing his head toward the corner room closest to the car. He stuck the key ring between his teeth, picked up both our cases, and barreled his way to our room. I followed, scrambling to catch up.

"I can carry my own bag, Ezra."

"Nnngghhgg aaa wooooggggnntt rrrr rrr."

"How could I negate an argument like that?" I oozed.

He stood at the door, so I took the keys from his mouth, grazing stubble when I did, and ignored the restless tumbling in my stomach because of it. I opened the door and held it open for him. He dropped the bags on the bed and I walked in after him. The room had wood floors that creaked underneath our feet, creeping me the flip out. The beds were updated with modern comforters, but they were about the only modern thing in the room. The fixtures and furniture hadn't been moved in sixty years, I could tell, though, I admit, it was all very clean.

I peeked my head into the bathroom and it was very, uh, pink. Pink tile on the floor and walls, pink tub, pink toilet, pink sink. Pink.

"We've got a Pepto-Bismol situation up in here," I said, before realizing the double meaning in that. My face grew hot. "I mean, uh, you know, like, not me or anything. I mean, *I* don't have a Pepto-Bismol situation." My hands gestured toward the bathroom in a circular motion. "The bathroom itself has a Pepto situation. You know, 'cause it's pink." Ezra stood at the end of the bed looking baffled. "Yeah, so, uh, I suppose I'll go look for Kai then," I said, making my way toward the door. *Again.*

"Jupiter," Ezra said softly, catching my forearm in a

warm palm, "stay. Shower. I'll go look for Kai."

"Oh, okay, yeah, that's a good idea," I said, flustered by his touching me.

Anytime his skin touched mine, my stomach plummeted at my feet. It felt like that time Frankie and I rode Space Mountain, but, you know, without all the puking. I told her chili dogs were a bad idea.

When the door closed behind him, I ran to my case and whipped out my soaps and stuff, a new set of unmentionables, another pair of cutoffs, and my T-shirt that read *You're suffering from a lack of Vitamin Me.* I practically skipped to Pepto and started the water, waiting until it got hot before switching on the shower. I stripped down and jumped in.

Since I was alone, I started to sing "YOLO" by The Lonely Island, because that was my go-to jam in the shower. The song was a cautionary tale of the dangers of a careless life. It included sage advice about investing in real estate with a low interest rate and sauna habits. It also had a dope beat. You really do only live once.

I washed my hair and even cleaned between my toes, something I never really did, if I was being honest. The water ran black for several minutes, so I rewashed every little nook and cranny until it ran clear. I turned off the water and kept singing at the top of my lungs while I dressed and dried my hair. I opened the door to let out the steam and leaned against the sink to do my makeup.

I rapped Kendrick's part while applying my mascara, but it didn't quite translate right since I always form an "O" with my lips to open my eyes better. I dug through my makeup bag and pulled out my vanilla extract. I wasn't allowed to wear perfumes because, you know, my parents, but my mom did let me wear vanilla extract, so I carried a bottle around with me.

I put a small dab of coconut oil in my hand and spread it over my palms to run throughout the length of my blonde curls to keep them in order. I flipped my head over to get the back then danced out of the room ass first and right into something solid. That something solid grunted. I stood abruptly, my blood racing.

Slowly I turned around to meet this intruder. It was Ezra. Of course it was Ezra. I closed my eyes, desperate to ignore the heat growing in my face, and looked up toward the ceiling.

"What fresh hell is this?"

Ezra leaned against the wall outside the bathroom, a small smile on his mouth. "Enjoying yourself?"

I felt my face flush again. "How long have you been listening?"

"Oh, right about the start of the second chorus, I believe… The first time."

"But you said you were going to go look for Kai!"

"I did!"

"Did you find him?"

"I did."

I buried my face in my hands.

"Kai?" I mumbled through fingers.

"Hello, Pavarotti," Kai answered from somewhere in the room.

"Somebody, please kill me."

"And deprive ourselves the pleasure of your lovely voice?" Ezra asked. "Never." I let my hands fall at my sides. "You sound nothing like Charo, by the way," he told me, entering the bathroom and closing the door.

I fell on the bed next to a very dirty Kai. "This is your bed," I told him, my voice muffled in the comforter.

"Okay by me. You can just share with Ezra then."

I sat up. "Don't do this," I begged.

"Do what?" he asked, feigning innocence.

"This," I said, gesturing to his whole body with rapid hand movements. "Dig in to me now that you know what I feel for Ezra."

Kai smiled in answer at me, letting me know he was definitely going to be digging in, then placed a hand behind his head as he flipped on the television with the remote with his other. The news started and my stomach fell a little. I'd forgotten about the fire.

"Have you heard anything?" I asked.

"Yeah," he said, flipping the channel. "They got it out. Nobody got hurt. Only a few trees fell. It's already old news."

I breathed a sigh of relief, flipping onto my back. My head laid near Kai's feet, his socks a shocking bright white in comparison to the rest of him. I crossed my bare feet on the headboard and let my hands fall toward the edge of the bed.

"This bed is kinda comfy," I said, bouncing up and down a little bit.

"You're a dork."

"I know."

"I'm starving," Kai said.

"Maybe after you shower we can all go grab something to eat."

"Sounds like a plan, Stan," he said, picking up his charging phone and messing with an app or something.

"I really like him," I whispered.

Kai sat up and threw himself beside me, tucking his hands beneath his chin. "Oh my God, like, tell me all about it."

"Shut up!" I couldn't stop laughing. Kai sat back against the headboard and picked up his phone again.

"So what? Lots of girls like Ezra," Kai said, shrugging.

I giggled a little bit. "Are you jealous of your cousin?" I asked him.

Kai signaled toward his admittedly pretty magnificent body, one that didn't look much different than his cousin's, by the way. "Does it look like I need to be jealous of Ezra?"

"Have you looked in the mirror today?"

He shook his head. "When I am showered and shaved, I am a beast, Jupiter."

"I concede the point, though you could use a little spoonful of humility," I told him.

Kai smiled. "Humility is for punks."

I laughed, but the laughter died slowly, much like the murdering clowns in my nightmares.

"I know lots of girls like Ezra."

Kai set his phone on the nightstand and looked at me. "Ezra is a different breed, though. He doesn't care about that stuff. He's a focused individual. He got his heart broken once and it changed him, kind of changed the way he handles stuff. I don't know. This shit is too deep for me."

"He's still hung up on Jessica then?"

"No, he's over her for sure, but I also know he told me it was pretty hard to get over her. Ezra seems to love people deeper than they love him."

Don't tell me stuff like that!

"And so he's *done*?"

Kai smiled, his eyes crinkled with the gesture. "No, not done, extremely selective."

I nodded.

Well, that rules me out then. Damn.

Seems I was going to be spending my time getting *over* Ezra Brandon on the trip instead of the opposite. You know, heh, heh, getting *under* him. <—I'm a grown-up. 'Cause that's the opposite. The opposite of over is under. I'm a punny genius. Not that I'd had any intention of getting under Ezra Brandon or anything. I mean, I was about as virginal as you could get. If it were two hundred years in the past, I'd have been first to be pushed in the sacrificial volcano. I wouldn't have even argued. That's how much of a virgin I was. Anyway, I just killed my pun. Shot it dead. In the street. Like a dog. He even did that thing that all bad puns do where they squirm on the ground in a fake seizure. That's how dead my pun is. Dead.

CHAPTER TEN

We'd all gone to dinner that night then straight to bed for an early morning departure. When we loaded up the car, I slipped a twenty in Ezra's pocket when he wasn't looking for my third of the motel then snuck away like a thief in the night, who, well, gave money away instead of stole it. I needed to go to thief school.

I did a little jig by my side of the car, channeling my extensive knowledge of Irish dance obtained by hours glued to **PBS Riverdance** specials, when the boys went to check the room for straggling belongings. Ezra emerged as I'd clapped the side of my boot in a stellar dance kick. There was a bra dangling from his index finger.

"Egad!" I said, stopping my victory dance. I loped to him and yanked the garment from his hand, tucking it underneath an armpit. I felt my face flush. "Heh, I, uh, must have forgotten it last night after my shower."

Ezra's brow raised in amusement, making me want to fall over in mortification, and stuck his hand in his pocket to pull out his keys. The twenty came with them. I started whistling and examining the edge of the motel roofline. Because whistling is inconspicuous. I saw it in a

97

cartoon once. It didn't really work out for that character, but I had high hopes.

"What the—" Ezra said. He held up the twenty between his index and middle finger. "Kai, is this yours?"

"Nah, man," he said, pulling back the front passenger seat to get into the back.

I whistled louder, studied more intently.

Ezra looked at me, his brows furrowed, his eyes serious. His mouth opened, presumably to speak, but I stopped him with a very convincing argument. "It's not mine! It's not mine!"

Nailed it.

"Gosh damn it, Jupiter Corey! What did I tell you?" he shouted, running around the front of the GTO. My heart started to race. He yanked me up by wrapping an arm around my waist and plopped me on the hood of his car. I gasped like a schoolgirl. Which is ironic, I know. *Note to self: Make Ezra angry more often.* He set the twenty by my hip then took my calf in his hands and began untying the laces of my right boot. I tried to yank it from his grasp, but he brought it right back to him.

"Don't. Move," he ordered, making my blood race through my veins.

He took the boot off and laid the twenty flat inside before placing it back on my foot and lacing it back up. I fought the urge to fan myself.

He leaned forward. "Don't try something like that again," his deep voice settled across my ears. He released my leg and let my booted foot dangle.

He picked me up again, his hands scorching, and set me down. He left me standing there, dazed and confused.

"Get in the car, Jupiter."

I stumbled to the car door in an Ezra-induced stupor and opened it slowly. Ezra was already inside and had started the engine as I sat down, closing the door behind me.

He backed out of the parking lot and made his way toward the on-ramp. Kai poked my shoulder, so I turned toward him. He wagged his brows at me, causing my face to flush hot as I fought a smile. It was gonna be hard to get over Ezra Brandon if he kept touching me like that.

"What's our next stop?" I asked him.

"Nashville."

"Nashville?" I asked.

"*Nashville?*" Kai asked as well, sitting up. He started pressing buttons on his phone feverishly.

"Yes, *Nashville*," Ezra answered, glancing at us like we were idiots, you know, 'cause we were. "Why do I feel like I just keep repeating things over and over around you two?"

You can repeat that car bit again if you want, I thought too quickly. *No! No. Bad Jupiter. Bad Jupiter.* I tried to turn my thoughts toward more innocent diversions, but it was really hard to when Ezra Brandon's hands, the very hands that lifted me not a mere ten minutes before, were resting so charmingly across his steering wheel. I took a deep sigh.

Then I sat up with a jerk. "Oh shit!"

Ezra fishtailed a little. "What?"

My face flushed warm again. "Uh, I just, uh, forgot to phone my sister last night."

"Damn it, Jupiter!" Ezra panted. He situated himself in his seat once more, pulling at his seatbelt.

"Sorry! Sorry! I'm really sorry!"

"Just call your sister before I lose control of the car again."

I smiled at him. His smirk came about but he fought it, I could tell, with everything he had. I found my sister's number and pressed the call button. I waited while it rang.

"You promised," she answered.

"I know. I'm sorry but I got sidetracked."

"But you promised," she said, her voice breaking up like she was holding back tears.

"Aww, Mercury, don't do that. You'll make *me* cry, and if I cry then Ezra will cry; we'll all be crying."

Ezra threw an annoyed look at me, but I ignored it.

"What's new there?" I asked her, trying to distract her.

"Nothing really. Have you been able to eat anything good yet?" Mercury and I were constantly scavenging for anything other than organic tomatoes. A bag of Cheetos in my house was worth two weeks of dish duty to the right person, and by right person, I mean Mercury.

"Yeah, actually, I ate a cheeseburger last night."

"Cheese and crackers! You heinous brat. Tell me all about it."

For the next ten minutes I described the cheeseburger I'd consumed the night before bite by bite, even going so far as to describe the various textures and temperatures of the pile of fries I'd hit Kai's hand over once when he'd tried to pilfer one.

"All right, gotta go, Mercury."

"You busy?"

"Nah, but I don't want to talk to you anymore."

"Okay, love you!" she said.

"Love you too. Remember, you're the hottest planet, baby."

100

"And you're the heaviest."

"Aw, man, I was trying to be nice, you punk."

"That's for not wanting to talk to me anymore."

"Fine," I said. "Bye, lint licker!"

I hung up before she could respond. I took a deep breath in satisfaction, my work done.

"Anyone want a cheeseburger?" Kai asked, making me light up inside.

"I should be a food critic, no?" I asked him.

He nodded with authority, which made me begin to question my life's plans.

"I might change my major," I told the car.

"What *are* you going to the University of Washington for?" Ezra asked.

He'd asked it so seriously, my whole body sobered. "Oh, I'm going to get a nursing degree as well as a nursing home administration degree."

Ezra did a literal double take, which I thought was only possible in cartoons. "*What?*" he asked.

He hadn't heard me apparently, so I spoke very slowly. "Me want to be nurse. Me also want to open a nursing home."

"I heard you, smart-ass, I just— I just can't…"

"What he's trying to say is that he finds this an incredible coincidence, because he too would like to work with the elderly," Kai chimed in.

"A geriatric physician," Ezra explained quietly, studying me.

"Well," I breathed, "that *is* interesting."

Ezra stared at the road ahead of him. "I want to start something sort of different," he continued.

"What's that?" I asked.

"I want to start a joint nursing home and preschool.

During the day the elderly could work side by side with the children, helping them, teaching them, giving them all something to work towards." He glanced at me, the fire obvious in his eyes. "Preschool-age children have so much to gain from being around them, and they give so much love in return. It's a win-win."

My breath sucked into my chest. It was a brilliant idea, literally brilliant. "That is an incredible idea, Ezra," I told him, thinking back on all my friends in my yoga class. They would have *loved* that.

"You think so?" he asked, that enchanting smile, the one that was so utterly Ezra's, gracing his face.

"I think it's genius, Ezra," I told him quietly, and I meant it.

"Thank you," he answered, making my heart skip a beat.

Please don't fall in love with him. Please don't fall in love with him.

CHAPTER ELEVEN

I slept right through entering Nashville, but woke in an unusual traffic jam right before the city itself, wrapped in that insanely soft blanket of Ezra's. I buried my nose in it and breathed deeply. It smelled just like him and I closed my eyes, memories of growing up with Ezra assailed my mind.

My phone dinged so I threw off the top of the blanket and reached for it. It was a text from Frank.

what are you doing? she asked.
I am riding in a car with boys
lucky
dude things have been insane
sounds right up your alley
usually it is
okay spill
i'm a criminal. wanted by the law.
lol whatever
i'm not pulling your leg, I told her.
all right then cool
we started a fire on the side of the road
yowza

we put it out and nearly killed ourselves doing it

damn gina

then we left to get something to eat and drink and while we sat there this local news broadcast reported that a grass fire was encroaching on the nearby pines off the highway

oh my gato

i know

then what, she asked.

we filed

your taxes? lmaobyatwe

stupid automobile

What? Frank texted.

Stub stepfather!!!!

Jupiter?

***stupid autocorrect I just meant that we fled**

what does lmaobyatwe mean, I asked.

laughing my ass off because you are terrible with electronics

touché one point to you

i gots to go buttercup love you and when they arrest you for arson remember to show them your left. it's your better side

love you too brat

see you on the flip, she said.

I tossed my phone in my bag.

"Who was that?" Ezra asked.

"Frankie," I answered, tossing a look behind me only to find Kai asleep, his big feet hanging out of the driver's side window behind Ezra.

Ezra fidgeted in his seat, his hands roaming the wheel, tapping at its edges. He let his elbow rest outside the window, thought twice about it, then brought it back in. He was unsure of himself. Ezra Brandon was unsure of himself! It defied logic. Perfect people were supposed to be so confident. Damn him and his endearing ways!

"It's really nice out today," he finally said. I looked out my window to avoid showing him my smile.

My pulse quickened. Ezra Brandon wanted to talk to me. Though he chose the weather, I didn't hold it against him. I ran with it instead.

"It really is. Nice clear sky, sun shining." I took out my phone and searched Nashville. "A comfortable seventy-nine degrees. Tonight it'll drop to seventy-three. Wind at two miles per hour. Humidity at a balmy fifty-two percent, but no chance for precipitation, so keep those umbrellas at home, folks. All in all, the makings of a great weekend. Back to you, Ken."

Ken smiled back at me. "Shut up."

"I'm sorry. Did you not want to talk about the weather?"

He laughed, really laughed, and my stomach sank into itself, flipping once and ratcheting up my already dangerous crush to an even unhealthier level. I took a deep breath. The tallies for making him laugh were starting to stack up and I was rewarded with that lopsided grin every time. Note to self: *Buy a book of jokes. Look into improv classes in Seattle. Up your quip game. Ignore how stupid all these ideas are.*

"Tell me a secret, Ezra," I asked him.

He swallowed. "I have none."

"Lie."

A signature grin. "None worth repeating."

"Another lie." I smiled. "All secrets are worth repeating," I whispered. I bit my bottom lip, waiting for it, but he said nothing, just glanced my direction and held my gaze for exactly three seconds. I know, because I counted.

"Tell me *your* secrets," his deep voice commanded.

It was my turn to swallow. "Like you, I have none."

"Lie," he accused as well, looking at me, seemingly through me.

"How do you know it's a lie?" I whispered, my heart in my throat.

"Because I know you," he said.

"You don't know me," I responded, blood rushing through my head, making me dizzy.

"I know you well enough," he said with a finality that made my stomach clench.

"Prove it then."

He didn't hesitate. "You don't like your hair, even though I think it's probably the prettiest I've ever seen. When the sun hits it, it turns this crazy gold hue. It's such a unique color, I don't even know what to call it. Let's see," he continued as if he hadn't just paid me the best compliment I'd ever gotten in my life, "you're funny as hell, but you don't realize it. You do this strange jiggle dance when you're happy and you think no one is watching. You actually argue with yourself out loud. You are fiercely loyal. You are often underestimated. You don't like attention, which is why no one at school really knew how extraordinary you are. You smell like a cake baking." He smiled. "And now I know that you like blankets," he admitted. My heart thudded at the declarations.

I gulped down the insane satisfaction I received from

his notice of me. Not because it was a boy noticing me. No, because it was *Ezra* who'd done the noticing. I didn't think Ezra noticed anyone, let alone me.

"I know a few things about you," I admitted to him.

"Do you now?" his deep voice crooned. "Go on then."

I sat up a little, pulling his soft blanket onto my lap more securely. Doing this made his face light up; I almost hyperventilated. I took a deep, steady breath. "You are kind. You always buy lunch for Jenny Miller because you know she doesn't have the money for it, but you don't let her know that you do it, preserving her dignity." His face showed surprise. He opened his mouth to speak, but I continued over him, knowing I'd lose my nerve if I didn't. "You are remarkably intelligent. You know all the answers in class, but you never offer them. I can tell because you wear them on your face. You don't feel the need to let everyone know this fact about you. I don't think you do this because you're ashamed, I just think it's in your nature to be humble. You draw a new meaningful quote on the bottom of your chucks every week, which means every week I'm looking up a new quote. I still haven't been able to figure out how you get them clean enough to do it, but you do." I paused as he stared at me. He knew where I was going, but I wasn't going to let him stop me. "You had a terrible accident last year that altered you. You retreated away from your friends and school."

Ezra shifted, his body language indicating he was done with our conversation, done with opening up to me.

"What happened?" I whispered.

He shook his head in answer.

"Tell me, Ezra."

"Stop, Jupiter."

I turned toward my open window, crossed my arms, and bit the nail at my thumb, staring into traffic. I'd treaded on some very sensitive territory with my big, clompy boots. I knew it was a sore subject for him, but I thought he could at least give me a little piece so I could figure out that facet of him, but I realized it was none of my business. I probably screwed myself out of any progress I'd made with him.

"I'm sorry," I told him, afraid to look his direction. "I shouldn't have said anything. It's none of my business."

"No," Ezra said, surprising me. I turned toward him. He shook his head back and forth. "I'm just not ready to talk about it. I-I actually want you to know. It'd be nice for someone outside my family to know."

"Oh," I said intelligently. I cleared my throat. "Well, whenever you want to unburden yourself, I'll be your sounding board, Ezra. I won't offer opinions. I won't offer sympathy. I will listen. Only listen."

He didn't reply, but that was good enough for me. I'd apologized and he'd accepted. I felt happier.

"Music?" I asked him, yanking up the cord.

"Sure."

I put on a list I'd created labeled "Nashville." Since I knew nothing about Tennessee, the list was basically a bunch of Elvis cover songs and *Arrested Development*'s "Tennessee."

"You're a dork," he said.

"I know," I agreed, laughing at my own stupidity.

The motel we were staying at was older, but again, clean and well kept. After we checked in, Kai and Ezra took a run around the property to work Ezra's legs. I noticed him wincing toward the last fifteen minutes in traffic, but pretended not to notice. They invited me along, but I thought I'd give Ezra some space. I didn't want him to feel like he was any less, so I let him work out his pain without a witness. Instead, I threw on my earbuds and laid in the sun by the pool, watching little kids in floaties practice their cannon balls. The big kids, i.e. the adults, did the same but in their muffin tops, wink wink. Also a floatation device, yet, for some reason not approved by the United States Coast Guard.

Afterward, I went back to the room and freshened up. We had plans that night. There was some club or bar or something Kai maniacally insisted we had to go to. Seriously, he was being a freak about it, so both Ezra and I gave in. Plus, Kai threatened to poison us in our sleep.

I'd asked him, "Why poison? It seems like a hard way to kill someone. They could wake up and fight you off. If they're already asleep, why not just, like, whack 'em on the head or something?"

He didn't think it was funny, but Ezra did and my heart soared into my throat.

I wore my brown suede mini and a white embroidered tunic with my boots, letting my hair lay free down my back. Ever since Ezra had told me my hair was pretty, I couldn't help but look at it in a different light. Ezra was good for the self-esteem. I looked casual but not too casual. I dabbed vanilla at my pulse points, reapplied my lip gloss, and stepped out of the bathroom to an audience of none.

I heard voices outside and thought they might be Kai's and Ezra's so I paced to the door, checking the peephole to make sure it was them before I threw open the door. It was, but before I had time to open it, though, Ezra pushed through, shoving me back. I tripped on something imaginary, because that's what I do, I trip on nothing, and fell smack on my bum with an *oof*.

"Jeez! Run me over, why don't ya!"

"Sorry!" Ezra said, picking me up by the elbow and righting me. "What were you doing there anyway?"

"I was looking out the peephole. I heard voices but wanted to make sure it was you guys before I just went sprinting outside."

Kai came in after Ezra. "Were you *spying* on us?" he teased, trying to provoke me if his devious smile was any indication. It worked.

"I was not!" I protested.

"Oh, I think you were," he argued.

Ezra looked at me like he just noticed me, making me feel uneasy. "What?" I asked nervously. "Listen, I was not spying on you. I have no clue what you two were talking about." His eyes wandered over my face.

"Whatever, Mata Hari," Kai insisted.

"You take that back!" I exclaimed before asking Ezra behind a hand, "Who's Mata Hari?"

Ezra crossed his muscular arms, the rolled sleeves of his plaid button-up stretched to the point I thought they'd pop at the seams. He lifted a brow. "She was a femme fatale of sorts. Spied for the Germans in the first World War."

"Oh," was my very clever response.

Ezra's hands fell at his sides. "So?" he asked.

"So what?"

"Were you listening?" he said. Just came out and said it! That bastard!

My mouth dropped open at the accusation. I turned and pointed to Kai. "You are a troublemaker." Then I turned to Ezra. "I was *not* listening to you." I crossed my heart. "Scout's honor."

"Were you even a *Scout?*" Kai irked.

"Well, no, but I did play 'Scout' Jean Louise Finch in our seventh-grade production of *To Kill a Mockingbird*, and that counts."

"That doesn't count," Kai argued.

"It does so! She is Finch stock. She is *honest!*"

Ezra placed a palm on his face. "I feel like the judge at a Spencer Pratt lookalike contest."

"Who's winning?" I asked.

"Jupiter!" he complained.

"Sorry. Are we done here? Are we ready to go?"

"Yes, get in the car, Jupiter," Ezra said, shooing us out.

Kai opened the door and ran to the car like a little kid, bouncing up and down like an imbecile.

Ezra looked over at me, shrugging his shoulders in question. "What is up with you, Kai?" Ezra asked, suspicion lacing his tone.

"Nothing, okay? Let's just go."

"You better not have any shit on you."

"I don't. God! Ezra!" Kai complained. "Why you always gotta ruin everything?"

I laughed, opening my door for him. "Get in, Kai."

He bounded into the backseat and I followed, pushing my seat back and getting inside. "What is this place we're going to?" I asked Kai.

He sat at the edge of his seat, scooting forward and laying his chin on his hands on top of the front bench. "It's a magical place of cash only and karaoke."

CHAPTER TWELVE

Santa's Pub was a double-wide trailer surrounded by a twenty-year-old chain-link fence. It was a dive bar. There were giant and varying portraits of Santas painted on the face and sides.

"Kai," I deadpanned when we pulled into the packed parking lot. "This is a dive bar. In a trailer."

"She's quick," Kai said to Ezra, chucking his thumb my way.

"Is it even safe?" I asked.

Ezra looked around for a parking spot. "All I see are pickup trucks with gun racks here, Kai. Maybe this isn't such a good idea."

"No!" he yelled, startling us. "No, we have to go in here."

Ezra studied him. "Are you going to tell us what exactly we're doing here?" he asked.

"We're here to have a good time, baby," he answered, but Ezra didn't look convinced.

Ezra found a spot near an alley whose grass reached the bumper of his car.

"If I die out here, Kai—" I let the threat hang in the

air.

"Hmm," Kai said thoughtfully, his hand on his chin. "You would be the one to go first, though, for sure."

"Ugh! Why?" I asked, offended.

"First off, you're a virgin," he rightfully accused. I acted as if what he'd said was ridiculous, my mouth gaped in mock offense, but I was afraid I might have oversold it judging by the looks on Ezra's and Kai's faces. "If there are stairs, don't go up them. If there's a noise, don't say 'Let's see what it is!' and if you get lost, don't ask for directions. You know, just to be safe."

Ezra smiled as he exited the car. I gave Kai dagger eyes and his smile fell. "Strike two, Kai. Strike two."

"What was strike one?"

"The Mata Hari joke."

Kai started laughing, so I left him behind in the car. Ezra was waiting for me at the trunk. "If you aren't comfortable here, I can take us back to the room."

"Nah, it's okay. You know, though, your cousin is a pain sometimes."

Ezra smiled, offering his arm as we reached the bottom of the porch steps.

I reached out but hesitated. My breathing deepened as I met his eyes. They searched me for something but betrayed nothing themselves. He smiled. "Does this count as stairs?" he asked.

My face bloomed red hot. "Stop," I begged.

"Come now, Jupiter," he urged kindly.

My hand slipped under his arm. I felt my heart race with the intimacy of it, but I almost stopped when he reached his other hand across his chest to rest on the hand wrapped around his arm. It was there, then, his warm fingers over mine, that I felt slightly faint.

Altogether too quickly, his hand left mine and I controlled a violent urge to grab his hand again.

A rough voice rang over a speaker inside, along with the clattering of beer bottles and the laughter of the pub's patrons. Ezra opened the door for me, and I stepped inside. Everyone stopped what they were doing for a moment before continuing on. That brief moment they studied me, made me aware of myself, which made for an exceedingly uncomfortable Jupiter. I tugged at the hem of my skirt and smoothed my hair.

I felt Ezra bend closer to me. "There you go, fidgeting again." He smiled. "You look beautiful, Jupiter," he said quietly into my ear. My heart raced.

"Thank you," I whispered back.

He led me over to a table in the back, nearest the bar, and studied our surroundings.

"We should leave," he told me, his eyes resting on several inebriated-looking guys staggering near the bar who seemed to be focused on us the second we'd sat down together.

"Just ignore them," I told him cheerfully, though I felt a little more than uneasy at the attention. "Look," I said, pointing at the makeshift stage, "karaoke."

He smiled at me. "The perfect place to showcase your singing abilities."

"Is that a dig, Mr. Brandon?"

He fought a smile but didn't win. He coughed it away. "What do you mean?"

"You imply, sir," I teased, "that this establishment is appropriate for *me* to sing in. I didn't miss the underlying meaning."

He laughed. "You assume too much."

"I do not! You mean to say that my voice fits well with

114

this double-wide trailer. You mean to insult me."

He leaned back, his arms tucked over his stomach. "You, Jupiter Corey, read too much into the things I say. I just thought it would be a good place to showcase yourself. Your superior ability should be much appreciated here."

I laughed. "There you go again, you double entendre-er!"

He smiled sweetly. "As you well know," he joked, "that is not a word, but let's assume for a moment that it is, shall we? A double entendre certainly means a double meaning, but it usually also assumes the second, hidden meaning is vulgar in nature and therefore does not apply here."

"Oh," I said, blushing. The heat crept up my neck and into my ears and when it reached my cheeks, I couldn't fight it anymore. My hands reached up to cover my face in mortification.

I felt Ezra's warm fingers once more wrap around my skin but this time at my wrist. He softly tugged my hand away. "Don't cover your face, Jupiter. It's a pretty shade you're wearing anyway."

I let my hands fall to the tabletop, Ezra's hand still wrapped around my wrist. Instead of pulling away, his grip shifted so that his thumb rested over my pulse point. He pressed there while watching my eyes.

"Your heart is racing."

I swallowed nothing. "So it is," I said, trying to pull my arm away, but his hold only tightened.

"You're innocent," he told me matter-of-factly.

My blush deepened and I tried to look away, but his other hand caught my chin, forcing me to look at him.

"Don't be ashamed of that," he told me, his eyes and

mouth bled dry of any humor, and he surprised me with his tone. His expression sobered. "Don't ever be ashamed of that, ever. Don't let anyone belittle you for it either."

Again, I gulped nothing, but managed to nod. His fingers dropped from my face and hand. As if a flip had been switched, I was privy to melancholy Ezra once again. We sat strangely in a pool of noise, but our table held none of it.

Finally, when enough time had passed, I decided to stand. I walked over to the karaoke girl and asked for a book of songs. She gave me the binder and a piece of paper with pencil and I returned to the table.

"Any requests?" I asked him.

"Whatever you choose I suspect will be sufficient," he said, smiling.

I smiled back. "Sufficient for?"

"Take your pick. This establishment," he teased, which I appropriately acted appalled at. "My amusement," he continued.

I perused the list and chose a song, shielded my paper as I wrote down my choice, stood, and turned it in.

"What are you singing?" he asked.

"You'll see," I said as a waitress approached our table.

"What'll it be, young'ins?"

"Water for me, please," I told her.

"The same," Ezra said.

"Big spenders," she cheekily replied.

Ezra threw a look at the door. "Where in the world is Kai?" he asked.

I just noticed he hadn't come in yet. *What is wrong with me?* "Crap! I don't know."

A look passed over Ezra's face. "We're so stupid."

"Speak for yourself."

"He probably only picked this place because of that chick he's been talking to online."

"What chick?"

"He has these girls he talks to online." Ezra looked pensive for a moment. "I think he's got one here in Nashville. I bet she convinced him to meet her here. I bet that's what's up."

I shook my head in disbelief. "He is so sly."

"No kidding."

"Should we go out and get him? Leave?"

Ezra sat up in his chair. "Nah, let him do his thing. Let's give him a little bit."

"Fine with me," I said, glad to have Ezra all to myself, but immediately there was an awkward pause and I rethought my earlier sentiment. I was frightened he'd find me boring, not worth talking to. "So—" I sang.

"Jupiter Corey!" we heard over the speaker.

"Oh, thank God!" I exclaimed. Something fell over Ezra's face, something reminiscent of curiosity, like he wondered why I was so eager to leave him. I bit my lip. He looked as if I'd hurt his feelings.

"Excuse me," I told him, standing, and meandering through the crowd to the karaoke stage.

I felt someone's heat behind me, which made me slightly uneasy. I turned around only to find Ezra there.

"Wouldn't want to miss this," he told me, smiling.

I smiled back but didn't answer him and stepped on to the stage just as The Cure's "Just Like Heaven" intro began.

The crowd screamed and began to dance on the floor before me, making my blood race with adrenaline. Ezra stuck his hands in his front pockets and stood a few feet in front of me, wearing a smile he couldn't hide. *Good choice*, he mouthed, to which I smiled then began the song which earned me another set of screams.

It started out great. I was having a blast, faking a British accent, and making Ezra laugh, but then something unexpected happened. Ezra's face turned from carefree to something altogether confusing, a look I couldn't decipher. Languidly his smile fell only to be replaced with a seriousness that made my skin crackle, my stomach plummet. I'd forgotten the poetry of the song's lyrics as they rippled around the two of us, flirting with unspoken words, unclaimed feelings, unuttered thoughts. Suddenly it was only the two of us as I promised to run away, run away with him.

But just as quickly as the room had fallen away from us, it came crashing back in whoops and hollers and cackled laughing, and the tender moment dissolved.

"Some idiot's doing donuts in the parking lot!" a guy yelled.

Both Ezra and I turned from him toward each other. "Kai," we said in unison and made for the door, stopping short on the deck, to see that, indeed, Kai was doing fast donuts over and over and over, hanging out of the driver's side window yelling, "I've been catfished! I've been catfished!"

A rotund woman hung out of the passenger window screaming, "Slow down, turbo!" But the "turbo" was drawn out in a thick, ridiculous accent. "Slow down, tuuuurboooow!"

"Kai! Stop!" I yelled as Ezra ran down the steps toward them, the tires squealing and the smell of burnt rubber hanging in the air.

"Ezra, no!" I shouted. "You'll get hit!"

But Ezra didn't listen. Instead, he went barreling into the ridiculous fray, a look of pure determination on his face.

When Kai saw Ezra approach, the color drained from his face as he tried to explain himself in sections as the loops of his donuts brought him closer to his cousin. "She's...not...a...she... She's...a...he!...I've...been... catfished!

"Slow down, turbo!"

"Oh for crying out loud, Kai. Stop the bleedin' car!" Ezra ordered.

I ran down the stairs and stopped near Ezra. "Kai, stop!"

A blur of "turbo" and "catfish" filled the night air around us as we continually yelled for him to stop.

"Santa's calling the cops!" someone yelled.

Adrenaline shot through my body. "Kai, gosh dang it! Stop! Right now!"

"That's it," Ezra said, running alongside the driver's side. He reached out, yanked open the door, and leaned in as the car spun. I started to panic, worried that if he fell, he'd be dragged beneath.

The car continued in circles, though slower, as Kai and Ezra got into a fist fight, Ezra running alongside the car and Kai belted into it. The entire scene was utterly ridiculous.

My hands went to my face, trying to think. I looked around and noticed a water hose near the side of the trailer. I ran to it and put the water on full blast, turning it onto the three idiots screaming and fighting among the squealing of tires, soaking them through. The car came to a sudden halt. It worked.

I stomped toward the boys, pushed Ezra off a bloody-nosed Kai, leaned into the car, threw it into park, and removed the keys without saying a word. They watched as I walked around the front and opened the other door to a gape-mouthed, wide-eyed passenger.

"Excuse me," I told Kai's catfisher, "but you're in my seat."

Kai's catfishing love interest stumbled out of the car. "You guys be crazy! Crazy!" And then ran off into the night.

I sat down in the soaked seat, one boot in the car, one resting on the lot itself. "Kai, please remove yourself from the driver's seat and pile into the back."

He had the decency to look embarrassed and obeyed without argument. Ezra sat down and closed his door. I silently handed him his keys and he started his engine.

Joyous claps came from the deck of Santa's Pub. "I give you a ten, baby!" a drunk boy yelled.

I gasped, turned toward Ezra, and pointed toward the deck. "A double entendre!"

He closed his eyes, two fingers pinching the bridge of his nose.

CHATPER THIRTEEN

Needless to say, the car ride back to the room was silent at first. We were all ready to burst, it seemed. Kai leaned his head on the back of the seat, his nose raised, his T-shirt pressed to his face to stop the bleeding. Ezra's knuckles strained white against the steering wheel, his jaw clenched in obvious anger. He was seething. I had to admit, I was more than a little pissed myself. Kai had ruined my moment with Ezra. Ruined it!

I flipped around toward Kai. "Listen up, buttercup," I told him. He snorted and shifted in his seat. "Obviously you're a few fries short of a Happy Meal, so I'm only going to ask one question."

"What?" he bit out.

"What is wrong with you?"

"Listen, I'd been talking online to this chick for six months—"

"Kai!" Ezra chimed in. "We don't care who that was. *I* don't care! Look at my car now! It's soaked!"

Iehgliuhelelhghg! (That was my actual thought.) "Seriously? That's what you focus on?" I asked Ezra.

"Look at this!" Ezra said, gesturing to the wet

upholstery and leather.

"Listen, I did what I had to do!" I yelled.

"It was a little extreme," he countered.

I scoffed. "A little extreme? A *little* extreme? Were you even there? You were running alongside a circling car, Ezra, battling your cousin, with a giant hanging out the passenger side screaming at Kai to 'Slow down, turbo!'"

Kai started laughing.

"Shut up!" Ezra and I yelled at him.

Ezra turned back to me. "I had it under control, *Jupiter*!"

"You didn't, *Ezra*!"

"I did too! He was starting to lag."

"I was not," Kai chimed in.

"Shut *up*!" Ezra and I both yelled again.

I took a deep breath. "Ezra, I was desperate. The cops were coming. I didn't think it would be wise for us to be under police supervision. Who knows what Kai would admit to?"

"*Hey!*" Kai said, offended.

"No offense, Kai," I said.

"Nah, you're right," he admitted.

"Ezra." I sighed. "I'm sorry, but I was desperate."

Ezra blew out a heavy breath, causing his hair to fly up briefly. He looked down at himself then over at Kai and me. "I'm sorry. I'm ju-just frustrated, I guess."

I raised a brow at him. "Let's just get back to the room. I just want this night to end."

Ezra drove us back to the motel, and we all barreled into the room. He went straight toward the bathroom and grabbed all the towels he could find.

"Call down to room service for more," he told us.

"Here, let me help," I said, and reached out.

"Don't worry about it. I saw a car wash with a wet-vac down the road. I'm going to vacuum all the water out. These are just for the leather."

"Let me go with you then."

"Whatever," he said, walking toward the door. He opened it, but stopped short and turned back toward Kai. "Your phone?" he asked, laying out his hand.

"No way," Kai said.

"Uh, yes way," Ezra mocked. "I have to leave here and I don't want you to have access to all your vices, you strange, strange weirdo." Kai laughed and handed over his phone. "Try to stay out of trouble."

"Same goes," he said as Ezra glided through the open door.

I followed him but yelped when Kai popped me on the butt. "Have a good time," he said with a wink.

I rubbed the welt. "Stop!" I whisper-yelled.

He started making kissing noises.

"Stop!" I yelled, glancing over my shoulder. "He'll hear you."

"Oh, Ezra," he wailed. "I love you, Ezra."

"Oh my God, I am going to kill you."

He laughed and followed me toward the door. I shut it on him before he could potentially ruin all my chances with Ezra, but he grabbed the handle and tried to open the door. I gasped, holding it closed with a boot on the wall, making Kai laugh harder. We struggled like that for at least ten seconds before I heard, "You comin' or not?"

I let go and Kai fell on his backside. It was my turn to laugh. "Sucker!" I threw over my shoulder before popping over the fence near the sidewalk outside our door, but I didn't quite make it over and ended up tripping over the top rail, landing on my hands and skinning my knees.

I laid on the blacktop trying to decide whether I wanted to go ahead and die of embarrassment there or try to play off my clumsiness with a giggle or something equally feminine. You know, a distraction.

"Dude, are you all right?" Ezra asked, offering a hand. I took it and he lifted me.

I stood tall even though my skin was screaming at me to cry. *Distract him with your feminine wiles!* Instead of the cute, whimsical giggle I'd intended, a garbled, strangled noise came out in its place. Ezra looked at me like I was nuts.

I cleared my throat. "Yeah, man, you know, I'm cool or whatever."

"Okay," he sang, obviously not believing me but choosing to give me whatever dignity I had left.

He released my arm and walked me to my side of the car, opening the door for me. I got in and sat down, buckling in. My boots squished in the water, mortifying me. When Ezra got in, water splashed everywhere, catapulting me down an embarrassment spiral.

"Oh my God," I exclaimed. "You probably regret so hard letting me on this trip." I fought the burning tears welling in my eyes.

Ezra started the car, putting it in reverse. He threw his arm over the back of my seat and turned to see if he was clear to back up. He stared at me, his eyes searching every inch of my face. It burned the skin there, heated it to the consistency of warm syrup, drugging me.

"Not even a little bit," he said, his own face devoid of any emotion, confusing me. He put the car into drive and pressed the gas.

We took off toward the car wash, my heart beating a

million thu-thumps a minute. We were quiet the entire ride, not even the radio to fill the silence. It was if he wanted to feel the tension that lay between us, with nothing to distract him. Every single weighted instant. I felt it. It was heady, heavy, alarming, but mostly it was torturous. A good torture, though.

We pulled in next to the wet-vac at the car wash and both got out. Ezra met me at my side.

"Why don't you ever wait?" he asked, reaching into his pocket for a few quarters.

"Wait for what?" I asked, a bit disoriented from the car ride, from the proximity.

"For me to open the door for you," he said, shoving in the quarters.

The machine bolted to life before I had a chance to answer. He looked at me a moment before ripping down the hose and leaning into the car. I walked to the other side, grabbed the hotel towels from the backseat, and set them on top of the car. I removed one and began wiping down the seats. We worked methodically, carefully avoiding one another, mindful that our hands never touched. Together we were a Molotov cocktail. A single brush would ignite us, I was sure of it, and who knew what the consequences would be?

I thought back to Ezra's touching my leg and foot at the beginning of our trip, thought back to the heat that pooled in my stomach when his fingers unzipped my boot. I stopped wiping altogether at the memory, stuck in that moment, it seemed.

Ezra noticed. "You okay?" his deep voice asked.

I shook my head to clear it. "Uh, yeah. Sorry," I said, moving the towel to the top of the seat.

The vacuum died and the silence was deafening.

"If you're tired," he practically whispered, "take a break, Jupiter."

"I'm not tired," I told him as I continued with the work.

Forty-five minutes later, we'd gotten about as much water as you could get out of the seats and off the floorboards. I stood and started folding all the wet towels on the hood of the car. Ezra came around, his keys jingling off one of the loops on his jeans, and helped me. When we were done, he tossed them on top of a plastic bag in the backseat. He stuck his keys in the ignition and turned on one of his playlists, then left the doors open.

"Let's let it air out for a few minutes," he said.

He sat on the hood, scooting back until he laid on the windshield, tucking his hands behind his head. I studied him there. His muscular legs strained against his jeans. He'd removed his button-up, leaving a graphic tee underneath.

"Come up here," he said as a small smile stretched across his beautiful mouth.

I rolled my eyes. "Fine."

I lifted myself up onto the hood next to Ezra, lying back against the windshield as well, and crossed my boots at the ankles.

"I dig those," he told the fluorescents above us.

"Dig what?"

"Your boots, dork."

"They were my mama's." I lifted one up for a second before dropping it back down. "They're comfortable as heck."

We were quiet for two songs.

"Christmas break," he began. His chest steadily rose and fell with each deep breath. "Our junior year." This was it. This was what I'd been waiting for. *The accident.* "Jessica and I were supposed to go to that party at Brian Fox's house. Remember it?"

"Vaguely."

"Did you go?" he asked.

I turned toward him. "I didn't exactly run in the same crowd, Ezra."

He nodded. "Lucky," he whispered. Another deep breath. "So we were supposed to go. Jessica was hyped." Since he was so much taller he was a bit higher on the windshield than I was and had to look down at me. "I went to parties, Jupiter, but I didn't exactly get anything out of them. To me it was just a bunch of idiots gathered up into a shared space vying for attention. Alcohol flowed freely. Drugs too. Always. I woke up that morning and right off the bat got into a huge fight with my mom over something. I can't even remember what. I left in my truck, deciding to head to Jessica's, you know, get out of my mom's hair, but she wasn't there. I texted her but she'd gone to the mall to get something to wear for that night."

"Like, oh my God, the mall?" I teased.

Ezra laughed. "Shut up. Listen."

"I am."

"So I went back home and my mom was pissed I'd left without telling her and for not picking up my phone. She'd been looking for me because she'd needed me to pick up my grandparents from the airport since they were coming in for Christmas. She had to send my brother instead. She was angry 'cause she felt I should have gone since he should have been studying for a final.

"Basically, she told me I couldn't go out that night, not only because I'd failed to pick up my phone, but also because her mom and dad were in town and she wanted the family together."

"But you didn't stay."

Ezra stared at me for a moment. "No, I didn't," he said quietly before continuing. "My mom and dad left with my grandparents to pick up dinner, and I was supposed stay put and wait for them. I was lounging on the couch when Jessica called."

"Uh-oh."

"Yeah, she was pissed. I told her she'd have to go by herself. She started yelling about how much time she'd taken to get ready and how much she'd spent to look good for the party and all this shit and that I better get my ass over to her house or she and I were through and all this crap. I was pretty angry at her threats but said I'd meet her there.

"She told me to be at the party at nine 'cause she didn't want to walk in by herself. I told her that would be cool and hung up. My parents and grandparents got home soon after that, so we all sat down and ate, talking and laughing. Time passed by so quickly I didn't realize nine had flown by. It wasn't until close to eleven that I realized how late I was. My grandparents and parents had just gone to bed, so I decided to sneak out and come back before they woke.

"I called Jessica a bunch of times, but she didn't pick up. I knew she was probably fuming, so I decided to head over there. When I got there, nobody would make eye contact with me. It was fecking weird. I caught sight of Brian in his kitchen and went over to him. I asked what was up, but he played off the question. I couldn't figure out what was wrong with everyone but chalked it up to their having been drinking the whole night.

"I searched the house for Jessica but didn't find her anywhere the general party was." He breathed deeply. "I decided to check upstairs." He looked down at me again. "Jess liked to smoke a little pot sometimes, and I figured she was holed up in some room with a couple of her girls." My stomach clenched. "She was holed up in some room, all right, but it wasn't with her girlfriends." I swallowed down the uncomfortable knot in my throat.

"Who was she with?" I whispered.

"Patrick Cooper."

Oh shit. Patrick Cooper played lacrosse with Ezra.

"I'm so sorry," I told him.

"They tried to cover themselves up, but they were so buzzed they failed. In so many words, I felt sick to my stomach. I fled the room, down the stairs, and through the party. Everyone avoided eye contact, and that's when I discovered they knew, but they hadn't said anything."

"A double betrayal."

"Yes," his voice said, seemingly far away. "I ran out of the house and vomited into the grass outside near a bunch of sophomores, but they just laughed at me, like I wasn't human, like I wasn't a *human being*.

"Jupiter," he said, my name hanging in the air around us. The way he said it made me feel closer to him than I'd ever felt before.

"Yes?"

"I left. Jumped into my truck, not bothering with my seatbelt, and tore out of there. I'd been in love with her. I really loved her."

"I know."

This surprised him. "You knew?"

"Yes."

"How could you know?"

"There were little things I noticed that probably wouldn't translate to anyone else watching."

"Like what?"

"Well, you used to, like, cull her into your body whenever you walked down a crowded hall, to protect her. You were hyperaware of her. One time I saw your head shoot up in class and I wondered what it was you'd heard. I followed your gaze and there she was." Ezra narrowed his eyes at me as if he was trying to figure me out. "Anyway," I continued, clearing my throat, "keep going."

Ezra swallowed hard. In preparation for the rest of the story, I thought, but I wasn't sure. The way he'd watched me while he did it made me curious.

"I was driving too fast down Salem and hit that curve near the ravine. You know it?"

"I do."

"I lost control and hit a large tree at the bottom of the ravine head-on. The engine was pushed into the cab, shattering both my legs in fifteen different places. I blacked out."

My hands went to my mouth. I remembered the news articles.

"They didn't find you for nearly twelve hours."

"That's right."

"Because no one knew you were missing."

"That's right."

"No one at the party called to check on you."

"Again, right."

"Your family was asleep."

"That's right."

"And because it took them so long to find you, you were in a coma for three days."

He nodded.

"And when you woke?"

"My parents were there. My siblings. My grandparents, but no one else."

"I think I get it now," I told him.

A deep, rumbling, sarcastic laugh crackled through his chest. "Do you?"

"Yes." I paused. "And Ezra?"

"Yeah?" he said, moving his hands to rest on his chest.

"If I'd been there, I would've checked on you."

Ezra took three deep breaths. "I know."

CHAPTER FOURTEEN

The next morning we were heading to Chicago. As if I wasn't nervous enough around Ezra, I had to come to terms with meeting his extended family. Ezra and I hadn't gotten back to the room until well after midnight. We'd found Kai asleep, so we did the same. Well, at least Ezra did, I think. I stayed up until two in the morning replaying everything Ezra had told me over and over, then fantasizing that our conversation had ended differently than just sliding off the hood and getting in the car. Instead, I imagined Ezra taking my hand and holding it. That's all I wanted to do. Just hold his hand.

Needless to say, waking up at six to get ready was kind of a drag. Me no likey four hours sleep.

I whined when Ezra leaned over me and nudged my shoulder. "Leave me here," I said and rolled over, tucking the pillow over my head.

"Get up, Jupiter," his soft voice uttered.

"Five more minutes, Mom."

"More like Daddy," he teased.

I laughed into the mattress. "Ezra, you're a dirty old man," my muffled voice told him.

I pulled the pillow down so only one eye showed.

"Get up, please," he said, sitting on the edge of the bed. The mattress sank a little and I slid into his side. The heat of his body made my heart race.

"Turn around," I ordered.

Ezra laughed. "What? Why? You're fully dressed. I saw you climb into bed last night."

My face grew warm, and I hoped he couldn't see my blush. "I-I know, but, uh, I don't want you to see me."

Ezra's face sobered. "Why?"

My face grew impossibly hot. "Because, I, uh, my hair probably looks crazy and I don't have makeup on."

Ezra pitched over me. He brought his face close to mine and searched my eyes. "What would you care if I saw you that way?" his deep voice asked. His question spilled over me, syrupy sweet and stunning.

I swallowed hard. *Oh, dear God. How to answer this question.* "Only, well, it's a little embarrassing."

Ezra sat up, gave me a coy smile, and said, "More embarrassing than falling on your face?"

That face grew so hot, I thought it would melt off. "Oy vey!"

I bolted up and hit him upside his head with the pillow I'd been holding. I drew back to hit him again but he maneuvered away quickly, yanking the pillow away with one swift movement. I grabbed its mate and swung at him. He ducked, so I missed, then he came up and knocked me in the side. We sparred back and forth, jumping from bed to bed.

Kai walked through the door as I was yelling I was going to annihilate Ezra, and we both dropped our pillows, standing on the beds like idiots.

"Oh, hello, Kai," I said, winded. I ran my hands over

my insane hair and stepped off the bed.

I calmly walked toward the bathroom, both boys watching me. Kai's expression looked knowing, and he winked at me. I ran my thumb across my throat in warning. I grabbed my bag and made my way to the bathroom to shower. I closed the door and looked at myself in the mirror. My hair stuck out at wild angles, of course, my cheeks were flush from the effort of our pillow fight, and my eyes as round as saucers. I looked like a giant Blythe doll someone had left under the bed for two years and forgotten about.

I ran the water and hit the shower, getting ready quickly and analyzing what had just happened between Ezra and me. Was it flirting? Or was it friends messing around? Was it friends flirting, but innocently? What was it?

When breakfast was over, we loaded up the trunk.

"Kai, I need you to drive," Ezra told his cousin, surprising me.

"Yes!" was Kai's immediate reaction.

"I'm only letting you drive because my legs ache from yesterday's fiasco and, frankly, I'm too tired."

Ezra tossed his keys at Kai and we all piled in, with Ezra in the back this time. Kai maneuvered us out onto 65 toward Louisville, Kentucky. I'd called my sister after breakfast and needed to text Frank.

Loser, I wrote.

Yes

What are you doing?

Waiting with baited breath for your text, of course. My whole life revolves around you

Shut up lol and it's bated not baited

Thank you Miss Mirriam-Webster you

gigantic nerd you

You're welcome

So did you kiss him

Jeez louise Frankie! Stop!

Pause.

Is pillow fighting considered flirting, I asked.

Does Carrot Top need to lay off the eyebrow waxing?

Stop, I'm being serious

Me too. It's too much. He overarches

I fought him with a pillow

Carrot Top!?

Lord help me with you, Frank

Okay, I'm serious now. were they feather?

I sighed. **I don't remember what does it matter**

Feather pillows weigh more and they land harder

Okay so?

I was just curious

Yeah but why?

Making conversation

I groaned. **One of these days, Frankie! One of these days!**

The truth is i don't know Jup I wasn't there so I didn't see what does your gut tell you?

It says "stop eating hamburgers, Jupiter, I can't take it anymore"

Nice. And what does it say to you about Ezra?

It says "that boy is whiplash personified" one minute I feel like he digs me but the next I feel like he barely notices me

Guys are strange, buttercup. If it isn't obvious to you, Jupiter, then maybe...

Maybe?

Maybe it's time to, you know, get over the high school crush thing

I felt my stomach plummet. Was she right? Frank, in all her surface idiocy, was usually pretty spot on when it came to boys, to many things, actually. I couldn't be friends with someone who didn't have depth. She had a sort of no-nonsense approach to boys. She'd always say if they were into you, their actions would let you know, and if they weren't? Again, their actions let you know. She didn't wait around, never pined, and she didn't tolerate boys who kept her hooked. If they didn't dedicate themselves, she cut the line. I'd always admired that about her, and she always encouraged that mentality in me.

"Letting a boy drag you along does nothing for *you*, which is the point, isn't it? It kills self-esteem and self-worth. If they don't bow at your feet, kick 'em to the curb, baby," she said time and time again to me.

I didn't respond to her. Better to put it off until later. Why resolve things in the moment when you can wait? That was my motto. *Wait until your problems compound and then rashly solve them.* It always works. Mostly. Well, sometimes it works. Actually, it never works. *Huh.*

While I procrastinated addressing my issues with procrastination, I was drawn toward the cars we were speeding by, a cartoonish zipping sound enveloping the cab.

"Scooby flipping Doo, Kai!"

"What?" he asked, smiling.

"Slow down!"

"Can't. Life in the fast lane."

I turned around and addressed Ezra. "Ezra, you're

136

okay with this speed?"

Ezra smirked and shrugged. "I know it sounds crazy, but Kai is a better driver when he speeds than when he doesn't. He's never once had an accident."

My hand went to the dash and I yelped as we narrowly swung around a slower driver. "Kai!"

"Listen, if you're too scared, you're welcome to sit in the back with Ezra. I'm sure he'll protect you."

My face flushed. Both Ezra and I gave Kai looks to kill, but all he did was laugh in response. I wished I had the ability to strike *real* fear over people. I'd seen Frankie do it at least a hundred times, but I could never quite accomplish the task.

"Just ignore him," Ezra told me. "He's an idiot."

Why? I thought, *because you don't want me back there? Or because you don't want me to feel uncomfortable? Why?!*

Kai whipped so closely around a man driving a pickup I could actually see individual hairs in the driver's stubble.

"Gah!" I screamed, as a very fitting "Ob-La-Di, Ob-La-Da" played through Ezra's speakers. "He had spinach for lunch!" Without thinking, I unbuckled my belt and tossed myself over the bench into the back with Ezra.

Ezra looked terrified. "What are you doing?"

I didn't answer him. Instead, I situated myself behind Kai and with trembling hands tried to buckle myself in. Third time's the charm, it hit home, and I cinched it tight. I look wildly at my right only to notice Ezra laughing at me.

"This isn't funny!"

"I beg to differ; it is just that."

I bit my lip to keep it from noticeably trembling. Ezra's

eyes flicked toward my mouth before his expression softened. "Aww, I'm sorry, Jupiter, but——" he said before his body slid hard into mine with an audible "umph" then back toward his side of the car, "he really is not a bad driver, as strange as that may seem." He said all this while casually holding his body stiff against the back of his seat to keep from sliding back and forth with each rapid jerk of the car. "Try to relax."

Deadpan was the look Ezra received. Dead *by* a pan was the punch I wanted to give Kai. And dead *in* a pan was what I would be when he finally crashed and we were all flattened like its namesake's cakes.

"Just wait 'til we get outside the city; it'll seem normal then," Kai offered.

"Oh my God!" I screamed. "The shoulder is not a turning lane, Kai!"

"It is in my world," he explained, one hand perched on the steering wheel as if he was on a leisurely stroll.

For fifteen minutes, we swerved in and out of lanes, round and around traffic, leaving their honking behind us in a blur of furious sound. My hands found the back of the front bench seat and stayed there the entire time. Occasionally I'd let out a small whimper of incredulity, making Ezra smile.

Eventually we found ourselves on the outskirts of the city and stuck between a staunch bit of forest flanking both sides of the highway. Apparently it was a soothing enough sight that it lulled me into a false sense of security. Not without incredible fight, trust me, I found myself drifting off, my forehead finally resting on the seat ahead of me, and that's the last thing I remembered.

Adrenaline is a sporty punk. She'll wear you down. I

had no fear of becoming a junkie. No, ma'am.

CHAPTER FIFTEEN

I was asleep. No, I was awake, but recently asleep, and I was in Ezra's car. I was awake, but recently asleep, and in Ezra's car, but I was in *the backseat?* I was awake, but recently asleep, in Ezra's car, in the backseat, and snuggled up against something hard and warm, Ezra's blanket around my shoulders. It smelled exactly like him, so I took a deep breath.

"Peter, you let me in? Even after that *one* thing?" I asked heaven.

"What one thing?"

"Gah!" I yelled, bolting upright, hitting the top of my head on the car's ceiling. I rubbed my newly forming bump. "Heh, heh. Uh, thanks for letting me sleep on *that,*" I said, gesturing to his chest with wild hand movements.

Ezra smiled at me and my heart fell into my stomach.

"So, are you guys, like, together or something?" we heard from the front seat.

We both turned to find a girl, maybe twenty-one, long brown hair, prettiest skin you'd ever seen on a person. A beautiful smile as wide as the Nile. I liked her

140

immediately.

"What? *No*," Ezra answered quickly, his words punching me in the gut.

"Cool," she said, eyeing Ezra as I would a cheeseburger.

An odd feeling struck me in the chest and gut and inexplicably I discovered that, in fact, I didn't like her at all. She seemed perfectly lovely, yet I didn't want her in the car with us. I wanted her as far away from us as possible. She with her mature face. She with that chic, iron-straight hair. She with that flawless skin. Ugh. I was suddenly aware of my intense jealousy. I'd been jealous before. I'm not an idiot. I knew the feeling, but this time it was so intense, it felt almost foreign to me.

I shook my head to clear it. "Excuse me, but *who are you?*"

She smiled and stuck out a sun-kissed, manicured hand. "Hi, I'm Ruby."

Reluctantly, I took it. "Jupiter."

Ezra leaned forward. "How—" he began, but she anticipated his question and threw a shoulder toward Kai. "I was thumbing it up north. Kai let me tag along."

Kai turned toward me, smiled and winked.

"You're a drifter!" I turned toward Ezra, my eyes wide. In a move I could only explain away as a temporary loss of insanity due to the stress of the situation, I channeled my apparent inner Oscar Wilde. "Dare I say, she could be a vagabond, Ezra!" I whisper-yelled.

"A *vagabond*, say you?" he teased with a grin that sank me back into my seat, a little hurt he was making fun of me. I know I sounded ridiculous. I didn't need the reminder, though.

"You seem cool," Ezra began, my heart racing, "but what Kai may not have told you is this is my car and I'm not comfortable with hitchhikers."

I sighed in relief and Ruby noticed. Her eyes narrowed at me so quickly I wasn't sure if she'd actually done it. She leaned toward Ezra. "I get it. I don't want to be *that* girl." She smiled a disarming grin, one made to devastate boys, and she knew it. "Just drop me off at the next exit?"

The boys lost their sanity for a moment as they ogled her face like morons.

"I've been driving with her for two hours while you slept," Kai explained, "she's fine."

Ezra sighed. "I guess."

You guess?

I frantically looked around me.

"What are you doing?" Ezra asked.

"Looking for the cameras." I patted my body. "Let's see, I'm the virgin in this scenario, that's painfully obvious. Kai's the moron that ruins any plot progress."

"Come on," Kai yelled, offended.

I turned to Ezra, his brow raised, suggesting a "bring it." "And you're the hot douche who sleeps with the killer and doesn't find out until you're in the throes of passion and she whips out a hatchet."

Ezra burst out laughing then shook his head. "You're an idiot."

"*I'm* the idiot?" I whispered.

"Who's the killer?" Ruby asked.

"Uh, you, obviously." I looked each passenger in the eye. "Everyone clear on their roles? Good. Break!" I said, clapping my hands.

For twenty minutes the femme stranger charmed the

boys by recounting borderline inappropriate, if you ask me, stories of her getting stuck in compromising situations. And surprise! She somehow lost an integral piece of clothing in each story! *Ugh! Gag me with a spoon.*

When we pulled into a gas station, I launched myself over the bench and pushed Kai out of the driver's seat so I could get out of the car. I wasn't gonna be the last person in there with her. The virgin is always the first to go. I barreled my way around two vacationing families and their gargantuan vans and bolted for the convenience store door. I was a woman on a mission.

I picked up a few things. "Funyuns, check. Twizzlers, check. Kit Kat, check." I jogged over to the refrigerators and grabbed a Mountain Dew, 'cause I'm classy like that, then headed toward the register. Just as I set my stuff on the counter, the door opened and in walked Ruby, followed by Ezra. He'd held the door for her. My stomach fell to the floor. I *was* the idiot.

"Be right back," the clerk told me and ran off to do something.

I listened as Ruby and Ezra, joined by Kai, meandered around the store. By the time the clerk returned to the front, they stood in line behind me.

"Oh my God, Jupiter!" Kai said, pointing at a trucker hat.

It read *Beam me up, Scotty.*

I rolled my eyes. "Hilarious."

"Is that funny?" Ruby asked him.

"Yeah, 'cause Jupiter's family are conspiracy theorists. They *believe*," Kai explained.

"Oh," Ruby commented, sarcastically, "that explains the name."

My face flamed hot, but I held my head high as if it

didn't bother me. Fake it 'til you make it, baby.

"That'll be seven thirty-seven," the clerk said.

"I don't know how you can eat all that," Ruby said, artificial saccharine oozing from every syllable. "I'd be as big as a house in no time at all." She laughed.

My face grew even hotter. When I get embarrassed, I get a little brazen. It's a flaw. I know, can you believe it? I have flaws. "You know what," I told the clerk, "throw this in there," I said, tossing a pack of Twinkies on the counter with the rest. "And this too," I said, picking up the trucker hat.

I paid for my crap and turned around, reached into my bag, and grabbed the Twinkies and the cap. I tossed the hat on my head as confidently as possible, fitting it snugly, and while staring at them from underneath the brim, unwrapped a Twinkie and took a gulping bite out of it.

"Mmm, good," I mumbled around a full mouth.

I took a deep, cavalier breath, overconfident in my badassery, but I guess my bite was too big. I began to choke. Coughing, I grabbed the countertop to steady myself, but the blockage wouldn't clear. I was starting to panic. I couldn't breathe! All three stared at me with wide, concerned eyes. I slapped my hands on the countertop several times, attempting to gain control over the situation.

"Jupiter?" Ezra asked, stepping forward.

Coughing like an idiot, I held up a finger for him to stay where he was. He obeyed. Eventually I caught a breath, swallowed whatever I had left of my bite, and with ragged pants, stood upright.

I looked down at Ruby's hands. Kale chips, a banana, and a bottle of water.

"Oh for Pete's sake!" I yelled. *I sound like James Earl Jones. Great.* A hand went to Ezra's mouth to keep from laughing. "See you in the car," I crooned.

Dejected, I stood by the car door because I didn't have the keys, and I refused to go back inside to get them.

I tested out my new rough voice. "Uh." I cleared my throat. "Uh, hello. Hello, hello. Jeez, I sound like a radio DJ or something." Two fingers went to an ear. "Jessie J comin' at ya! You're listening to ninety-seven-seven, all the hits from the seventies, eighties, and nineties! This segment brought to you by Preparation H. 'Relax. Your relief is waiting.'"

"Uh, Jupiter?"

I jumped and a hand flew to my chest. I turned around, tried to act cool and casual, leaning an arm against the car. "Oh, hey, Ezra! What's up, bro?"

He stuck his keys in his door and swung it wide for me. I climbed in and sat in the back, tucking my hat as far over my face as possible. Ezra got in and sat beside me, which surprised me.

"What was all that in there?" he asked.

"What was what?" I asked.

"What prompted chokageddon?"

"I don't like her."

Ezra pretended to act shocked. "No!"

I fought a smile.

"You just don't know her," he said.

"Neither do you, jackass. We literally woke up three hours ago with her in the car. And Ezra, how come every single one of her stories somehow ended with her without her shirt, or bra, or panties? I mean, come on, man!" I sat up and stuck out my chest, looping the end of my hair over and over. "Like, oh my gosh! Like, I don't know how, but my shirt was just gone! My panties were just gone! Can you *believe* it?" I fake giggled. "And Twinkies? How do you eat those? Me? Why only kale chips for me, of course. I'm not a lard ass like you, Jupiter."

Ezra smiled at me in obvious pity.

"Don't look at me like that."

He laughed. "Like what?"

"Like I'm just some silly female who has jealousy issues!"

Ezra shrugged his shoulders. "*Well?*"

"*Oh!* Oh my gosh. My *gosh*, Ezra."

"What, *Jupiter?*" he teased. "She seems fine. I think it's just you."

"Have you lost your mind? She's a stranger! Didn't your folks ever warn you of stranger danger?"

"I'm not ten anymore," Ezra explained.

I took in his broad shoulders and hands. *No, that you are not*, I thought.

"Fine. Whatever. It's your car. I'm just along for the ride," I huffed, crossing my arms and burying myself deeper into my seat. "I'll just be over here with common sense, my only friend, it seems."

I rested my knees on the back of the bench and pulled the bill of my ridiculous trucker hat down, but then remembered what it said and ripped it off, tossing it at my feet. Ezra leaned over and picked it up, dusting off little pieces of grass from the floorboard that had attached itself to the top.

Ezra placed the hat on his head and turned toward the window, mumbling something.

"What?" I asked, pissed.

He turned toward me but didn't say anything.

146

Eventually the heat of his gaze ate through my resolve and I looked into his eyes.

"You're not just along for the ride, Jupiter, and you know it," he said, pinning me with his stare and making my heart pound.

Wisely I said nothing, and not just because all the moisture had left my mouth. There wasn't a response I could think of that would have thrown me out of the buffoon stage in which I was so deeply entrenched. I felt suddenly immature. I knew I was jealous. I'd always thought I was above such impulses, but I wasn't. I really wasn't. *Must change that. Grow as a person, Jupiter. Grow.*

"Sorry," I whispered.

"Don't ever be sorry for being you, Jupiter."

"I'm not. I'm just sorry for not giving her a proper chance. You're right. I'll just chill."

He smiled, removed the cap from his head, and stuck it back on mine.

Kai and Ruby started walking back toward the car. Kai stuck his head through the open driver's window. "You okay there, Mama Cass?"

I laughed. "Shut up and drive."

They both got in and buckled up.

We set out on the road, and I was on a mission to be cool to Ruby.

"So, Ruby, where did you grow up?" I asked.

"In Cincinnati," she replied without turning around.

"That's cool," Ezra said. "I've never been to Cincinnati."

She turned around with a large, bright smile on her face. "You should! You and Kai should come visit me when you're on break, you know, when I get back that way. I'll take you all around. Show you the sights," she offered.

I bit my lip. *You should come too, Jupiter! I would love to show you around as well!*

"That'd be nice," Kai replied, smiling at Ruby as if she hung the moon.

Thank the Lord, Ezra didn't say anything.

Ruby looked ahead of her at a passing sign.

"You know what might be fun?" she asked.

Ritual sacrifice? I thought.

"There's this little swimming hole with a ten-foot waterfall about half an hour east of here. Not a whole lot of people know about it. If you're game, we could make a little detour and check it out?"

I began to panic a little. I was eager to get to Chicago, to settle in somewhere, even if it was only for a few days. And, to be honest, to get rid of Ruby and her mysteriously disappearing clothes.

"I'm down if you are," Kai said, looking back at Ezra.

"Sounds fun," Ezra chimed in, disappointing me. He turned my way. "What about you?" he asked.

I took a deep breath to control my anxiety. "Uh, yeah, that's fine," I answered, trying for breezy, but failing miserably if Ezra's furrowed brow was any indication.

"It's only a few exits up, Kai," Ruby told him.

We drove half an hour away from the interstate toward this supposed waterfall then turned onto a winding, admittedly gorgeous, pebbled drive past a sign that read Muscatatuck Park. Our tires crunched against the rock. The trees still held their summer leaves, green and rich and utterly different from Florida. They canopied over the drive, protecting us from the sun and the elements.

"Pretty," I said absently. "How do you know about it?"

I asked her.

"Oh, it's a funny story," she squawked before falling into yet another story about her losing her clothes on some random skinny-dipping trip with a bunch of random friends. She mentioned these friends' first names so casually, as if to imply we should know them, or to lend them some believability, I wasn't sure. Her intentions were strange. I knew it. I knew girls. I knew something was desperate about her, but I couldn't quite put my finger on what it was.

She led us to some random little offshoot of road and we followed the somewhat rocky terrain until our car could go no farther. Eventually, and much to my relief, we were forced to exit the car.

"It's this way." Ruby indicated with a hand.

"Just a minute," Ezra said, heading back to the trunk. He popped the hatch and disappeared through its open frame, rummaging for something. His head emerged and he closed the trunk then locked it, bright yellow plastic ribbons hanging from his hands.

"I'll just mark the trees," he said.

"Oh, that's not necessary," she said. "I know this place like the back of my hand."

Ezra smiled. "I don't doubt you do, but if it's all the same, I'd feel better."

"Whatever you like," she said, but her forced smile held a tinge of pissed-off girl. *She's up to something*, I thought.

Ruby set off at a brisk pace, easy for her tall frame, and Kai followed along like a lost puppy. Ezra fell behind them to stay with me.

"You can go on," I said, as he tied a ribbon around a tree trunk. "My legs are short." I giggled. "I'll just follow the ribbons."

"Uh, no," Ezra said. I waited but he offered nothing else.

We walked for at least ten minutes in silence before I couldn't take it anymore.

"Bets on what piece of clothing Ruby loses first?"

"Stop," Ezra said, but laughed anyway. He opened his mouth, then shut it, only to open it again. "Cash? Or favors?"

I smiled. "I was gonna say cash, but a favor seems a much more fascinating prospect now."

"All right, Corey, spill. What do you want from me?" he asked.

My face flamed a bright red. *Oooh, lawd, boy, if you only knew!* I cleared my throat to regain some sort of composure. "Well, uh, let's see how about, if I win, you let me see what's in that bag of yours."

"I don't know what you're talking about," he said, wrapping another ribbon around a tree.

"I think you do."

He switched tactics. "There's nothing to show."

"Ha! You're lying, Ezra! You shut that case with a finality that told me you were hiding something and I, being the curious kitty that I am, really, really, *really* want to know what it is!"

"Haven't you heard? Curiosity killed the cat."

I wagged my brows. "What are you saying? You'd kill me if I found out?"

"No," he said, "but *I* would die of embarrassment. That counts."

"Oh my gato! Now I *have* to know!"

He laughed nervously. "Pick something else," he said.

"No."

"Come on, Jupiter, pick something else."

"Fine," I huffed, scaling over a collection of boulders.

Ezra stuck out his hand to help me down. "Thank you," I told him, sliding my hand into his.

When I did this, when his warm palm met mine, I forgot what we were talking about. We stood, both of us silent, staring down at our connected hands. Eventually Ezra let mine go and continued walking, but not before squeezing my fingers so slightly I barely registered it, but it was there. I knew it. Because I was aware of even the minutest cells in my body when I was around him. It was an awareness of myself I'd never felt around anyone else but Ezra Brandon.

He cleared his throat while tying yet another ribbon. "And the favor?"

"I want you to read something, Brandon."

"Um, just read something?"

"Well, read something out loud." I followed his lead and cleared my throat, cleared the hesitation. "To me. Without questions after."

He laughed. "Okay, I guess."

"Can you do a British accent?" I asked.

"Huh?"

"Nothing."

I have to fess up to something. In eleventh grade, after reading *Sense and Sensibility*, when I remembered that Ezra's last name was Brandon, I almost swooned with giddiness. Why, you ask? Because I was a fan of the incomparable Jane Austen, and Austen, of course, conjured the enigmatic yet strangely steady Colonel Brandon. In other words, Ezra Brandon's personality doppelgänger, and that astounded me. It was like this blinding moment of profound perception, like Austen knew a previous version of Ezra personally or something. Both are quiet, constant, gallant, and unapologetically masculine. They are both remarkable yet unassuming representatives of their gender. Colonel Brandon is the sort of character most readers find underwhelming at first glance, but when Austen peels back his layers, she reveals the most extraordinary person, much like Ezra.

I sighed like an idiot.

"So, um, I know what favor I'd like," Ezra said quietly, as if he were afraid of his own voice.

I sidled next to him as we continued walking. "Oh yeah? What's that then?"

"When we get to Seattle, you have to remain my friend."

I didn't know what to think of his "favor." It was confusing because I didn't think he would have cared one way or another if we stayed friends. Ezra wasn't in the habit of being active socially, as you well know.

"Define friend," I begged, sort of desperate to know what his definition was.

"You are strange," he commented, but continued. "You know, someone to hang with, someone to study with, watch films occasionally, maybe grab a bite to eat?" He ran the palm of his hand over the back of his neck. "I don't know."

"Is this because I'll be the only one you'll know in Seattle?"

He laughed, but I didn't think he found it funny. "You overanalyze the shit out of things sometimes, Jupiter."

"Well?" I asked.

"No, okay? Damn. I just thought it would be cool if we stayed friends with one another is all."

I felt stupid. I don't know why I questioned everyone's

motives all the time. I mean, I kind of knew why, but since I was aware of it, I hoped to outgrow that part of myself, but obviously it bubbled up, and usually at the most inopportune times. My family was weird, I was weird, everything about me was weird, and I was constantly called out on it. Naturally I became defensive, and usually by calling out motives aloud. Nothing made people more uncomfortable than having to answer for their behavior.

"Sorry," I told him. "Of course I'd love to hang out with you in Seattle, but that can't be your favor. I'm not letting the fact of whether we remain friends in Seattle hang upon the stripping abilities of a hitchhiker named Ruby."

Ezra laughed and meant it this time. "Deal. Let me think of something else then."

"What are the terms?"

"What do you mean?"

"I say she loses the bra first," I said.

Ezra blushed, making me giggle. "I feel like an idiot, but her shoes?"

"Boring!"

"Listen, I'm trying to win, and logically, losing the shoes seems the most feasible option."

"Fine. I'd say let's shake on it, but I need to know what I'm risking."

"Okay, let me read your texts to Frankie." I didn't respond, didn't know how to really. "I know you're talking to her about me, and it's driving me crazy not knowing what's being said."

I felt my face sober, but my heart started to race at the mere thought of him reading those texts. "Have you lost your damn mind?" I finally asked.

"I take that as a no?"

"That's a big hell to the no!"

"Come on, man."

"Okay," I said, and his face lit up. I was going to enjoy this next bit, "but only if you let me see what's in the bag."

"No way."

"Exactly."

"All right," he said, tying another ribbon, "then karaoke. On a date of my choosing."

I smiled. "Deal."

CHAPTER SIXTEEN

Ezra and I arrived at the waterfall shortly after Ruby and Kai, thankfully before she started undressing. We stood at the top of what looked like a ten- to twelve-foot waterfall cascading into a deep blue pool of water roughly fifty feet wide and thirty feet long and half surrounded by a rust-colored beach that met bits of nature that climbed up a steep hill. The pool fed into a ravine through a small crevice on the opposite side where a rock face surrounded the other half of the pool and shot straight up to where we stood near the waterfall's edge, similar to The Narrows in Zion. The water fell aggressively enough to churn the base, creating a gorgeous repercussion against the rock face. The water foamed and frothed where the fall met the calm. I itched to jump in.

It was a sight for the ears as well as a sight for the eyes. Ezra bent forward toward me, and my belly felt much like the stirring water below. "Unbelievably beautiful," Ezra commented in my ear.

I felt like I'd swallowed my tongue and so nodded my answer.

Ruby broke the moment in half with a happy girlish squeal, something I knew boys found attractive if Kai's reaction meant anything, but could never bring myself to duplicate.

"Oh my God! Let's get in!" she yelled over the deluge, reaching under her shirt for her bra clasp.

I grabbed Ezra's arm, confident in my triumph, but she threw a wrench in my short-lived victory by simultaneously toeing the heel of a sandal. We both braced ourselves. It would be a race to the finish. With one shoe gone, she threaded her arm through the loop of her arm strap as she shoved the heel of her other sandal off and, much to my dismay, kicked it off to the side before she even got the other arm through.

"No!" I shouted at the sky, then fell to my knees. *Goodbye, Colonel Brandon monologue!*

Ezra could not stop laughing at me as Ruby jumped over the drop. Silly Kai shoved his shirt off his head and joined her, shouting something as he fell.

"You won!" I cried out.

Ezra bent over me, holding out his hand. I took it and he pulled me so quickly up to his side, my head swam. An unsubtle reminder of how strong he was.

"Shall we?" he asked, gesturing toward the falls.

I bent to unlace my boots and tugged them off, walking a bit to tuck them into the V of a low tree. Without thinking, I ran straight for the edge of the falls, past a surprised-looking Ezra, and tossed myself over, turning toward him at the last second to catch an expression of wonder and something like to amazement. I winked as I disappeared behind the mantle and over the brink, in every sense of the expression.

The fall was exhilarating. Three seconds of pure adrenaline, free falling to the sound of rushing water, and suddenly I couldn't remember a moment before that one, at least not with the same eyes. It was as if the look on Ezra's face started everything new again. No one had looked at me like that before. It felt so final, so adult, like a line drawn in sand, but heated to an impossible temperature, and solidified into glass. A once malleable life calcified into two definite pieces composed of "what was before" and "what was after." No longer was I Jupiter Corey, daughter, sister, child. I was Jupiter Corey, adult, with adult thoughts and adult feelings.

I blasted through the cool water feet first and my body felt paralyzed for a moment. I wasn't prepared for the cool temperature, but quickly shook the shock, bobbing to the surface with an involuntary shout, stupefied by newly open eyes, open ears, and an unexpectedly open life, the haze of girlhood somewhere at the bottom of that chilled pool. The possibilities were unexpectedly endless.

I'd surfaced in time to see Ezra tumbling off the edge of the falls down toward me, his arms and legs flailing to keep himself upright. His smile was infectious, and I found myself copying him. He shot through the water next to me, disappeared for half a minute, then popped up beside me, tossing his hair to the side to shake the water out of his eyes. He was utterly adorable. His expression was open and was one of pure happiness.

He swam nearer, his face a foot from mine. "Totally worth coming out here," he said.

I looked around at my magical surroundings. "It's pretty amazing."

"Come on, guys!" Kai yelled from the shore, making

his way up the sloped nature path to jump once more.

Ruby was already at the top of the hill.

I turned back to Ezra. "Should we?"

Ezra looked around him back toward the falls. "No, not yet," he said. "Come here." He grabbed my arm and we waded over to the falls themselves.

He guided me around the falling water and up onto a little alcove buried behind the cascading water.

"Oh my God," I whispered.

We stood upon the ledge, the water echoing around us. Tiny, varying rivulets of water spilled down the alcove's walls in a symphony of dripping song, the sound magnified by its secluded recess. It was a place where wondrously only two people in the world could exist at once. It was surreal, the stuff of literal dreams. I knew I would never forget that place, never forget the feeling I was experiencing, and who I was with for as long as I lived.

Ezra reached out his hand and caught the fall, interrupting its flawless veil for a mere moment, but it was a moment it would never get back again, frozen in those precious seconds despite its ability to immediately forget the brief intermission, because I was there to witness it, like we were influencing history forever in that tiny, dazzling, exclusive world.

"It's seductive!" I yelled over the din of water.

Ezra shook his head, letting me know he hadn't heard me. He edged closer and leaned his ear near my mouth. I swallowed, afraid to repeat myself in such an intimate way.

I tried to shrug it off as if it was nothing. Ezra stood, balanced himself next to me, gripped me by the shoulders, and bent his mouth to my ear. "Tell me," he ordered.

I swallowed. "It-it's seductive," I told him.

He pulled away and his eyes met mine. He stared at me with the most serious expression and my heart raced, beating so harshly in my chest I was convinced he could hear it even over the cacophony. Finally, and with obviously great difficulty, he turned his gaze to the water and dropped his hands to his side.

Before I had the chance to feel my disappointment, he whipped his stare back toward me and mouthed something at me, but I couldn't read his lips. He grabbed my shoulders and brought me in so closely my chest rested against his panting one. We were so close I could feel the heat of his breath on my face. His eyes searched my own for something and my blood pumped furiously once more through my head, chest, and stomach. His eyes betrayed a furious war battling within him. *He's going to kiss me*, I thought. His hands raised to my hair and he ran them through its wet length, pulling it to the ends. The sensation of Ezra's hands on my hair was more than I thought I could bear, until, that is, his fingers found the tops of my ears. Silently, he rubbed the tips between his thumb and index fingers, his eyes studying what he was doing as if he'd forgotten everything else around him. He closed his lids like he was memorizing the feel of my skin. I was learning the roughness of his fingertips, the temperature of his unbelievably powerful hands.

I felt like I could tip over at any moment. In a daze, I began to pitch forward, so I grabbed one of his forearms with a hand to steady myself. This startled him back to the present and he pulled away so quickly it left me stunned.

"*What?*" I asked, confused.

He shook his head and pointed toward the outside edge of the falls and guided me out, falling into the water without looking back, so I followed him, diving through, and coming out near the shore. He whipped out of the water so fast I couldn't keep up.

"Ezra, wait!" I yelled, but he ignored me. "Wait!"

"Can't," he said, sounding a little desperate.

I fought to gain footing up the hill to follow the path. Being fully clothed and sopping wet didn't help. By the time I reached the top, I was out of breath but ran after him anyway. "Ezra, jeez, calm down! Can you just stop?"

He was at least twenty feet away before he ceased walking, his head hung low, yet he didn't turn around. He lifted his head, his hand brushed across the back of his neck. His hair clung everywhere his touch hadn't disturbed.

"What did you say to me behind the falls?" I asked, advancing toward him.

I reached him. His jaw was clenched, his forehead pinched in frustration. His T-shirt plastered itself against his chest; his jeans hung on his hips.

"What did you say behind the falls, Ezra?"

"Get your boots, Jupiter."

"No."

He looked at me, narrowed his eyes. "Fine," he said, turning toward the waterfall's edge, straight for my shoes. I followed him closely.

"Tell me what you said back there and I'll leave you alone about this. It'll be like it never happened," I told him.

He shook his head, his teeth clenched. I grabbed his arm, made him look at me. There was something in his expression. "Instant regret," I whispered to no one, making my stomach drop to my feet.

I let go of his arm and sprinted up the incline to the tree that held my boots. Absently, I noticed Kai and Ruby weren't anywhere around. I yanked the boots from their resting place, leaned against a nearby boulder, and shoved the shoes back on. *Don't cry. Don't cry. Get to your phone. Call Frankie. Get to your phone. Call Frankie. And don't cry!*

The hill was steep and in my manic state, I wasn't being as careful as I should have. I slid, my hands catching on the rocks below. I saw the blood dripping before I felt it, but I ignored it. I spun around, desperate to find the first ribbon. *I could have sworn it was right here*, I thought.

"They ripped them off," Ezra said quietly, shocking me. He was leaning against a tree at the bottom of the incline, dripping water to the earth below.

"Kai wouldn't do that," I told him.

"You're right, he wouldn't," Ezra said, "but I'm guessing Ruby would. I'm also guessing she let him lead the way."

Ezra glanced toward my hands. "Jesus, Jupiter. What happened?" he asked. Without hesitation, he tugged off his T-shirt, drained it by twisting it, then tore it in two. "Let me," he said, gently taking one of my hands and examining it. "They're covered in dirt."

"Who cares," I told him, feeling dejected.

He didn't respond, only took me by the elbow and led me back to the pool, and made me dip my hands into the running water. Gently, he examined the cuts.

"Not too deep, but when we find the car, I've got an antibiotic ointment I want to put on them. This water isn't stagnant, but I don't want to run the risk."

I'd had enough. "Just stop it."

He looked at me. "Only trying to help."

"Who cares about my damn hands? It's just a few scrapes. We both know you're avoiding addressing what happened in there," I said, pointing at the falls.

He took one hand in his and wrapped a scrap of his damp T-shirt around my palm then did the same for the other.

"We need to find the car," he said.

"And kick Ruby to the gosh damn curb."

"Agreed."

I couldn't help myself. "Told you so."

"Yes, you did," he said maturely, avoiding the bait. I rolled my eyes.

"Do you have any idea where to go from here?" I asked.

"That way," he said with such authority I believed him.

"Tell me what you said," I ordered as we walked into the woods together.

"No."

"Why not?"

He breathed deeply. "Because. Just no."

"So you like ears," I told him.

His face flamed bright red. "Please let this go."

"I'll let this go when you tell me what you said."

"I will never tell you what I said."

I raised a brow. "Then I will never let it go."

"You like to torture me."

I *like to torture* you?

"Whatever you said, why'd you say it then?" I asked, curious.

"Y-you do things to me, and I couldn't fight it

anymore," he admitted, rubbing the back of his neck again.

I was shocked and flattered by this. Flattered because it was obvious now that he found me attractive. Shocked because I would *never* have been able to even remotely guess he struggled with anything where I was concerned.

He stopped, studied his surroundings, then picked back up again. I followed.

"What are you fighting, Ezra?" I asked him.

"Instinct."

"Oh yeah? What does your instinct say?"

"Run," he said, deflating me. Then my blood boiled.

"What bullshit!" I told him. "People follow their gut when their mind *stops* getting in their way." I pointed to the waterfall several hundred yards behind us. "What you did back there, *that* was your true instinct. And now your mind is meddling where it doesn't belong."

I pushed forward ahead of him, not really caring if I was going the correct direction. Eventually I'd have to hit road and I'd follow it down to Ezra's car, or a bus, whichever came first. I was determined. Determined, that is, until Ezra yanked me back toward the direction he was following.

"I'm not letting you walk off, Jupiter. Stick by my side. No matter how pissed you are at me."

For several minutes, I stayed quiet, but then the silence began to irk me so, to keep myself from talking to Ezra, I began to hum, to keep me busy but also, hopefully, to irritate him. Keane's "Somewhere Only We Know" spilled between my lips, softly at first, but picked up as the song progressed and I gained a little confidence. Soon I found myself engrossed in my little song, examining the world around me, and seriously determined to wipe my slate clean. Any lingering doubt I had in letting my crush go was settling within the walls of the waterfall alcove.

When I got to Chicago, I was going to leave a note for Ezra thanking him for the lift and would purchase a ticket to Seattle with the little money I had saved.

CHAPTER SEVENTEEN

Sure enough, Ezra led us to his car. Well, what was left of it, anyway.

"Where's Kai?" I asked, panicking.

Ezra and I ran around and found Kai unconscious near the trunk.

"Kai!" I yelped, falling near his side. Kai stirred, his eyes droopy. "What happened?" I asked him, cradling his head in my lap.

"What took you two so long?"

"Ruby tore down all the ribbons," I explained.

Kai took a deep, frustrated breath. "She clubbed me over the head with a rock."

I turned his head around to check out the damage. It wasn't too bad, really, just a little blood. The bump was significant but manageable.

"Can you sit up?" I asked him.

He leaned forward and Ezra helped him sit all the way up then leaned him against the tire. "I can't believe she did that," Kai said, bringing his hand to his temple.

"Who? Ruby? The complete stranger who couldn't keep track of her clothing?" I sarcastically bit out.

"Not now," Ezra said, examining his cousin's head. He stood and pulled his cell phone out of the trunk. There was a huge dent there where Ruby had tried to get in.

I didn't think she realized with those old cars you couldn't get into the trunk without the key. I stood and peered inside.

I gasped.

"What?" Kai asked.

"She ripped the inside to shreds, man."

I could hear Ezra on the phone with the police. I bent down to Kai's level, literally and figuratively.

"Why did you leave in the first place?" I asked him.

"We saw you both slip behind the waterfall and Ruby figured you two could use some privacy, or so she said. Stupidly I thought she wanted to be alone with me too."

"Kai," I breathed out, exasperated. I fell beside him, leaning against the car door.

"How could she do this? She was so hot."

I snorted. "Seriously, Kai."

"Did those few hours we had mean *nothing* to her?"

I laughed. "Get it together, Kai. Look at your cousin's car."

He groaned. "I know. He's going to kill me."

"If it's any consolation, he's already in a foul mood. I can't imagine it could get any worse."

"Whoa, really? Why?"

I examined his bump again. The bleeding had almost stopped. "We, uh," I cleared my throat, "we had a sort of strange, intimate moment back there, but then he, like, bailed. I ran after him like a little lost puppy and demanded he *fess up, buttercup.*"

"And?"

"He did that sullen Cullen crap."

"Ah," Kai offered. *Helpful.* "Can I just—"

"No."

He eked out some sort of sound suggesting I should listen.

I sighed. "Fine, spit it."

"Can you just trust me on something?"

"Who? You? The great judger of character? Kai the common sense guru?" He laughed then moaned in pain, grasping at his head. "Go on then."

"I admit I don't have the best judgement of very many things, but Ezra I know. Give him time, Jupiter."

My head dropped low as I considered what Kai was telling me.

"Do you know something I don't?" I asked.

"I know enough," he answered, "but that's all you'll get out of me."

I needed to talk to Frankie. Then I remembered I'd stuck my phone underneath the seat and Ruby saw. "Shit!" I stood up, opened the door, and threw my hand beneath the seat in the back. "Damn, she got my phone." I gasped. "That beyotch! And my hat! And my bag of goodies!" I stuck my head out to look at Kai. "She is a scandalous hooker! Kale chips, my ass!"

"I'm really sorry about that," Kai apologized.

I climbed out, closed the door, and sat next to him. "It's okay, at least my bags and laptop are okay. Thank God for old cars, huh?"

He nodded. We sat in silence for a moment.

"Dude, this is the trippiest trip I've ever been on in my entire life," I told him.

"Bet you wish I'd kept Mary Jane around, huh?"

"I've never even touched the stuff."

"What in the world! How is that possible? Aren't your

parents from, like, another dimension?"

"Shut your mouth, high Kai. We're organic, but not *that* organic."

He started to laugh but sobered when he saw Ezra hang up.

"Cops'll be here soon," Ezra said.

Kai panicked. "I thought you were just filing a report or something! What if they finger me for the fire?"

I leaned forward. "Yeah, ya stool pigeon. We don't want no gumshoe 'round here." I threw a thumb Kai's direction. "Bugsy here can't do another turn in the big house. A couple of goons promised revenge. It'll be the meat wagon for him for sure!"

Ezra's stony expression told me he wasn't impressed with my 1920s gangster vernacular, which was a shame, because I was a dame packing some serious idiomatic heat.

He held out his hand for me to help me up. I refused it, which would have sent a powerful message if I hadn't forgotten that my hands were scraped up and consequently my standing from a sitting position had all the finesse of a turtle on its shell. Eventually he gave up waiting for me and slid his hands underneath my arms, lifting me like a toddler. *Dang it.*

Ezra grabbed his first-aid kit and a new T-shirt from the trunk and carefully unwrapped my hands. More delicately than I thought possible for a boy with hands Ezra's size, he placed squares of antibiotic-treated bandages across my palms then wrapped them both in gauze.

"Keep your mouth shut about the fire, Kai, and you'll be just fine," Ezra threw over his shoulder.

When the cops got there, Kai acted so sketchy the

police demanded to search the trunk. Thank God they didn't find anything. Ezra tried to explain away Kai's insanity by blaming the situation and eventually they took us seriously. They took statements from all of us and promised to send copies of the reports to Kai's parents' house for insurance purposes.

"I'll get you a new phone as soon as we get to Chicago," Ezra promised once the police left.

I sighed. "It's all right, dude."

"No," Ezra said more forcefully than I thought necessary. "It's my fault that pyscho took it. I should have listened to you."

"I hate it when you're reasonable."

He bit back his smile. "I'll even replace your hat."

"Don't push it," I told him, pointing a finger in his face.

This time he smiled. "Get in the car, Jupiter."

"What did you say at the waterfall?"

"Get in the car, Jupiter."

"What's in the bag?"

"*Get in the car, Jupiter!*"

CHAPTER EIGHTEEN

The seats were all torn up, so we had to lay blankets across them, which, of course, I didn't mind at all being the blanket hooker that I am and all. We hit the road, downgrading Kai into the backseat once more. He didn't complain.

"Can you text Frankie for me?" I asked Ezra.

"Sure. What do you want to say?"

"Don't tell her the phone was stolen. Just say that I lost it. She'll believe it. Tell her I'll call her later."

Ezra texted Frankie at the stoplight right before the entrance to the highway. The phone buzzed before we'd even had time to access the on-ramp. Ezra brought the phone up to his face.

"It's her."

"What did she say?"

In a deadpan tone, "I don't believe you. You've kidnapped her. Don't even bother. She's not worth anything. Drop her off at the nearest corner. Unless you own a circus. In which case she might prove useful. She can grow a beard with the best of them. Stick her on the trapeze."

"Shut up," Kai said, laughing. "She did not say that."

"Here," Ezra said, "read it."

I sighed. "That's *exactly* what Frankie wrote," I confirmed without even looking at it.

"Only four hours until home." Kai sighed. "I don't think I've ever wanted to be in Chicago as badly as I do right now."

"Miss your mommy?" Ezra teased.

Without skipping a beat, Kai said, "As a matter fact, I do." He looked at me and smiled. "I'm a mama's boy."

"*No,*" I jabbed.

"Make fun all you want, but you're going to love her as much as I do." He stared at me hard, making me a little nervous. "But she's mine, you hear me? Mine!"

"Fine, Kai's mama is his alone," I stated for his benefit.

"Do you miss your mom?" I asked Ezra.

He shifted in his seat. *So that's a yes then.* He tossed his long side-swept hair to the other side of his head. *Huh. He looks a little like Jesse Rutherford without the tats. Never noticed that before. The shaved part of his hair needs a little trim, though,* I thought. Then my thoughts went somewhere else entirely. *No! Bad, Jupiter.*

"Yeah," he said quietly. "I really love my mom."

My hands flew up trying to find something to steady myself on because I was dangerously teetering on the precipice of Swoonville. Ezra looked at me like I was nuts, which brought me back down to earth. *Ope! Moment gone.*

The rest of the drive to Chicago was fairly uneventful. Kai was in pain from the Ruby fiasco (whom I was right about!), and Ezra was still mopey about the fatal waterfall mistake with me, which was a real boost to my ego, let me tell ya.

I'd thought more on what Kai had told me and wondered if I really should give Ezra some time. I knew his history. I knew he'd had some life-altering crap barrel down at him at the speed of light flushed from an airplane called My Girlfriend is a Cheating Wench. He would never play lacrosse at the college level because of it. He could barely drive a few hours without his legs aching. Lean and muscular though they were, it made no difference. From what I understood, it was a bone-deep thing. Many things went bone deep for Ezra. I was beyond confused.

Thanks to our little waterfall adventure, we were late to arrive to Chicago, and almost as soon as we passed the city line, Kai's phone rang. He glanced down then brought it to his ear.

"Hello, Mama."

I heard a woman's muffled voice on the other line. I turned to look at Kai's happy face.

"Around half an hour." More indistinct chatter. "Okay, love you too," he said, then hung up.

"What's your mom's name?" I asked him.

"Rosie." He smiled.

"Aww, that's such a great name."

"It is. It suits her."

I turned to Ezra, realizing something. "What's your mom's name?"

A crooked smile spread across his lips and it made me smile. "Holly."

I turned to look out the window, satisfied with our exchange. "Do you love your mom?" Ezra asked me.

"Like the dickens," I told him, and he smiled at me again.

172

Half an hour later we pulled onto Lake Shore Drive and my stomach dropped. Though the water was so different from what I was used to in the Keys, it didn't matter. I was so happy to be near it. It was a bolster to my heart. I stuck my face out the window to feel the humid air against my skin.

I breathed in deeply. "I missed the water."

Kai laughed. "Not exactly Florida, though."

I grinned. "It doesn't matter. I never realized how much I needed to be near it."

"Makes you a little homesick, no?" Ezra asked.

"Maybe a very little."

We pulled into some sort of underground garage and parked next to a line of incredible classic cars.

"What are we doing here?" I asked.

"This is my uncle's garage. He restores cars here," Ezra explained.

"You live in this high-rise?" I asked Kai, remembering the sheer number of floors that kept climbing up and and up into the sky of the building.

"Not this one," Kai absently remarked.

"But you live in a high-rise?"

"I live in a vintage building a little south of here."

"I would have gone there but thought it'd be better to take the car here first since Kai's dad has a mechanic who could fix the damage Ruby did in time for us to head out next Monday."

We all piled out of the little GTO that could. I stood and stretched my whole body. I felt pretty relaxed up until I noticed Ezra eyeing my body like I was something to eat. My face got hot, so I bent back into the car to hide my face and to get my boots since I'd taken them off for the ride. I rested a hand on the top of the car as I slipped on each boot, trying so hard not to look Ezra's direction because I felt his stare and it was heavy enough to speed up my breathing.

I heard Kai and Ezra mumbling something to each other then heard the trunk pop open. I stood when I felt like my face was no longer the color of the forbidden apple. I dared to glance a peek at Ezra. And that would be one forbidden apple, let me tell ya.

"We're walking," Ezra told me. "Are you cool with that?"

"Yeah, that's fine." I took in our collective luggage. Ezra's and Kai's bags had rollers on them. Mine didn't because it was made in 1973 or something stupid like that. "Uh, how far is it?" I asked.

"About three blocks from here," Kai answered, lifting up the handle of his case.

I studied my heavy case, resolved to my fate. "Okay, that shouldn't be too bad," I told them with an overenthusiastic smile, which Ezra for some reason found hilarious.

He walked to the far wall on the opposite side of the cars and pulled two bungee cords off a latticed metal grate bolted to the wall. He walked back to us and laid his own bag flat, rested my case on top of his, and fastened it tightly.

"Swell, baby," I said without thinking. My face burned that bright red again and I had no way to hide it. "Not that you're my baby or anything," I tried to cover. His face looked so hurt it made my chest ache. "Uh, well, not that you wouldn't be a great baby, you know, to someone. Someone else that's not me. I mean, I know you're not my baby... Back. Ribs. I want my baby back, baby back, baby back." Kai looked at me as if I'd sprouted horns. I started to hyperventilate and covered my face with my hands. "Oh God, make it stop."

"Stop saying the word baby, you freak," Kai said, wrapping his arm around my neck and playfully driving his knuckle into the top of my head. I shook him off.

Ezra pushed the rolling case out with his foot and started to roll it up the steep incline to reach street level. I started to go after him to help, but Kai reined me back, wrapping his arm around my neck, his hand around my mouth. "Let me spare you from yourself. Just chill."

I nodded my head, and he released his hand. "You're hot, but you're a dork. Follow me."

Kai walked up the hill and caught up with Ezra. I followed at least ten feet behind, mortified, and not feeling comfortable at all knowing I was about to meet Ezra's aunt. My feet felt heavy as I followed both boys. It was too awkward for me to walk with them. It was also too awkward for me to walk behind them. The ultimate catch-22. *Screw it*, I thought. *Just own it. Look at the buildings or something.* I'd started to but was struck at the resemblance between Ezra and Kai, besides their hair color, and watched them instead. They had the same gait, same build, same height, even the same laugh. The only difference was the slightest hitch in Ezra's walk when he'd hit pavement with his left foot. It wouldn't be noticeable to anyone else, really, but it was to me. I suddenly hated Jessica West for giving that to him, despite how indirect the blame was. I felt a little more in tune to Ezra's struggles watching him walk with his cousin. I felt something unfamiliar deep in my gut. I didn't know if I liked it.

He slowed and came to a complete stop, his gaze never leaving the sidewalk below him, though. Kai kept walking. I sort of galloped a bit like some *My Little Pony: Friendship is Magic* doll, then remembered myself. When I stepped next to him, he continued. We didn't talk, but we didn't need to.

Kai's "house"—and I use that term loosely—was nestled in a vintage 1920s apartment building on Scott surrounded by other equally imposing high-rises.

"Damn, Gina," I said under my breath.

Kai hugged the brick. "Matilda!"

I didn't ask.

The lobby was all posh marble, and the elevator was true to the age of the building with those sliding metal accordion door things. We all piled in before Kai pushed the top-floor button.

"Ground floor: perfumery, stationery, and leather goods, wigs, and haberdashery, kitchenware, and food...going up!" I sang in my best *Are You Being Served* impression.

I looked at Ezra, the corner of his mouth turned up in a crooked smile. "Are you free, Miss Brahms?" he asked, shocking the hell out of me.

I gulped, my eyes going wide. "I-I'm free." I tried to play it cool but couldn't succeed. Frankly, I was stunned he got the reference. It was obscure. And not really cool obscure either.

I turned toward the doors of the elevator, afraid to look at him anymore, and clenched my teeth, afraid I'd call him "baby" again or something. I lost even the smallest amount of mojo I possessed when he was around me. When the elevator dinged, the door slid open, and Ezra leaned across from me, the sleeves of his hoodie brushing against my stomach, leaving goosebumps behind as he opened the accordion grate. I stepped out onto more marble and looked up and down the hall. There were only two doors and they were on opposite sides of the hall. Kai led us to the door on the far left and with every click of my heel on the floor, I was very aware of my wrinkled clothes, my shorts, still a little damp, and my unmanaged hair. My only comfort was that both boys were in as bad of shape as I was. Poor Kai had a knot on the side of his head that was turning a little blue.

"We look like we all got into a fist fight right before we got here," I told them.

Kai sighed. "I know. Mom is going to freak."

I swallowed my nerves and they settled like a rock in my stomach. "Is she, like, particular about clothing and stuff?" I asked, taking a mental inventory of my thrift store clothing I packed.

Ezra laughed. "Nah, Rosie is salt of the earth. She will, though, instantly worry that we got mugged on the way up here."

I breathed a sigh of relief as Kai stuck his key in the door, but before he could even turn it, it whipped open.

"Oh my God! I thought you would never get here!" a boisterous, short, plump woman with shoulder-length black hair exclaimed. Her smile faded from ecstatic to concerned as she tugged Kai's head to her level. "What in the Sam Hill happened to you, Kai Brandon?" she yelled, a thick southern accent coming to the forefront.

So this is Rosie. She was unbelievably beautiful, eyes bright blue. Her cheeks matched her name with two deep dimples in each one. She exuded wonderful from every inch of her short frame.

"Sorry, Mama. I didn't want to tell you until we got here, didn't want you to worry."

She let go of his face and placed her hands on her hips. "With you I'm always worryin', boy. Are you okay?"

"I'm fine. Tell you the details later."

Her mouth screwed into something incredulous. She shook her head and sighed a sigh of exasperation, then looked around Kai and noticed Ezra. She gasped and jumped up and down like a cheerleader. "Ezra! Baby boy! Get over here!" she yelled and reached for him then hugged him fiercely.

Everything she did was loud and full of energy, but it was so charming. She was the type of person whom everyone was drawn to, the type whose heart was always open and always ready to give. I knew it the second she opened her door. It was no wonder Kai loved her so much.

Ezra stood from their hug and placed his warm hand on my lower back, sending a thrill of butterflies. His fingers bit into my skin making me shiver all over. They slid up to the curve of my side and fit every arc, every bend there, but they were tense, like he was fighting an urge he didn't want to fight. Neither did I. My breaths came a little faster and I memorized the intensity of those fingers as he brought me forward. His hand left the skin there, leaving it cool and starved for his touch again.

I was shot out of my thoughts when Rosie leaned for me, wrapping me in a generous hug.

"And you must be Jupiter!" she told me, leaning back, keeping my hands in hers and spreading them wide so she could get a good look at me. She shook her head. "Girl, you are just a devastating little thing! Mike, get in here!" she yelled over her shoulder. "Come look at this girl that somehow survived a road trip from Florida with these hoodlum boys!"

My face bloomed bright red.

"Rosie!" Ezra exclaimed, looking a little embarrassed.

She narrowed her eyes at Ezra then down at me and something changed in her face, like she was seeing something she hadn't noticed before, trying to determine what we were to each other. *Join the club. We got ourselves a little sitch-i-ation. Maybe without all the hair gel, though.*

"What's all the hubbub about?" a man asked, rounding a corner into the entryway. *Hubbub. I love old people.*

He looked so much like Ezra and Kai, maybe just a little shorter, and of course older. He smiled at me then turned toward his son. His hand went to his head as it shook in disbelief.

"Kai. Kai. Kai. You've been wrestling with pigs again?" he asked.

"Had a little incident," Kai divulged. "I'll tell you all about it later."

Kai's dad hugged and slapped him on the back and did the same with Ezra. Two more ridiculously tall boys spilled into the entryway, curious as to what was going on. The one right behind Kai's dad looked about thirteen, maybe fourteen, and was a spitting image of Kai, save for a little lighter hair. He peeked around his dad's shoulder with the sweetest smile I'd ever seen. Another boy stood behind him. He looked around my age and could have been Kai's twin. He had hazel eyes, though, instead of Kai's blue and his nose was a little longer.

All six pairs of eyes were looking at me at once. I felt my heart speed up. "Uh, hi, I'm Jupiter," I said, tossing up a hand in hello.

They didn't say anything and I started to get nervous,

biting my bottom lip, trying to fight the burn rising up my neck. Then all at once they were talking.

"So nice to meet you, Jupiter. I'm Mike," Kai's dad greeted with a smile, his hand out. I shook it and then he introduced Kai's brothers.

"This is Van," Mike said, pushing the younger one forward. He offered his hand and I took it. "But we call him Bear. And this is Milo," he said, introducing Kai's middle brother.

Milo stuck out his hand and I shook it. "Nice to meet you," he said, smiling at me with that charming smile all the Brandon boys possessed.

I giggled. "Nice to meet you too," I told him.

It got quiet again, so I began to examine the ceiling.

"Well, no sense standing here. Let's get in the kitchen!" Rosie broke the silence. We all pushed forward through the hall at once. I got swept up in the crowd of giant boys. I looked over my shoulder at Ezra and he smiled at me from the rear of the group.

The house was incredible. There was a main hall that emptied into several rooms with giant glass doors that were spread wide open. I caught sight of a library, some sort of gigantic living room lined with floor-to-ceiling windows that peered out onto the buildings all around. There was some sort of study and then at the end of the hall, through an elaborate arched doorway, was the kitchen. On the floor was a black-and-white checkered pattern and on the walls, large marble subway tile. It was a sea of marble, copper, and high-end appliances. For lack of a better phrase, it was really, really, *really* pretty. *I want!*

Through speakers in the plaster ceiling spilled Harry Belanfonte's "Jump in the Line." I burst with laughter when Rosie began to shimmy to the stove, a hand touching the opposite elbow of a raised hand, back and forth, back and forth, with a little rumba step.

"I made jambalaya, darlins! With a sweet potato pie to finish," she shouted over the music and stirred a pot on the stove. "Go on and sit!"

A few boys, I don't know which ones, it was too hard to tell at that point, rushed me over to the table and settled me in the center of a long bench. They all filled in around me. I was literally surrounded by boy. I looked left and up to take in a very friendly Milo then turned to my right and up to take in a tired-looking Kai. Bear sat at the end of the table as did Mike on the opposite side. And Ezra was directly across from me. He watched me closely. It made my heart flip-flop. Luckily, Rosie came to the table with a giant, steaming pot and distracted me. She set it dead center on an iron trivet. I had to lean up to see Ezra, and even then I could only see his eyes. They crinkled as if he was genuinely smiling. I fought the urge to push the pot aside so I could actually witness it.

Rosie tucked in beside Ezra next to her husband. "Pass your plates!" she said cheerfully, and they happily obeyed.

Milo took mine before I even had a chance to catch up with them and handed it to his mom.

"My mom is an excellent cook," Milo's deep voice told me.

I glanced at him then at Rosie. "If it's half as good as it smells, Rosie, it'll knock my socks off, I'm sure."

Rosie blushed prettily and I wished I could wrap her up and put her in my pocket. She passed a heaping plate of food to me, causing my eyes to bug. She laughed.

"Sorry, used to serving teen boys," she offered in

explanation. "Eat what you can, doll."

The table was loud as everyone served themselves a buttered roll that smelled like heaven itself and poured their drinks.

"Boys," Mike said, and the whole table died down, their heads bowed. I copied them as Mike began to thank God for the food on their table. When he was done, the table erupted once again. I sat there a little shell shocked by the noise made by this gigantic man family. I looked across the top of Rosie's pot at Ezra. His eyes were crinkled and his shoulders were shaking. *God! His punk ass is laughing and I'm missing it!*

"So you're headin' to school with Ezra, are you?" Rosie asked, taking a bite.

My fork still sat in my hand. I hadn't made a single move since I sat down. The table got quiet again as they waited for my answer.

"Yes, ma'am," I answered.

To be honest, I was intimidated by the boys around me, which was a new one for me.

"That's a mighty good school. You must have been an excellent student then."

I smiled. "I try, I guess."

"What luck you two decided to go to the same school," she said, fishing for information.

"It was a cool luck of the draw, for sure," I told her. "I didn't have a ride up there. My parents aren't the most conventional sort, and I would have had to get creative if it hadn't been for Ezra."

"Are you and Ezra dating?" Milo came out and asked.

"Oh no, we're definitely not together," I told him, trying hard to control the blush stretching across my face and the hurt of that knowledge from penetrating any

182

deeper into my heart.

I looked over the pot at Ezra and his eyes bored into mine then he looked at Milo. "No, I'm just giving her a ride is all," he told his cousin.

I was disappointed in him. He had to have known how badly that would hurt me. Kai looked at Ezra and shook his head lightly. He looked at me then patted my knee tenderly under the table to comfort me. I picked up my fork and took a bite.

"Oh my God, this is amazing!" I said without thinking.

Rosie sat up a little and smiled, bolstered by my compliment.

"How old are you?" Milo asked me.

I swallowed.

"Eighteen," I answered.

"*Interesting.* I'm fourteen," Bear told the table. He smiled at me. "Four-year age gaps mean nothing anymore, you know."

Kai snorted and choked on his food. I hit his back to help a literal brother out. "Yep," I answered, not sure what else to say.

"Demi Moore and Ashton Kutcher had a *sixteen*-year age difference," Kai's youngest brother told me, wagging his brows up and down.

It was my turn to choke. "Aren't they divorced?" I asked him between gasps of breath.

"Still," he responded. "I heard it was good while it lasted."

Mike laughed into his plate, mumbling *hormones.*

"Bear, you need a cold shower or somethin'?" Rosie asked him. She looked dumbfounded.

"*Mom!*" he gritted, his face turning bright red.

"I'm seventeen," Milo told me.

I turned his direction. "Cool. Senior this year?"

"Yeah," he said, throwing his hair out of his face and grinning at me.

I looked over at Kai. "I know," he explained.

"They're all yours," Rosie told Mike.

CHAPTER NINETEEN

"I've got a sweet little bedroom for you," Rosie told me after I rang my sister and parents, letting them know I'd gotten to Chicago. We walked to a corner bedroom where the boys' rooms were. "Ezra's already put your bag in here. There's a private bathroom as well." She took me by the shoulders and smiled. "Make yourself at home, honey. Holler if you need anything at all."

"Thank you. For dinner. For sharing your home with me. Thank you," I told her.

She winked at me. "Darlin', I like you," she said. She began to close the door, then remembered something. "P.S. If you put your ear up to the vent near the bed there you can hear everything said in the room where the boys are sleeping." I laughed. "It's how I find out all the dirt and dole out punishments accordingly. They're always scratching their heads on how I find out. Haven't put two and two together. You're welcome," she told me and closed the door.

The room faced out onto a busy Chicago street. I couldn't hear the bustle below, but I could see the streets full of headlights and the sidewalks crowded with people.

There was an energy there I had never experienced, and I liked it. It was intimidating, but I liked it.

I bent to unzip my case to get my shower stuff and T-shirt to sleep in when I noticed the vent. *Oh, go on then.* I leaned next to the bed and bent my head to the vent.

"...up about it," Ezra said. I recognized his voice immediately despite how tinny it came through.

"Milo, please," Kai said.

"Yeah, if she's gonna like anyone here, it's gonna be me," a smaller voice shouted. *Bear.*

Collective laughter rang through the vent.

"Dude, she's the perfect chick," Milo said.

There was a pause and a bed creaked.

"You don't even know her," Ezra chimed in.

"Fine," Milo conceded, "but she is definitely hot as hell."

I dusted off my shoulder then rolled my eyes at myself.

"What happened back at that waterfall?" Kai asked, ignoring his brother.

"Don't want to talk about it, Kai."

"Well, I want to talk about it," he insisted.

Another pause. "Nothing happened."

"Liar, liar, pants on fire," Kai accused.

"Listen, will you just drop it? I-I'm not sure what happened. I'm trying to figure it all out."

My heart beat into my throat.

"Wait, do you dig Jupiter?" clueless Milo asked. "From what you said at the table, you acted like she was just a friend."

"She *is* a friend," Ezra explained.

"You're good," Milo chimed in. "I'll give you that, but you left your answer open and since I'm familiar with your insane ability to avoid a question, I need you to clarify, Ezra. Are you *just* friends?"

There was a loud thud in the room and I missed his answer. *Poop on a stick!*

"Fine, whatever," Milo said. "I'm making a move then, 'cause girl is fine as a dime."

"Can you just stop regurgitating crap?" Kai asked Milo. "Please, your stupidity is starting to infect Bear."

"Hey!" Bear shouted, his voice breaking.

"I'm gonna hit the showers," Ezra said. "Y'all chat it up like a couple of chicks."

I heard him stand, walk, and a door shut.

I got nothing out of eavesdropping. How is that possible? If Frankie were here, she'd would have gotten every detail imaginable because that's her luck. I get squat crap. I grabbed my shower stuff and hit up the bathroom, showered, and dropped into the Brandons' guest bed. I wished I'd had my phone. I wanted to text Frank right away. I also would have fallen asleep to the album *The Miseducation of Lauryn Hill* because I didn't, no, *couldn't* think anymore, and needed a badass chick to tell me what I was worth.

"Good night, nurse!"

CHAPTER TWENTY

I woke up to a light knock on my door then looked out the window to see if the sun was out and was startled to see tall buildings bathed in streetlight instead. It was still really dark, though. I went to grab my phone then remembered I didn't have one.

I stood up, pulled my T-shirt over my bare thighs, and cracked the door a few inches. I peered out into a softly lit hallway.

"*Ezra?*" I rubbed an eye, trying to wake up. "What time is it?"

He stood there, his hair a mess, wearing a pair of track pants and no shirt. I opened the door a little farther but still stood behind it. It was uncomfortable, but there was no way I was going to open it fully.

"I see you've brought a six-pack," I joked, gesturing to his stomach.

He smiled down at me. "You're funny."

"What time is it?"

"Three."

"In the morning?"

He rolled his eyes. "No, the afternoon."

"Sarcasm? Really? Is that why you woke me? I need every second of beauty sleep I can get."

He looked taken aback. "What are you talking about?"

"Nothing, what's up?"

"No, tell me what you mean by that."

I sighed. "I didn't mean anything by it, really. Bad joke."

"You know you're beautiful, right?" he asked. I swallowed. "If you didn't, you should."

"Th-thank you."

He shook his head as if to clear his thoughts. "I couldn't sleep. I needed to talk to you."

"Um, okay. What's up?"

"Can I come in?"

"Uh, well, I'm not wearing pants."

His eyes bugged. I would have found that hilarious if I'd been holding a full deck. By deck, I mean fully clothed. As it was, I was short a spade. And by spade, I mean pants.

"Let me slip into the covers and you can come in. Just, uh, just give me one second."

I closed the crack in the door and headed for the bed.

"One," he said. The door creaked and I panicked.

"Wait! Wait! Wait!" I scrambled. "I'm not in. I'm not in!"

I was greeted with laughter on the other side.

"That's not funny, jackass." I sat on the edge of the bed and pulled the covers over my legs. "Okay, come in."

"Are you decent?"

"Yes, dummy, come in."

"Because I wouldn't want to come in if you weren't decent. Even the slightest peek at your leg might send me into a tizzy."

"You think you're so funny," I huffed. "Now, come in."

He stuck his head through. "Whew," he sarcastically bit out as walked in. He closed the door behind him and sat across from me.

He didn't say anything for a moment.

"Ezra, if you don't start talking soon…"

"You'll what?" he asked. He grinned and moved closer to me.

I scooted back, fighting laughter. "Will you stop? What did you wake me up for?" I whined that last bit to encourage spillage.

He sat back. "Milo has a crush on you," he said like he was dropping some bomb.

I needed to pretend I didn't already know. "Huh, okay, that's not a big deal." *Nailed it.*

"*Not a big deal?*" he asked me. He was unbelieving. I must have been a terrible actress.

I let out a frustrated laugh. "No, it's not, Ezra."

"It's a huge deal!" he whisper-shouted. "Milo is relentless. He won't stop until you're in love with him. He's just *like* that. Milo always gets what he wants."

My face fell into my hands and I dragged them down. "Ezra, did you seriously wake me up at three in the morning to tell me your cousin has the hots for me?"

His neck tinged pink. "Well, *yeah.*"

I furrowed my brows and sniffed the air twice. "You smell that?"

He looked around, smelled nothing. "Smell what?"

"That bullshit you just fed me. Seriously, tell me, Ezra. Right now. Why did you really come in here? What is keeping you up?"

He took three deep breaths. "It's strange having a

mega crush on a girl who doesn't play games."

My jaw dropped to the floor. "Um, excuse me, I am a flipping master at Monopoly, sir."

He smiled. "Stop it."

"I can't," I told him. "I'm digesting the bomb over Baghdad you just dropped, and I feel like you might not have even said it. I feel like I might still be asleep."

He reached over and pinched my arm. It hurt.

"No, I'm up like a toddler at dawn on Saturday."

I was still and we were quiet for at least two minutes.

"Digested?" he asked.

I nodded my head. "You like me."

He swallowed. He took another deep breath, like he was screwing up the courage to reveal something. My hand went to my chest, and I leaned toward him.

"I have never liked anyone as much as I like you, Jupiter, and I don't think I ever will."

When I realized my eyes welled with tears, my cheeks burned in embarrassment. He brought his hand up and caught a falling tear with his thumb. He leaned in and brushed my hair back away from my face.

I sniffed and smiled at him. "That's something." I laughed. "That's more than something. That's probably the best compliment I've ever been given, Ezra." Two more tears fell and I giggled at myself. "I'm an idiot."

He cocked his head to the side and studied me. "No, you most definitely are not."

I picked up the sleeve of my T-shirt and wiped my eyes dry. "How long have you liked me?" I asked him.

He shook his head and stared out the window, running a hand through his hair and off to the side.

I poked his leg. "How long, Ezra?"

"Since two months before graduation," he told the

window.

I balked at that. "I don't believe it."

He looked at me. "Believe me, Jupiter." He turned back toward the window. "It took me a very long time to get over Jessica, over what she did to me, over what happened to my body, over the loss of lacrosse, over my changed heart." He turned to me again.

"One day I just sort of snapped out of my haze. It was during class. I looked around me and there you were. You were this bright, beautiful light. You were gut laughing at something Frankie said and your hair swung forward, touching your knees. I noticed you didn't do anything unless you could do it with your whole heart, and I just found that so attractive. I don't think I'd ever been so drawn to someone in my life. You just gave off this energy, and it was like I saw you, really saw you. You weren't funny, cool Jupiter Corey anymore. You became *Jupiter Corey*. Funny, cool, unbelievably interesting, want-to-flunk-all-my-classes-just-so-I -could-follow-you-around, gorgeous Jupiter Corey.

"And I *never* had that with Jessica. *Never*." I followed the line of his throat as he swallowed. "I've wanted you so bad."

His words weakened me and I fell back onto my pillows, unable to hold myself up anymore. "C'mere," I told him, and he slid beside me on top of the covers.

"I've liked you for years, Ezra."

"Liar."

I shook my head back and forth slowly. "Years," I whispered.

I turned to him and he followed suit. I walked my fingers up his arm and defined shoulder and let them find his hair. I threaded them through and held them there.

"When you walked into a room, Jupiter, you got all of me. I didn't care who I was with or talking to at the time, I ignored them. You got my attention. So watching Milo with you today and occasionally while driving with Kai, I burned," he said before clenching his eyes shut, "no, seethed with jealousy."

His words went straight into my heart and settled there, like I swallowed a shot of something strong and drugging.

"Why didn't you ever say anything? Why haven't you made a move this whole trip?"

"Because I'm a chickenshit," he admitted behind a devastating grin.

I laughed. "Underneath that cool bravado?"

"Lies the heart of a pansy," he said, smiling.

"Why?" I asked.

He breathed easily, more easily than I'd seen him since we left Florida. He reached for a strand of hair and coiled it around his finger over and over. It sent shivers down my body.

"It sounds stupid," he explained.

"Try me," I sleepily demanded, dazed by his touch.

He took a deep breath and dropped the strand of hair. "At the waterfall, with the stone below us, the water around us, I felt like we were the only two people on earth and I forgot about my stupid rules for a minute. You were beautiful, and I couldn't take being near you anymore without being able to touch you. Like I was either going to touch you or approach the cliffs of insanity. I skated that fine a line.

"It's felt unnatural going all this time not placing a hand on you whenever I felt the urge. I kept having to remind myself you weren't actually mine, even though I looked—*look*—at you like you are. That's the problem, Jupiter. You have unimaginable power over me."

He gulped and his brow creased as if it had been difficult for him to admit that to me. Ezra didn't like to lose control. A light clicked on. All the times he wouldn't let me drive, or even Kai, really. The fact he wouldn't let me pay my part for gas or the rooms. The ribbons on the trees. Admitting his vulnerability for me. It was a control issue.

"I promised myself the night I woke up from my accident," he continued, "that no one would ever have that kind of authority over me again. So, when I took notice of you that day in class, when I started wondering what you were doing, who you talked to, what your life's plans were, and if you ever thought of me, I realized I was giving you power and it was a fearsome thing, Jupiter, because the hold you were beginning to take over me was infinitely stronger than anything I had ever felt with Jessica, and if that were true..."

"Then this fall would *really* hurt," I finished.

He closed his lids briefly then stared hard into my own. "Not hurt, Jupiter, *wreck*."

"That's what's haunted you these last two years," I stated.

He nodded, his handsome face relaxed. He leaned closer and dragged his thumb over my forehead and down my cheek, resting his palm on my neck. It fit over my entire throat and sent a thrill through my head and stomach.

"Do you have any idea how badly I've wanted to touch your skin?" he asked.

"Not as long as I've *wanted* you to touch my skin," I

whispered.

He looked at me and I could tell he saw me, saw every facet. "You'd have needed only to ask, Jupiter," his deep, soft voice promised.

My heart beat furiously. My pulse raced with the statement.

I closed my eyes. "What did you say at the waterfall?" I asked, bracing myself for rejection. It was an old habit.

He dragged his hand down from my neck, his fingers splayed across the top of my chest, and I opened my eyes. He had to have felt my Benedict heart in all its treasonous pounding.

"I said I couldn't endure another minute without knowing what you felt like."

All the breath escaped my lungs in one full rush. Something passed over his face, something different, foreign to me, something liken to desperation, I thought. Both of his hands found the sides of my neck.

"I'm going to kiss you, Jupiter Corey," he told me, his hands trembling.

I took short, shallow breaths. I'd forgotten how to breathe. My hands went to his wrists. "Ezra, I-I've never kissed anyone before."

His eyes narrowed. "How is that possible?"

"No one has ever placed their lips on mine?"

His shoulders shook in a silent laugh. "Surely guys have asked you out. Have you seen your face?"

I smiled. "I have, and don't call me Shirley."

"You're an idiot." He laughed, kissing my cheek.

"No, not a single boy has ever asked me out."

"What nimrods."

"I think I'm just a little, you know, too much, maybe."

"No, you're not too much. You're the perfect amount

of awesome, actually, and that's intimidating to guys."

"Not to you, though."

"No, you intimidate the hell out of me. It took me months to gather up the courage to talk to you. On the last day of school, I'd known I'd blown it and I got pretty depressed. Then I remembered I'd see you at graduation and promised myself I'd talk to you."

"Thank God Molly Carrington moved away."

He smiled. "No shit." He sighed. "You were so freaking hot that day."

My cheeks flushed. "Oh my gato, you are such a liar. I went there with wet hair! My mom tossed my graduation outfit. I had to pull some crap together to try and look halfway decent."

"Dude, you didn't look halfway decent, you looked full-on decent. It was all I could do not to fall on my knees and worship at your feet."

"Oh, Ezra." I giggled.

"*Oh, Ezra,*" he mock teased.

"Stop it!"

"*Stop it!*" he falsetto mimicked.

"*Ezra,*" I pretended to whine.

He laughed. "Fine. After you asked for the ride? I couldn't conjure up enough grit to say anything to you over the summer. Crippled by fear and intimidation. How's that for proof that boys are only scared of you?"

"Boys are just soft little kitties after all then?"

"We are, but we don't like to admit it," he said.

"I won't ever bring it up again, Felix."

"Thank you."

He gave me that crooked smile again, his eyes crinkled when he did it, and I found that such a fantastic thing to look at. I pushed my fingers through his hair then down to his neck. His skin was warm and sent tingles through my own. His vein pulsed under my fingers.

"Nervous?" I asked him.

"Anxious," he admitted. "Excited. I've been waiting a long time to taste you."

I swallowed down the fluttering butterflies. "Don't *say* things like that."

"Why?" he asked softly.

"Because it drives me berserk."

He leaned in and gingerly kissed the side of my jaw. I gasped. I felt him smile against my skin.

"I can feel your heart beating against my chest," he said before kissing a line down and around to the base of my throat. I panted to the point of hyperventilation. "*Slow*," he ordered, a hint of satisfaction in his voice.

I tempered my breaths, and my head began to clear.

"Stay still," he told me, running his fingers down my throat.

Ezra gently pushed my chin to expose my neck, kissed the dip between my collarbones once and moved up to my ear. My hands found his shoulders when his mouth found my earlobe and he drew it between his teeth. I began to pant again. He laughed low and deep into my ear.

"Jupiter, how are you this sexy?"

He didn't give me time to answer because his warm tongue found my earlobe again, rendering me speechless. Before I was ready for him to, he abandoned that punch-drunk place, leaving it cool and neglected. He kissed along my jaw and up a little, stopping at the corner of my mouth before drawing away to look at me. I wanted to scream at him to keep going.

He cupped my face in his hands and drew a thumb

across my bottom lip, pulling it down a bit before letting his hand slip back to my jaw. He smiled a lazy smile at me, his teeth white in the moonlight, his heavy-lidded eyes doing something to my insides, a feeling I knew I was immediately addicted to.

"I'm going to kiss you this time," he told me. "I'll go slow," he assured me.

I nodded, afraid to speak.

He leaned into me, pressing his entire body against mine over the covers, but his heat fell through to my legs, belly, and chest anyway and it brought a sweet kind of relaxation. Tentatively at first, he pressed his warm, soft lips to mine, his breaths mixing with mine. I thought I'd died and gone to heaven. Slowly, he brought the kiss deeper and I followed his lead, sinking farther into him until I thought I'd go mad if I couldn't get closer. I wrapped one hand around his neck and in his hair and drove the other's fingertips into his bare back.

One of his hands stayed at my neck and jaw but the other moved down to my hip and lower back, crushing me into him. His tongue met my bottom lip, licking the length, and I found myself opening up for him. This time my tongue sought his and when I found it, Ezra groaned into my lips. We traded back and forth like that for what seemed like hours, and like an exceptional bottle of wine, we only got better with time.

Unfortunately the sun began to crest the buildings above, shining morning onto the bed, reminding us where we were.

"Oh my God," I said, my voice hoarse, "the sun is rising.

He kissed my mouth to stop my words until it was his turn to speak. "Why aren't we ten years older with our own apartment?" he asked, making me giggle.

He kissed my neck and collarbone.

"You have to go," I told him, gasping when his mouth found my shoulder and bit down lightly.

"If I didn't love and respect my Aunt Rosie so much, I would put a chair in front of that door and hole up in here with you all day, leaving teeth marks all over your neck."

"Promises, promises," I wheezed, out of breath from his comment, the make-out session, both.

He buried his face in my neck then skillfully bit my collarbone. He slid off the bed, his hair sticking up at all angles, and I couldn't help but smile at him.

"Bed head?" he asked.

I stood up on the mattress to peer into the little square mirror above the dresser opposite the bed and I almost laughed out loud. I turned to Ezra and pointed to my own hair.

"Look at this mess," I whisper-yelled.

He wasn't looking at my hair, though. I followed his line of sight to my legs and blushed the deepest crimson I've ever blushed. I pulled my T-shirt down.

"Oops," I snickered. "Sorry."

"Stop," he said, reaching for my hands. He pulled them out so he could get a better look. I discovered I was wrong—I *could* blush a deeper red.

The T-shirt wasn't indecent or anything. It came to just below mid-thigh, but the fact I wasn't wearing any shorts made me self-conscious. Ezra let out a shaky breath then ran his hands down his face, stopping over his mouth.

"I gotta get out of here," he said. He kissed my cheek and opened the door, closing it so softly I barely heard it.

I imagined him creeping down the hall and back into Kai's room. I laid back down with the biggest shit-eating grin on my face.

"How am I supposed to sleep after that?" I asked no one.

CHAPTER TWENTY-ONE

I was too keyed up to get back to sleep. *The four hours I got will just have to suffice,* I thought. I jumped in the shower again to tame that fake Christina Aguilera Afro thing I had going on, only mine was real. I was in such a good mood I sat in the shower rapping some sick lyrics of my own creation and shaved my legs just in case Mr. Brandon wanted to cop a feel of those bad boys.

When I was done, I wrapped a towel around my body and got out my blow-dryer. While experimenting with Frankie we discovered my curls were best tamed right after they were dried. Like, the curls were big enough naturally that while still warm from the dryer, as long as I pinned them up like I'd used a curling iron, and let them cool completely while pinned, they would fall and look like a professional blowout. The effect was marvelous, darling, but took forty-five minutes, which I didn't usually have.

But that morning I did, so I carefully pinned big curls to my head and while they cooled down, I cleaned up my eyebrows and applied my makeup. I took extra time pulling together a fantastic outfit and threw together a few choice pieces of jewelry, got dressed, and pulled on my trusty boots. I searched through my bag for my bottle of vanilla and found it on the bottom of the case, of course. Since I didn't hear the house stirring at all, I decided to kill some time and rearranged my bag for optimal fittage. In the bathroom, I dabbed a few generous drops of vanilla on all my pulse points.

I put my hands over my pinned curls and felt they were cool enough so I pulled the duckbill clips and let the curls fall, setting them with a little hair spray and a little hair serum to smooth any strays. I turned my head over and shook them out, letting them tumble down my back. The effect was exactly what I wanted.

I sat on the edge of the bed, reading for a few minutes, when I started hearing voices drift into the kitchen down the hall. Doors opened and boys spilled out when the smell of bacon permeated the whole apartment.

My blood started to race knowing I'd be seeing Ezra soon. I was so eager yet so hesitant, my stomach that strange mixture of anticipation and queasiness. I started to doubt whether what happened last night was really as I remembered it. I knew enough of boys from Frankie to know they often got some twisted sense of buyer's remorse after a night of *pasión*. Not that hands really went anywhere but around the facial/shouldery area. I started to lose it, overanalyzing everything that happened, then recalled the words Ezra gave me. He wasn't a liar. He was a boy, no, man of integrity, and I needed to give him a little credit.

I stood, checked my reflection, touched a jittery hand to a door handle and pulled open the door. I stepped out into the hall and closed the door. There was one thing I didn't take into consideration when I stepped out, and that was that the open kitchen was settled across the main hall, perpendicular with the hall my room was in, and everyone had the perfect view of me as I took the fifty-foot walk. And they watched. All of them. All four boys. Mike and Rosie glanced at me but returned to their business. I almost turned around and sprinted back toward the room but knew how ridiculous that would look, so I owned the walk.

I was slow at first, but picked it up with as much pep as possible. *Confidence!* The speakers in the kitchen blared something young, letting me know one of the boys picked the station.

It got all quiet as all of them, save for Rosie and Mike at the stove together, their backs to me, stared my direction. I checked behind me. There was nothing. *Hot dog! This is for me! Well, well, well.*

All of them were still in their PJs and I hesitated again. I was halfway down the hall. It was too late, so I kept going. I'd thought they'd have gotten control of themselves, but all four boys were frozen where they stood.

I reached the kitchen and waved. "'Allo, govnas!" I greeted, hoping to wake them up a little.

It worked, they all scrambled around, back into their morning routine. All except Ezra. Wonderful, beautiful Ezra. He smiled at me and bit his bottom lip to keep from grinning too widely. He made a little twirl motion with his fingers, asking me to turn around, so I did. I curtsied, 'cause I'm a gosh dang lady, when I met him face to face again.

Nice, he mouthed.

He still had on his track pants, but he'd thrown a T-shirt over his Adonis chest and abs, which was a crying shame, but I had to respect his acknowledgment of a social norm, you know, because it's a social norm and lest be thrown into the dregs of society. Jeez.

Out of the corner of my eye, I noticed Kai. He looked at me, then back at Ezra, then back at me, and put it together at a Joey-from-*Friends* kind of pace. He pointed at me and Ezra at the same time, smiling like an idiot. We ignored him.

Ezra patted the area next to him on his side of the bench at the table where he was reading the paper like he was a grown-up. I walked over to him and sat with my back to the table so I could swing my legs over modestly because I was wearing a skirt. He looked right through me, it seemed, and I froze in place. He leaned imperceptibly my direction and inhaled.

"You smell good enough to eat," he whispered, making my stomach drop.

I threw my legs over the bench and swiveled around, maintaining an appropriate distance from him so as not to alarm the parental units of the shenanigans we'd gotten up to during the night.

Acting as apathetic as he could, Ezra said, "Coffee, Jupiter?"

"Thank you, yes," I said. "I'd love some."

He leaned over me, his chest brushing against my arm, and flipped a coffee cup in his hands, settling it in front of me on an agate coaster. He grabbed the French press in the center of the table and poured a cup for me.

"How do you like it?" he asked me.

I bit my lip to keep from laughing, shattering all pretense of maturity. Ezra's cheeks flushed red when he realized the suggestion, and I giggled, resting my forehead against his shoulder trying so, so hard not to laugh out loud. We both choked down our amusement as Milo and Kai joined us at the table.

"What's so funny?" Kai asked.

"Oh, nothing," I told him. "Ezra was just getting me coffee."

Kai looked at my coffee cup then at Ezra. "Heh, heh. Yeah, *that Ezra*. Such a trip," he teased.

He shook his head, leaned over, and started to fish through the paper, landing on the sports section, and plucked it out, setting it in front of him.

Ezra cleared his throat. "Cream? Sugar?" he asked.

I didn't know. I'd never really had it before.

"Both," I told him to be safe.

He put both in, took a small spoon from a pile next to the coffee pot, stirred my coffee for a few strokes, handed it over to me, and encouraged me to keep stirring. When I didn't feel any more resistance from the lumps of sugar, I picked up the cup and took a trial sip.

HOLY MOTHER OF MOSES! It was amazing. I kid you not, the nectar of the gods.

Like it? Ezra mouthed.

"You have just created a monster," I warned.

"Jupiter!" I heard across the kitchen, startling me. I spilled a little coffee on the table. Ezra took his napkin and wiped it up for me.

"Thank you," I told him. "Good morning, Rosie!"

"Mornin', child!" She came around the middle island toward the table, a spatula in her hand. "Sakes alive, girl! You look prettier than a glob of butter melting on a stack of pancakes."

"Thank you!" *I think.*

"You like bacon, baby?" she asked.

"Does Kai like girls?" I answered.

She laughed. "So what you're saying is you like bacon now, but once it comes to the table, you'll change your mind 'bout it and want ham instead," Rosie chimed in.

The whole kitchen erupted into laughter including Kai, but his smile fell quickly. "Hey, a pig's a pig," he bit back.

Rosie slapped Kai on the back of the head and walked away, rolling her eyes and shaking her head. "Come on!" Kai said, laughing. "Can't stand the heat, get out the kitchen!" he said, mimicking her accent perfectly.

"Hey, respect your mama," Mike said, flipping something.

"Don't worry," Rosie said sweetly to Kai, "one day you'll learn. One day you'll meet a pretty girl and you'll wrap yourself around her finger. I'll watch with pure glee as she runs you around in circles."

Kai looked shell shocked and swallowed hard.

"Where are you boys going to take Jupiter today?" Rosie asked, pulling something from the oven.

"What about the aquarium?" Bear suggested.

Ezra laughed. "We live in the Florida Keys, Bear."

"So?" he asked, confused.

"What about the Chicago Shakes?" Milo asked. He shrugged his shoulders. "It's near the Pier, but who cares?"

"What's Chicago Shakes?" I asked Milo.

He smiled a brilliant smile at me. "The Chicago Shakespeare Theater."

"That's cool!" I said.

"He only wants to go because he's got a paper due the first week of school next week on *Othello*. Our prep school makes all the new seniors read the play over the summer, and he didn't have time," Kai dug in.

Milo's eyes blew wide.

"Milo!" Rosie said, whipping around. "Is that true? Did you not read *Othello*?"

Milo bent across the table, making like he was going to get up. "Your ass is grass," he told Kai under his breath then fully stood. "Ma, don't worry, I'll read it this week. I swear," he tried to appease.

I watched as Milo buttered up his mom, and she fell for it hook, line, and sinker. She was putty in these boys' hands, I could tell.

"Listen," she told everyone, "make sure whatever you do, you guys get back by five."

"What for?" Kai asked, scanning the paper.

She placed a large platter of French toast on the table. She looked exasperated. *Note to self, being a mom to boys is aggravating but a blast.*

"Kai, I have the library fundraiser here tonight. You know this, boy! The caterers will be here by three. I want you all out of the house until five, but home in time to shower and dress. Your tuxes are in your closets, pressed. Do *not*, under any circumstances, walk into this house five minutes until seven. Guests arrive then, and I expect you all to be dressed and ready to go, with smiles on your pretty faces." She looked at Ezra. "I had one of Kai's tuxes pressed for you as well, Ezra."

I swallowed. *Was I expected to be here? Surely not.*

I smiled up at Rosie. "Uh, Mrs. Brandon?" I asked.

She rolled her eyes. "It's Rosie, baby. Or Mama. Whatever," she said, then offered a gorgeous smile.

"Um, what time does this party end?" I asked, trying to figure out what I would do while they threw this fundraiser thing. I wanted to see Chicago but didn't want to walk the city on my own at night.

"Not sure, honey. They go pretty late. Does that make you uncomfortable, babe?"

"Oh no," I said to reassure her. "I just didn't know what time I should come back to the house."

Her confused face matched Bear's. "Whatcha talkin' 'bout, honey?"

"Uh," Kai chimed in, his voice a bundle of nerves, "Jupiter, my mom would like to cordially invite you to a fundraiser we're throwing at our house. We throw one every year. It's a formal affair."

Everyone stopped what they were doing and stared at Kai.

"Kai!" Rosie yelled. "My God, boy! You get sorrier and sorrier every day."

He laughed. "I'm sorry, Mama. I just forgot to tell them."

Ezra leaned into me and whispered, "More like smoked it away."

I would have found that hilarious if I wasn't a little panicked that I didn't have anything decent to wear.

Rosie noticed my face. "Now, don't worry. It's no big thing. Did you bring anything?"

"I really didn't," I told her. I felt all the color drain from my face.

"Okay, don't get hysterical now. We've got hours yet."

She got up to get a big plate of bacon and set it next to the French toast. Kai reached over for a piece, but she slapped his hand away.

"Ow!" he said, rubbing his hand.

She sat down as Mike brought over a big platter of scrambled eggs and settled in next to her.

She snapped her fingers. "I got it! Melissa!"

The boys nodded their heads as they filled up their

plates. Ezra offered eggs and I nodded, still a little stunned by the morning's progress. He filled my plate for me.

"If I don't do this," he said in my ear, "the rest of them will wipe the platters clean and you'll miss out."

I turned and smiled at him. "Thank you," I told him.

I picked up my fork and took a bite of eggs after we prayed. "Um, Rosie?"

"Yes, baby?"

"Who is Melissa?"

"Oh, she's the corporate lawyer who lives across the hall. She's 'bout your size. She's sweet as cherry pie and a good friend. She'll be more than happy to help out, I just know it. I'll call after breakfast and we'll head on over there."

"She's also hot as a tamale," Kai mocked his mom's accent.

Mike looked over at Kai and Kai shrank into his side of the bench. Mike was the silent, calm type, but it worked for him.

"Kai Brandon," Rosie said sternly.

"Sorry," he said, looking remorseful.

"Should I look up matinee times of *Othello*?" Ezra asked the table.

I looked at Ezra and he smiled. "Definitely," I told him.

CHAPTER TWENTY-TWO

After breakfast, Rosie called Melissa the corporate lawyer across the hall and yanked me to her door, chatting me up and making me laugh. Rosie was the *best*.

She knocked on Melissa's door a few times and quicker than I would have thought, Melissa pulled the door open with flourish.

"Welcome!" she said, making way for us to pass.

"Melissa," Rosie said, dragging me through the foyer and main hall to the main living room, "this is Jupiter!"

I took the hand Melissa stuck out to me. "Hello!" she said. "So nice to meet you."

"It's a pleasure," I told her, returning the pleasantry.

Melissa was my height with gold hair cut at the shoulder. She wore it wavy and ultra chic. It made me want to bolt out the door to the nearest hairstylist.

"I hear Kai, and I quote, *left you up the creek with no paddle?*"

I laughed. "Yes, he did."

"Come on," she said playfully.

She and Rosie walked into the main hall and I followed. Melissa's house was similar to the Brandons' floor plan, but she decorated it so eclectically it felt different. I followed her into the master and around a corner, through a kick-ass bathroom that would have been my favorite room in the house, if it had been mine, and into a giant walk-in closet.

My eyes followed rows and rows of expensive-looking clothing and shoes and suddenly I wondered what the hell cases Melissa fought. She didn't look any older than twenty-eight or so, and I thought she must have come out swinging after college. It damn near made me whoop with pride. She awakened a rivalry in me, a healthy kind of contest. *Success looks good on women*, I thought.

"You like clothes?" Melissa asked.

"I like clothes just fine," I admitted, "but you know what really tickles my pickle?"

"What's that?" Rosie asked, rummaging through Melissa's closet.

"Textures. I'm a touchy-feely kinda gal."

"Oh my God!" Melissa yelled. My eyes blew wide. "I know the *perfect* outfit for you then." She ran to one corner of her closet. "I bought it about a month ago in New York while arguing a case. No, after I *won* a case." She pulled out a zippered bag and hung it on a hook to unzip it. As she did, she said, "It's by Max Gengos. It's so unconventional I knew I couldn't really wear it anywhere often, but I couldn't help myself."

She took a silky, creamy white skirt and top from the bag and held them up in front of me, shoving me in front of her floor-length mirror. Rosie and Melissa stood beside me, trying to imagine what I would look like in it, I guessed.

"Oh my God, it's perfect," Melissa said.

I dragged the fabric through my hands and resisted

the urge to moan. It was a heavenly feeling. My fingers caught a tag at the end of a sleeve.

"Melissa, you haven't worn this yet?"

"Oh not yet, hadn't found an occasion to. Why?" she said, cocking her head to look at the tag.

It was a seventeen-hundred-dollar outfit.

"Melissa, I can't wear this! Don't get me wrong, it's beautiful, really beautiful, but I can't wear something this expensive, especially if you haven't worn it yet."

I started to push the top and skirt back at her, but she only scoffed at me. "I don't care about that kind of stuff, Jupiter. Trust me when I say I bought this so it would be worn, and if you take it on its maiden voyage then I would be honored."

"Oh my gosh, I don't know," I said. "Why don't you wear it tonight?" I asked.

She sighed. "I would have but I forgot about it and bought something else. I have my heart set on my newer dress. Just wear the Max Gengos, Jupiter. I really don't mind."

She'd convinced me. "Are you sure?"

"Very," she said, smiling wide. "Here, go try it on in the bathroom while Rosie and I pick out shoes for you. What size are you?"

I gulped. "Um, an eight."

"I'm an eight and half, but it'll work."

I left the women in the closet and undressed in that kind stranger's bathroom. I looked at the inside tag of the top. Fifty-one percent silk, forty-nine percent wool body. One hundred percent silk charmeuse lining with silk organza tipping. I ran my hands over the top of the fabric. It was without a doubt probably the highest quality garment I would ever put on.

The skirt was tight fitting and came to about three inches above the knee, but there was a high slit over the left thigh. Despite it's mature fabric, the style was very young looking. They were so well made you couldn't even see the zipper closure. The top was fitted and long sleeved, and slightly cropped, with two peekaboo squares under each shoulder that left an inch or two of fabric between the collarbones.

I felt dizzy remembering Ezra kissing me at the dip between my collarbones earlier that morning. My face flushed a bright red, my skin growing hot. It felt very appropriate for a piece of fabric to cover that part of my body, as if it belonged to Ezra now and I wanted to keep it that way.

When I gained a little bit of my self-control back, I opened the closet door and stepped inside. Both women gasped.

"Is that a good sign?" I asked, a little embarrassed.

"It is a *very* good sign." Rosie giggled. Her hands went to her face. "Jupiter, Ezra is going to keel over when he sees you." That burning in my cheeks returned. Rosie laughed at me sweetly. "Oh, please, child, nothing gets past a mama. Nothing."

"Here," Melissa said, gesturing for me to sit at a vanity chair in the corner of her closet. "Try these on," she said, and handed me a pair of simple black, closed-toe, ankle-strap stilettos.

I shoved them on and stood, walking to the mirror. The effect was a little dramatic. I almost didn't recognize myself. Rosie took the bulk of my hair and pinned it all to the side. Melissa pretended to lick her finger then placed it on my shoulder. "Tsst!" she teased.

I laughed and smiled at her. "You're very kind to lend

this to me."

"Think nothing of it, Jupiter. Thanks for doing it justice."

I looked back at my reflection again and noticed I no longer just felt like an adult woman, I *looked* like one too.

CHAPTER TWENTY-THREE

Since we'd all eaten like pigs at breakfast, none of us felt like lunch before the twelve o'clock showing of *Othello*. The show had been sold out for weeks, but somehow Kai's dad pulled some strings and got five tickets in the gallery. When we'd found our seats, I felt slightly dizzy. Heights + Jupiter = nervous, hyperventilating Jupiter, carry the difference and you get giggly Jupiter.

"You okay?" Ezra asked, placing his hand on my lower back.

His touch calmed me. "Fine," I told him.

Bear walked to the fifth seat in our row, then Milo, myself, Ezra, then Kai. We all sat at once.

I leaned into Ezra's side and whispered, "We're smack dab in the middle. Guess there'll be no making out for us," I joked.

Ezra stared hard at me and I felt my stomach plummet. He brought his mouth up to my ear. "Maybe nothing obvious," he said, shocking me as his tongue found the side of my neck to taste my skin.

He sat back as if he hadn't just licked my neck, and laughed at something Kai said. I blew out a shaky breath and wiped the palms of my hands down my Elvis Presley miniskirt.

"Do you like Shakespeare?" Milo asked at my side.

I turned to him and smiled briefly.

"My love is as a fever, longing still
For that which longer nurseth the disease,
Feeding on that which doth preserve the ill,
Th' uncertain sickly appetite to please.
My reason, the physician to my love,
Angry that his prescriptions are not kept,
Hath left me, and I desp'rate now approve
Desire is death, which physic did except.
Past cure I am, now reason is past care,
And frantic mad with evermore unrest,
My thoughts and my discourse as madmen's are,
At random from the truth vainly expressed;
For I have sworn thee fair and thought thee bright,
Who art as black as hell, as dark as night."

"Bloody hell," Kai said with an awful fake British accent, making Bear laugh.

Milo swallowed. "I'll take that as a yes."

I smiled at him. "You would be correct."

"That sonnet is rather dark," Ezra said, pulling me away from Milo's ridiculous expression.

"It is," I confirmed, "and yet it's still my favorite."

He looked at me. "And why is that?"

Kai and his brothers listened in.

"Because it proves that love is blind. If it was in 1609, it always was. It always will be."

"Is that a good thing?" Ezra asked me.

"It is neither good nor evil. It just *is*."

216

Ezra bit his bottom lip thoughtfully. "That's sort of a profound observation," he finally said, leaning closer to me.

The entire theater, including Kai and his brothers, seemed to dissipate into nothing around Ezra and me. It was us and only us.

"I'm sure I can't be the only one to have made that connection. There's no such thing as an original thought," I told him.

"It doesn't matter, though, does it? Because it's original to you. Right now. To us."

I smiled at him. "Is it?" I asked.

"It is." His gaze dipped to my lips and he swallowed, idly meeting my eyes once more. "Are you? *Blinded?*"

The house lights dimmed all around, plunging us into sudden and deep darkness. I leaned into him, the dim bolstering me, pressing lips to his ear.

"Are *you?*" I quieted.

I felt him smile against my cheek, his hand going to my knee. "I'm blinded, all right, but not deceived."

My words stuck in my throat at his surprising compliment, so I pulled at his collar and kissed him so softly at the base of his throat I was afraid it might not have registered, that is until his hand squeezed my knee.

I sat up when his hand left my leg and faced the front, thankful the black hid my secret smile, and waited for the stage lights to come on and the actors to do their thing. I felt his burning stare on the side of my face for several seconds before he turned and did as I did. I shifted in my seat, placing my forearm on the armrest, and crossed my legs. His left hand found my right and he dragged it over into his lap, turning my palm up for him to study at his leisure.

The tip of his thumb traced the outline of my hand when Roderigo and Iago took the stage and the scaffolding lights turned on, bathing us both in a dull light. It was just enough for me to watch his face as he memorized my hand twice then moved his investigation to my wrist, bringing it to his mouth to kiss once.

His fingers traveled the length of my forearm to the inside of my elbow and pressed there. I thought he'd keep going but instead he lifted his arm and brought it around the back of my seat. To the casual observer nothing would seem suspicious, but under closer scrutiny, they would have seen his thumb making lazy circles at the back of my neck, distracting me from the extraordinary performance on the stage.

Two can play at this game, I thought.

I let my arm fall from the chair rest. Excruciatingly slowly, I ran my fingers across the outside seam of his jeans then slid my hand onto his thigh and let it lie there. I felt the muscle tense for several minutes and almost burst out laughing. My thumb followed every movement against the top of his leg that he made at the top of my neck.

He caught on soon enough and squeezed my neck so I squeezed his thigh in turn. Both our bodies shook as we tried not to laugh. Milo and Kai stared at us, baffled as to why we would be losing our shit during Iago's monologue to Roderigo professing his hate for Othello. We both started to double over, but neither took our hands off our prospective game pieces, which only made it worse. Neither of us would let go. It was the world's worst yet *best* game of chicken.

Milo cleared his throat, warning us. We both sat back and moved our hands from one another. When my hand

218

was finally free, I swiped at my eyes to clear the evidence of my teary laughter. I sighed once then coughed, silently both agreeing to shape up or risk getting shipped out.

During intermission, we all spilled out into the lobby. We huddled in a circle at first, then decided to walk so we could stretch our legs.

"Uh, what the hell happened in there?" Kai asked us.

My cheeks burned and I ducked my head, peering out of the huge glass windows that circled the entire theater onto the pier.

"I don't know what you're talking about," Ezra said, shrugging off Kai.

"What was so funny anyway?" Milo asked.

I snorted but saved it with a cough. "Coming down with something?" Milo asked in a concerned tone.

"No, no," I answered, "just clearing my throat."

His brows furrowed. He suspected something was up. And he was right, but Ezra and I needed to have a little discussion before we went blabbing to the whole world what that something was.

"*Ezra?* Ezra Brandon!" we heard over our shoulders. We all turned toward the voice. "Oh my God! I knew it was you. How crazy is this?" a tall, leggy brunette squealed.

She sprinted our direction and threw her whole body on him, wrapping her legs around his waist and hugging him around the neck. Ezra grunted and settled his hands at her waist.

"Cameron," he choked out.

She slid down his body bit by bit, drawing out the contact. I was hit by a wall of jealousy. It was such a heady sensation, I felt myself falling back a bit. Milo caught me by the elbow and smiled down at me.

"Clumsy?" he asked, poking me with a finger in the ribs.

I tried to play it off with a casual smile. I only hoped it translated. "A little," I told him.

"How long's it been?" she asked. "A year?"

Ezra had the decency to look a little shell shocked. His cheeks pinkened as he pushed her body away from his. "Yeah, about a year," he confirmed.

"How long have you been in town?" she asked. "Why haven't you called?"

He rubbed the back of his neck. "Just got into town last night," he told her in explanation.

Cameron turned to Milo and winked at him. I watched him duck his head after a quick wave of his hand.

"What's up, Cameron?" he asked.

"Nothing much," she answered. "You ready for school to start? You here for that *Othello* paper too?" She laughed.

"Something like that," he offered.

Cameron turned to Kai and Bear. "Hello, boys! What's shakin'?"

"Not much," Bear said.

Kai didn't answer but offered a smile devoid of teeth and a raised brow. He didn't like her. If Kai didn't like this Aphrodite reincarnate there must be something going on.

She threaded her arm through Ezra's and dragged him down the hall. Kai and his brothers kept up with them as they all talked. The walkway was only so wide so I was forced to follow them like a Justin Bieber Insta account, with shame and humiliation.

Milo fell back with me, which I was grateful for.

"That's Cameron," Milo offered without question, thank God.

"Oh?" I asked, trying not to sound too curious.

"I'll introduce you when she comes down from her Ezra high," he teased, not realizing how badly that hurt me.

"Okay, cool," I somehow regurgitated, despite the frog in my throat.

"They hooked up last year at Kai's graduation party."

Oh my God. I do not want to hear this. "Oh, that right?"

"Pissed me off too. I mean, at the time it pissed me off. I'd had a crush on Cameron since freshman year. Of course, Ezra didn't know this then, but it still hurt. After that, she wouldn't even talk to me unless it was to inquire after lughead there."

Yup, didn't want to hear this. "That really sucks, Milo. If it's any consolation, she's a fool not to see you." He got that dreamy-eyed look on his face again. "Don't worry," I said, patting his arm, "whoever she is, she'll come along soon enough," I reassured him, while also trying to draw that line in the sand.

It didn't work.

"At the fundraiser tonight, will you save me a dance?" he asked.

What was I supposed to say? *Uh, can't, Milo. Sorry, I dig Ezra. You know, the one who distracted Cameron?*

"Sure," I told him. "I've got the perfect song."

"What song's that?" he asked, trying to flirt.

Lock it up, Jupiter. Lock it up! I tried to think of the most unromantic song ever written. "Uh, R. Kelly's 'Ignition Remix'?" I *immediately* regretted that suggestion.

Milo's eyes blew wide. *Shiiieeeeet! I done messed up!*

Should have gone with "I Believe I Can Fly."

Needless to say, intermission threw ice on the friction Ezra and I'd created.

Toot, toot! Beep, beep!

CHAPTER TWENTY-FOUR

After the play, we all congregated outside the front of the theater in a giant circle. Somehow I got stuck beside Cameron, the Amazonian. Next to her, I felt like an Oompa Loompa. *Doom-pa-dee-do!*

"Jupiter, this is Cameron," Milo introduced. "Cameron, Jupiter."

"Hi," I said, waving at her.

"Hi, nice to meet you," she said.

She had friendly eyes and a nice smile. I wanted to dislike her, but I couldn't. She didn't know. *Ezra doesn't even owe me any kind of explanation, not really. It was last year.*

"Nice to meet you as well," I told her.

"Ezra says he's giving you a ride to Seattle?" she asked. "How lucky you're both going to the same school."

All the boys watched our exchange with rapt attention. I looked over at Ezra. His face seemed a little stricken.

"Yes," I answered her, yet eyed Ezra, feeling a little sick to my stomach. "He's my *ride*." I turned back toward her. "Fortunate indeed."

"Are you going to the party tonight?" she asked.

"I am," I told her.

"Cool," she said, glancing over at Ezra. "Where are you staying?"

I felt confused. "With the Brandons," I explained.

She looked taken aback but quickly recovered. "Oh! Oh, cool."

I nodded my head and folded my arms around my waist. "Yup."

I felt myself checking out.

"It should be a pretty fun party." She laughed at some private joke. "You'd think they'd be a bore, being a fundraiser for the library, but Rosie knows how to throw 'em, right, Ezra?"

We both looked at him. He forced a smile. "Uh, yeah."

"Have you decided what you're wearing?" she asked, trying to keep the conversation going. "I have no clue. Guess I'll be raiding my closet. Or *maybe* I'll do a little shopping, scare myself up a little black number or something."

"Shopping is never a bad idea," I told her, trying to sound lighthearted.

"Isn't that the truth!" She grabbed my arm, startling me. "Oh my God! I have the best idea! You can come with me."

"Oh, I don't know about that," I said, but she interrupted me.

"Come on," she urged. "It'll be fun, I promise."

"Actually, Cameron," Ezra spoke up, "we're headed for a late lunch right now. We'll catch you later?"

Her face fell in obvious disappointment. "Okay, that's cool. Yeah, see you tonight."

"Come on, guys," Ezra said, leading us down the pier.

"See you tonight, Cameron," I said, waving goodbye.

"Bye, Jupiter!"

When we were a few yards away from Cameron, Ezra turned to the group. "Where do you guys want to eat?" He glanced at his watch. "We've got an hour to kill before five."

Milo looked at my face, at the heartsick I knew I was probably wearing like a bright yellow afghan. "Naw, man, count me out. I'm beat. Just want to get a few winks in before we have to get ready," Milo said. "What say you, Jupiter? Want to walk with me?"

Milo was my human life preserver.

"Yes!" I said too enthusiastically, then checked my tone. "That sounds perfect, actually." Milo started walking in the direction of his house so I followed. "See you guys in an hour?"

"Jupiter! Are you sure you aren't hungry?" Ezra asked.

I turned and gave him a watery smile, hoping he didn't see how sick I felt. "No, really. Still kind of full from earlier. I'll see you back at Kai's."

I sprinted ahead a little to catch up with Milo. I glanced over my shoulder. Ezra stared my direction, his brows pinched.

"You're in love with him," Milo said matter-of-factly.

"No!" I insisted.

Milo smiled and rolled his eyes, reminding me so much of Rosie. "Yes, you are."

I shook my head emphatically, but it lost steam and petered out into me bawling into my hands.

"Oh my God, I think I am."

Milo wrapped an arm around me as we walked. "Why'd you let me carry on like that about Cameron?"

I took a deep breath and wiped away the tears. "We're not exactly talking about it yet," I explained. "If I'd stopped you, you would have known something was up."

"How long have you been seeing Ezra," he asked with an intense edge I chose to ignore.

"I've seen him for as long as I've known him, but we only started *hanging*," I said, using finger quotes, "last night."

"Last night!" Milo shouted, making me laugh a little.

"Yeah, he came into your guest room around three in the morning and just sort of declared that he was into me, like, *really* into me, and we spent most of the morning kissing our faces off."

Milo made a disgusted pout. "Okay, okay. No more needs to be said."

I laughed for real. "Listen, I'm not crazy. I know Cameron showing up probably doesn't mean anything to Ezra, but the way he handled her, the situation, made me feel a little queasy. It just felt wrong for him to let her jump on him and then, instead of explaining to her who I was, he just mentioned that he was giving me a *ride*? It makes me feel like he's trying to keep his options open, and that doesn't settle well."

Milo looked pensive. "When you put it like that," he said.

"Oh my God! *You agree with me?* Now I feel full-on sick."

He laughed. "I'm just saying I can see your side to things. Let's get back to the house, take a little nap, and get ready. You can have a heart-to-heart with Ezra, and it will probably get all straightened out."

I sniffed back tears. "Okay," I told him.

He squeezed my shoulders. "Feel better?"

I smiled. "I do. Thanks, Milo."

"You're welcome."

"Cameron's an idiot," I told him.

"Tell me something I don't know," he said.

Milo and I went up to his apartment. Rosie looked surprised to see us without the others, but we explained that we were more tired than hungry and she waved us off, content to return to her party preparations. As soon as I reached my room, I laid down with the intention of only sleeping for twenty minutes at the most.

A knock at the door woke me. I turned over to look at the clock by the bed. It read six o'clock. *Damn it!*

I tried to clear the sleep from my throat. "Yeah?" I croaked out.

"Jupiter, are you still asleep?" Ezra asked.

"Uh, yeah, sorry. I'll get up and start getting ready," I told him.

"Can we talk?" he asked.

"Yeah, I want to chat it up real badly, but can it wait? I only have an hour."

"Sure," he said, sounding disappointed.

It got quiet. "Ezra?" I asked.

"Yeah?" he answered.

"I promise. Just give me an hour."

"Okay," he said, sounding better.

I rushed to the bathroom to pee and brush my teeth. I ran a hand up my leg to make sure my morning shave still held up, which it did, and inspected the ol' mane.

"Whoa, Nelly!"

The nap did her in.

I grabbed my curling iron from my bag and sectioned off my hair, re-curling and setting the curls with a duckbill clip again to cool. I washed my face, applying moisturizer, primer, and makeup, then rifled through my bag for a pair of underwear that wouldn't show through Melissa's skirt, but also wouldn't make me want to kill myself. It was a fine line.

I came up with a pair that satisfied all requirements and put them on. I dabbed a little vanilla on my pulse points and let my hair down, turning over and spraying it lightly with hairspray. I flipped back over and shook out the whole thing.

I glanced over at the clock. Seven fifteen. *Dang.* Carefully, I dressed in Melissa's borrowed outfit, wishing I'd eaten when I had the chance, because there was no way in hell I was going to let any food or drink anywhere near her expensive clothes. I sat at the edge of the bed and strapped on the stilettos. I stepped in front of the mirror in the bathroom.

"That'll do, Pig."

I cracked open the door and a multitude of voices poured down the hall. I was late. Pretty late. I wondered if that would offend Rosie. I made a mental note to apologize to her when I found her. Based on the volume of the voices, I doubted she had time to worry about why I was late, though. The hall where my room was, was dark to discourage guests from wandering down into the private bedrooms, I assumed.

As quietly as I could, I edged through the hall, trying not to trip out over the fact that Melissa's stilettos cracked against the ancient wood floor like a judge's gavel with every step I took. Eventually I reached the wide main hall where there had to be at least a hundred people mingling about, talking with one another.

Music rang through the house and I noticed Rosie had chosen a modern playlist, or had allowed one of her boys to pick it out. That seemed more likely the case. Taking a deep breath, I stepped out of the shadows of the hall and out into the light. Half the room turned my direction to see who had emerged from the dark. I resisted the urge to raise the middle of my forearm to my nose and cackle, "I *vant* to drink your *blud*!"

Many of those eyes turned back to their conversation, but some turned toward the kitchen, as if they saw or heard someone or something I didn't.

They followed someone crossing through the main hall, looking back and forth between me and whomever else distracted them until I saw who they'd been staring at.

It was Ezra. In a tux. Ezra in a bleeding tux.

Ho.ly. Ca.nno.li. *Sign me up!*

Why? Why do you have to be so hot?

He was staring at me, almost through me, and my stomach flipped over and over again. He walked with purpose toward me and people took notice.

When he reached me, he stood at least two feet away and I reveled in the fact I didn't have to strain my neck to look into his eyes. He stuck two fingers at his collar and pulled, running his fingers across the front.

"Jupiter," he said, his voice deep, almost hoarse.

"Ezra," I countered.

"I—" he began, but didn't, or couldn't, finish.

His eyes raked me from my toes, perusing slowly, all the way to my face. It did things to my belly. I tried to take a deep breath in that moment but couldn't pull in enough air. I rocked my weight from one foot to the other and that's when I noticed Kai had moved toward us, watching us. He raised a brow at me, trying to hide his smile, and gave me the okay sign with his fingers. I looked next to him and saw Milo. His face looked pale and wounded, which speared me in the gut for a minute.

When I looked back at Ezra, he'd moved closer to me, leaning against the wall I stood near.

"You are the most beautiful woman I have ever met in my entire life," he told me. His tone was severe, though, like he was struggling with something.

"But?" I asked, leaning a shoulder against the same wall to face him.

"But *nothing*." He laughed without humor. "I'm not leaving anything out, Jupiter."

I felt my neck heat to an impossible warmth then as it crept up my face. He saw it and he liked it if his smile was any indication.

"I'm having difficulty with something," I told him.

"What is that?" he asked.

"Why did you tell Cameron you were giving me a ride to Seattle?"

"Because she asked."

"And that's all you offered?"

"Yes."

"Why?" I asked, feeling the heartsick come flying to the surface again.

"Because we hadn't discussed anything yet and I didn't want to start calling you my girlfriend around my cousins without talking to you about it first."

"It wasn't because you hooked up with her last year at Kai's graduation and you were trying to keep your options open?"

"Absolutely not," he answered, a look of revulsion on his face.

"Okay," I said, processing what he'd said.

"Are you?" he asked.

"Am I what?"

"With me? Exclusively?" he pressed. He took one step closer to me.

His shoulders strained against Kai's borrowed tux, his hands tucked into the crooks of his arms. I studied his fingers and wondered if he would put them on my skin soon. I swallowed the thought; the idea tasted too sweet to pass up.

"What exactly would a girlfriend of Ezra Brandon be?" I asked, stepping forward. Only a few inches separated us.

"She'd be kissed," he said, pulling back the fabric of my top slightly and pressing his lips at the dip between my collarbones. "Touched." He ran his thumb across my bottom lip. "Told things." He leaned in and whispered in my ear that he'd want me always. "Worshipped," he continued. Ezra ran both his hands through my hair, tilting my head back, and kissed a line up my throat that made me almost fall over. He caught me and held me upright. "Cared for," he told me. He paused and swallowed hard. "Loved," he said with finality as the palm of his hand found the top of my chest and pressed deeply but gently.

I felt my eyes water. "She'd be all those things, would she?"

"To name a few," he teased.

I took a deep breath and stared into the eyes. "My name is Jupiter Corey and I'm Ezra Brandon's girlfriend," I told him. They were words I didn't think I'd ever get to say, words I could not have enjoyed more.

He smiled as he placed his hands at my jawline and walked me backward into the dark hall. All pretense aside since Rosie's guests could no longer see us, he kissed me deeply, his lips bruising mine, his breath hot against my face, his hands exploring my shoulders, hair, and neck.

We heard someone clear their throat in the main hall. "Um, Ezra?" Kai or Milo, I wasn't sure, asked. Ezra's mouth pulled away except for a feather touch. His lips slightly parted and his hands gripped my face. He groaned, frustrated beyond belief, and I seconded the motion. His eyes opened but his lips stayed.

"Don't you dare move," Ezra whispered against my mouth, his voice echoing against my skin.

As if he knew what I needed, he pressed me against the hall's wall, a hand on my hip, squeezing the bone there, his body pressed into mine.

"What's up, Kai?" Ezra asked as coolly as possible.

I didn't know how he could speak so calmly when his mouth inched over my throat. *You're burning me up from the outside in.* It was a slow, violent heat. I swallowed and his eyes followed the movement.

"Sorry, man," Kai said, a smile in his voice, "but Mama and Melissa want to see Jupiter."

"Tell them to buzz off," Ezra said, finding my mouth with his again.

Kai laughed. "That's not gonna fly," he said. "Meet me in the kitchen or they'll come after you personally."

Ezra pulled back, taking my bottom lip with him briefly. He looked at me with those lidded eyes, so I lifted myself on my toes and kissed each one.

"Oh God," he said. "Why are we here?" he asked me.

I giggled softly. "Because you love your aunt?"

He sighed. "True, but right now I don't like her very much."

I playfully pushed him. "Come on," I said, grabbing

his hand.

"Uh, Jupiter," he said, yanking me back lightly.

"Huh?"

"You, uh, might want to, uh, check your hair and maybe your lipstick."

He followed me to the guest room and I flipped on the light. We both adjusted to the sudden brightness. I stepped into the bathroom and leaned over the mirror. He leaned against the jamb of the door, looking suave as shit, and staring at me.

I smiled at him. "Don't I wear your kiss well?" I goaded, trying to clean smeared lipstick off my face.

"You wear it so well I can't stop looking at you."

"Don't then," I whispered, smoothing away the messy parts of my hair.

I turned around once I'd reapplied my lipstick and removed evidence of my first application from his mouth. I gripped his chin in my hand and rubbed my thumb across his bottom lip.

"I don't like it," he told me.

"Like what?" I asked, leaning across from him against the opposite jamb, our knees and legs mixing together.

"There's no smoking gun," he told me, his hands tucked into his pants pockets. He gestured to my face and hair. "No proof that my lips ever met yours, that my tongue ever tasted your skin."

Two fingers went to my swollen lips. "I can feel you. Still."

He stood tall, unbuttoning his fitted jacket, and gripped the edges of the trim above my head with both hands. I looked up at his straining fingers.

"If it were up to me, you'd feel me here," he spoke, barely brushing his lips against mine before breaking away, "always."

I reached up to kiss him again, deeper.

He stopped me by sedately leaning back against his side of the doorway, a knowing smile on his face.

I smiled back. "Rosie?"

He let out a deep breath, looked toward the bed, then back at me.

"Don't tempt me," I murmured low, as if his glance were a question.

"No," he said, with resolution. "Don't tempt *me*." He stood from leaning and grabbed my hand. "Come on, partner in crime."

Ezra led me down the dark hall, his hand firmly in mine, and into the dazzling lights, sounds, and voices of the party. He walked in a relaxed, detached way, the only real indication that anything had happened between us in that dark hallway was his thumb circling the bottom of my palm.

I looked around at the crowded rooms and noticed a lot of younger people our age with their parents. *Must be Kai's old and Milo's current classmates*, I thought. I moved my eyes to the entrance of the living room and caught Cameron's stare set on where Ezra held my hand.

Her gaze went to my face. She startled then gave me a pleasant, albeit forced, smile. She waved, so I lifted my free hand to wave back. I left my face as open and kind as possible at her. I hoped it worked.

Ezra dragged me into the kitchen where Kai and his brothers and a handful of other handsomely dressed people, including Melissa and a man, all stood.

The group stopped their conversation to watch us come through. My face flamed knowing they had to be aware what we'd been up to now that Ezra held my hand

234

so brazenly in front of them.

"Jupiter!" Melissa exclaimed, hugging me around the shoulders. She pulled back. "You are stunning!"

"Thank you so much," I told her. "Clothes make the girl and all that."

"No, honey," Rosie chimed in, "the girl makes the clothes."

"Thank you, Rosie."

"Looking a little worse for wear there, Ezra," Kai taunted. "You doing okay?"

"I'm fine," Ezra answered, but the indifferent facade broke when he started straightening his jacket again, pulling at his shirt sleeves, and running a hand through his hair.

Kai's shoulders shook trying to prevent himself from laughing. I stared out the kitchen windows suddenly interested in the buildings outside.

"Jupiter looks sick tonight, right, Ezra?" Kai continued on, crossing his arms over his chest.

Ezra looked down at the floor, his hands in his pockets. "She looks great," he confirmed.

"She really does, doesn't she, Milo?" Kai asked his brother, like a jackass.

Milo didn't answer.

"Like a hundred bucks," Kai interjected.

"I think the expression is 'like a million bucks,'" Bear corrected him. He was so adorable. I pinched his cheek playfully and a blush swept across his face.

Kai looked at Ezra. "No, I stand by what I said."

Ezra's throat started turning red and a hand went to the back of his neck. I didn't fully understand what was going on, but I knew I was missing something. This was more than Kai just trying to embarrass Ezra a little in front of his extended family. Everyone got really quiet, wondering what was actually happening. I don't think Kai realized it, but he was making me just as uncomfortable.

Milo slipped away from the chatting group. My eyes followed him as he approached the wall-mounted pad that ran the music running throughout the house. R. Kelly's "Igniton Remix" began to play. I burst out laughing as the young in the house *ooooh*ed.

"You are hilarious," I told Milo.

"Hey!" he yelled over his hollering classmates, dancing in the main hall. "It was *your* request." He walked around me and grabbed me by the wrist. "Come on," he told me, "you owe me a dance."

Ezra's brow pinched in confusion. *Don't worry*, I mouthed as Milo led me to the dance floor packed full with half the guests at the party.

"Make some room!" I shouted, my arms wide. "Y'all 'bout to be schooled!"

For some reason people thought that was funny. *They just don't know!*

I channeled the gutter-ball dance from *The Big Lebowski*. Milo and several others around us couldn't stop laughing. *What is wrong with these peeps? Don't they know I am an excellent gosh damn dancer?*

"Pipe down, player!" I shouted at Milo over the music. "You've never seen moves like this!" I said, popping my hips out.

Milo played along, trying to keep his laughter from taking over. As we shimmied around the floor, we'd created a pocket of people around us, including Ezra and Kai, both with tears in their eyes. *What is so funny?* I wanted to shout. I contemplated their reactions as I thrust my hands in pointed movements above my head and out all around. *Could I be a horrible dancer?* I asked myself as I ran in place. *That can't be it.*

When the song came to a close, Chuck Berry's "You Never Can Tell" spilled over us. I almost squealed in excitement.

"You?" I shouted at Ezra, pulling him toward me with an imaginary rope.

He smiled as he playfully Travolta twisted in front of me, taking Milo's spot.

"Dance good," I told him.

We *Pulp Fiction*'ed the crap out of that song without skipping a single step. Tarantino would be proud. Possibly aghast. Later, I would think both.

The rest of the night, we all flung and flailed around each other, taking the occasional water break in the kitchen to rehydrate. Kai tried his hand at Michael Flatley's Lord of the Dance. It was the kind of dancing that, had I been drinking, the next day I would have told everyone I knew what a talented Irish dancer he was. Since I was sober, though, I still planned on telling everyone I knew. I absently noticed someone taking video of him and made a mental note to find out who it was. He could never run for president.

When it got late and most of the older people left, leaving their young to their youthful indiscretions, the lights were turned low and the music followed suit with lots of slow dancing and idle hands. When I say idle hands, I mean that the boys' rambled and the girls' slapped. Periodic *ow*s rang out around us.

Ezra and I were in the kitchen, resting our feet. We each laid on a bench, feet to head, staring at one another from underneath the table. I'd ditched my shoes in my room about halfway through the night and stared down at my painted toes. Ezra craned his neck to see what I was looking at.

He smiled. "Did you make those feet pretty for yours *truly?*" He acted flattered. It was a ruse, but it made me happy anyway.

"Cointainly!" I answered and offered a foot for him to examine.

He grabbed it, his thumb resting in the arch, and massaged. I glanced at the clock on the stove. It read two in the morning.

My eyes began to droop. "Tryin' to make me sleepy?" I asked.

"No, Jupiter," his voice, rough from the night, answered. "If it were up to me, neither of us would ever sleep again."

I looked at him, curious. "Why?"

"Every second I get with you I want to be awake, that's why." He smiled and reached for the other foot. I gave it to him, suddenly very alert. "I don't think I've ever known anyone as alive as you. I want to absorb anything you're willing to lend." He rubbed my foot. It looked as if he was working up to something, so I stayed silent. "After the accident, something died in me, Jupiter, and you revived it. Colors are brighter, foods taste extraordinary, music sings brilliant, views dazzle. You are excitement and harmony all in one, Jupiter. You've weaved yourself so well through me there's no tearing you out. I don't *want* you out. You fill those strange, empty places. You make me happy."

"In the Aeroplane Over the Sea" poured through the speakers onto the surface of the table and spilled over our bodies. I took my foot away and slid beneath the table. My fingers tugged at his rolled shirt sleeve since he'd abandoned his jacket, and I pulled him below with me. I held his face in my hands, studied his expressions, his skin.

"I'm happy when I'm with you, Ezra," I told him.

"You are?" he asked, a worry line forming on his forehead.

I laughed at his obvious insecurity. "I am. I'm happy without you, too."

"Thanks," he told me, laughing.

"Let me finish." I giggled. "I mean, I'm a happy person, but with you? It's elevated tenfold. It's a sweet peace with you."

His brows drew together as he swallowed. "Jupiter, I-I have something to tell you," he began, but Kai came swooping into the kitchen, interrupting us.

"What are you two doing under there? You're both a bunch of weirdos," he claimed, bustling through cabinets, searching for something. "You guys hungry? I'm freaking starved. Everyone's pretty much left except for Cameron, and I have a feeling she's just hanging around here for—" Kai stopped talking. He turned toward us.

My expectant expression changed something in his.

"Heh, heh. Uh, you know what?" His voice rose with every word. "I just remembered something. I, uh, I have to get something from my room," he said.

It would have been halfway believable if he hadn't escaped the kitchen while prowling like the Pink Panther.

"What's up with him?" I asked.

"It's Kai," Ezra offered.

"True." I yawned.

"Let's get to bed."

"You wanted to tell me something, though."

He sighed and ran his hands through his hair. "Don't worry. We can talk in the morning."

I studied his troubled face. "Are you sure?"

He forced a smile. "Yes. Come on," he said, dragging me from underneath the table.

He walked with me down the hall to the guest room, kissed my cheek, and I went inside, closing the door behind me. Peeling off my borrowed outfit, I hung it up in the closet, threw on the most comfortable pair of yoga pants and T-shirt I could find, brushed my teeth, and fell into bed. Just as I was drifting to sleep, I remembered that I'd never gotten my phone replaced that day. I'd have to call Mercury and Frankie by landline again in the morning.

CHAPTER TWENTY-FIVE

Knock. Knock. Knock.

There was the faintest knock on my door, causing my heart to leap to my throat. I smiled. *Ezra,* I thought. The room was too dark to see the analog clock over the room's fireplace mantel. It was still pitch black outside when I looked out the window.

Slowly and as quietly as possible, I crept out of bed, smoothed down my clothing, and opened the door with a giant smile. Immediately it fell.

"*Cameron?*" I said, surprised. I looked into the hall around her. It was empty. "What's up? You okay?"

"Yes," she said, "can I come in?"

I hesitated. Did I want Cameron to come in? Not really. Did I really have a choice, though? "Uh, sure," I reluctantly allowed, moving to the side.

She brushed past me and sat at the corner of my bed. I left the door cracked open, letting her know I didn't want her to get too comfortable.

"What's going on?" I asked.

"I found out something, and I think you should know about it," she stammered.

"Okay, just say it then," I urged her, patting her hand.

"Well, it's just… it's hard to say it, but, well," she said, sitting up, "I overheard Milo and Kai arguing at the party."

"Oh, I see," I said, not really seeing.

"They were fighting back and forth about a bet between Milo and Ezra, actually, and Kai was pissed about it."

"*Okay*," I said. "It was probably nothing. It seems like they have a healthy sense of competition between them all."

Cameron shook her head. "No, Jupiter, it was about *you*."

"*Me?*" I asked. My heart started to pound. "What are you talking about?"

"Milo bet Ezra that he could get you to sleep with him this week before you left for Seattle."

"What the *hell?*" I asked, feeling shocked.

"And Ezra said that he could sleep with you *before* Milo."

My throat went dry; I shook my head. "No, Ezra wouldn't do that."

Cameron's hands flew up, palms out. "Hey, I'm just the messenger, but that's exactly what Kai and Milo were arguing about. Milo was pissed that Ezra was making ground and Kai was berating him for being an ass and making the bet in the first place."

I stood up and walked to the door, holding it open for her. "Cameron, it's late. I'm sure what you heard was a misunderstanding. Thank you for your concern, though."

She nodded sullenly and stood as well. She shuffled toward the door but stopped right in front of me.

"I know what I heard," she whispered and tiptoed down the hall toward the main living space.

I was torn between knocking on the boys' door and demanding answers or going back to bed, because it was, in my mind, a ludicrous possibility. I closed the door and climbed back into bed, edging toward the wall with the vent, listening for signs of talking, but heard none.

"I trust him," I said out loud to no one. I looked at the vent. *Then why are you listening here?*

Feeling guilty for even entertaining the thought that the bet existed, I burrowed into the center of the bed and pulled the covers over my head. Doing something I hadn't done in a very long time, I prayed for peace and got it a few minutes later.

I didn't remember falling to sleep, but I do remember waking up.

"Dude, stop making it a bigger deal than it is!" Ezra practically yelled through the vent.

I sat up, my heart racing, and scrambled down to press my ear to the vent.

"It *is* a big deal," Kai accused. "It's a shitty bet."

"I'm winning, aren't I?" Ezra asked.

There was a pause. "How is that supposed to make it okay, Ezra?" Kai said.

"It's *Milo*," he told Kai. "I couldn't let Milo win. It would crush her when she found out."

"And when *you* win?" Kai asked. "What happens then?"

"Let me worry about that," Ezra answered. "I'll figure something out."

"Just be careful. She's a cool chick," Kai said.

I heard his door open and footsteps sound down the hall.

Son of a gun! Cameron was right!

Blood boiling, I threw the covers off and rushed to the bathroom to get ready then grabbed all my stray belongings and stuffed everything in my suitcase, not caring to pack with any finesse at all. *Get your crap and go!* After a quick glance around the room, satisfied I wasn't leaving anything, I grabbed two sheets of stationery from the corner desk and sat down.

Dear Rosie,

Please forgive my abrupt departure. I apologize profusely. Ezra will be able to explain better than I will.

Thank you so much for your incredible kindness and generosity. It was amazing to stay with you. You're an incredible hostess and you made me feel so welcome here.

Thank you again and again.

Best wishes,

Jupiter Corey

P.S. Please let Melissa know how thankful I am to her for letting me borrow her outfit.

I waved the thank-you note back and forth so the ink would dry then pulled out the second sheet of paper, a quote from Shakespeare bleeding from the tip of my pen.

Dear Ezra,

"For I have sworn thee fair and thought thee bright,

Who art as black as hell, as dark as night."

- Jupiter

I stuck Rosie's thank you in a bright pink envelope that

went with the cream stationery and wrote *Rosie* on the front. The other, I held in my hand as I stood from the desk stool, and strolled toward the door with my bag in hand. As quietly as I possibly could, I left the room and walked next door to the boys' room. My heart pounding in my chest, I bent and slipped Ezra's note under the door.

I moved down the remaining hall, past the bustling kitchen, propped Rosie's thank-you note against the base of a vase on their foyer table, and discreetly opened then closed the front door behind me.

I bolted for the elevator and jumped inside, pressing the button for the lobby floor. The ride down was long, the tears I'd been holding burned to spill out. When the elevator doors opened, I hefted my bag and ran for the main building doors, throwing them open.

When the outside air hit my skin, when the morning sun fell across my face, and when my boots hit Chicago sidewalk, I finally let go of everything I'd been holding in.

I cried all the way to the bus station.

CHAPTER TWENTY-SIX

Ezra

I can't wait to see Jupiter, I thought as I dried myself off. I took the quickest shower possible just so I could see her as soon as possible. I searched through my bags, spotting my HAVE YOU SEEN THE BRIDGE? T-shirt and pulled it on along with a ratty pair of jeans. Not wanting to bother with shoes, I stomped barefoot toward the door, eager to wake Jupiter. I stepped on a piece of paper, peeled it off my heel, and threw it in the trash. Milo and Kai never kept a clean room.

I practically sprinted to Jupiter's door and knocked softly. I gripped both triceps with my hands and bounced up and down on the balls of my feet, anxious for her to answer. I knocked again, a little louder.

"Jupiter?" I whispered.

She didn't come to the door.

"Jupiter," I spoke a little louder. My hand gripped the doorknob. "I'm coming in," I told her. "I hope you're decent. But not really. Just kidding." I laughed. "Really, though, I'm coming in. Fair warning. One. Two. Three!"

I said, opening the door.

My smile fell. The room was empty. *Damn, she beat me*, I thought, and headed for the kitchen.

I needed to talk to her, but I knew everything would work out. It had to. Everyone, including Cameron, was running around the kitchen getting breakfast ready.

"Morning, Aunt Rosie," I said, kissing her cheek and stealing a piece of bacon from her platter.

"Oh, child!" she said, slapping at my hand, and making me laugh. She didn't stay mad for long and gave me a sweet smile. "Morning, Romeo." She looked around me. "Where's Juliet?" she asked.

I looked around the room. "I thought she was in here."

"No, darlin', we haven't seen her anywhere."

I glanced at my cousins. "Haven't seen her," Kai said, reaching for a blueberry waffle.

"*Milo?*" I asked.

"I swear," he said, holding up his hands. "Haven't talked to her since last night."

I could feel my heart batter at my ribs. "She's not in her room," I told them.

Cameron studied her plate. I remembered that piece of paper and put it together. I ran for Kai's and Milo's room and dug through the wastebasket, pulled it out, and held it in front of my face.

"No! No, no, no, no, *no!*" I bellowed, throwing a fist into a wall.

I walked with purpose back to the kitchen and slammed Jupiter's note on the table in front of Cameron.

"What did you do!" I yelled at her.

She began to cry. I thought Rosie would shout at me to be kinder, but she only stood there, her mouth gaping.

Milo stood up. "What are you yelling at her for?"

Pointing at her with as much vehemence as I could muster, teeth gritted, I told him, "Jupiter is not in her room. She's gone. And she left me this." I slid the paper over to him to read.

Kai, Rosie, and Bear leaned over to read the message.

"For I have sworn thee fair and thought thee bright. Who art as black as hell, as dark as night?" Rosie asked. "What does that mean?"

Shame inundated my face and chest. "It means that the stupid thing Milo and I did got back to Jupiter, that's what it means."

Rosie looked at me, her brows already narrowed in anger. "What stupid thing?"

I sank against the tabletop. "I'm too ashamed to even tell you."

Rosie dropped the platter of bacon and sausage she'd been holding onto the table. "Somebody better start talking, and it better be now," she said, folding her arms.

I cleared my throat, but Milo spoke over me. "We made a bet," he explained.

My uncle came into the kitchen, shuffling his slipper-clad feet, his hair a mess on top of his head, and making a beeline for the coffee.

"Mornin', honey," he told Rosie, clueless to the drama unfolding before him.

"What was the bet?" Rosie asked. Milo's face turned bright red. "Milo!" she shouted.

Uncle Mike finally caught on and sat down at the head of the table.

"Well, you know guys," Milo offered vaguely.

I rolled my eyes. "Milo bet me that he could get Jupiter to sleep with him before we left for Seattle."

Rosie's face looked livid, as did Uncle Mike's. "And I bet him that he couldn't."

"No," Kai corrected, making my own face heat up. "Ezra bet that he could do it before Milo could."

"That's not true!" I insisted. "I bet that Milo couldn't do it, because I could win her over first, *not* that I could sleep with her first."

Rosie's face turned the angriest shade of red I'd ever seen.

"Let me get this straight," Uncle Mike said with an eerily quiet tone. "You," he said, pointing at Milo, "bet that you could get Jupiter to have sex with you by the end of the week?" He pointed at me. "And you thought that you could get her to become interested in you before Milo succeeded?"

Thoroughly embarrassed, I nodded, but added, "I only did it because I wanted to keep her from making a mistake with Milo."

"Wrong!" Kai said with bravado and a mouth full of waffle. He swallowed. "You did it because you like her but refused to act on it before because you're as yellow as a daisy but the mere idea of Milo getting with her scared the crap out of you."

I didn't answer. Wouldn't answer.

Rosie stood up, took Milo's fork and plate from him, and placed it in the sink. She leaned her hip into the lower cabinets of the island.

"Never, not even in my wildest nightmares, would I have thought that you were capable of something like this, Milo."

The blood in Milo's face drained into his neck. "I'm sorry, Mom."

"That means nothing to me right now, Milo," she

replied.

"What kind of a man would make a bet like that, Milo?" Mike asked him.

Milo kept his mouth shut as Mike looked on him with sad disappointment.

"Cameron," Rosie addressed, "did you speak with Jupiter about this?"

"Yes, I did," she said, her hands folded in her lap.

"What exactly did you tell her?" Kai asked.

"I, uh, I told her," she cleared her throat, "that Ezra and Milo had a bet going on who could bag her first."

I folded my arms, sinking into myself. "*Why?*" I asked her.

Tears bubbled up in her eyes. "Because I was jealous."

"Dear God," Mike said, burying his face in his hands.

"I'm so sorry," Cameron told the room. "I thought telling her about the bet would be the perfect thing to get her out of here."

Kai looked at her as if she'd grown two heads but fixed his expression. "Okay, well, Cameron?" She looked over at him. "I'm thinking you should go ahead and get yourself home."

She nodded, tears falling down her face. "See you in class, Milo," she said, then stood, and walked toward the kitchen alcove. Before she left, she turned around and said, "For what it's worth, I am sorry."

We all waited until the front door closed then all turned to Aunt Rosie when she sighed. "Milo, I don't really know what to do with you right now. Go. Get in the shower. Your dad and I will be in there in a minute to talk to you. "

"Yes, ma'am," he said, going to his room.

"Ezra," Rosie told me, "I suggest you do some

growing up. Maybe not become entrenched in bets where intimacy with a girl is considered a boon? Maybe have a little bit more respect for women?"

My face grow hot. "Aunt Rosie, I really meant what I said. I had no intentions like that toward Jupiter, I promise. I only got caught up in the threat that Milo might succeed and panicked."

"Except now that poor girl is hurt, isn't she?" Mike asked.

My gut ached and twisted. "Yes, sir."

"What were you plannin' on doing when she fell for you? Let her down easy?" Rosie asked.

"I-I don't know, really."

"Again, a lie," Kai said, taking a big bite of bacon, his conscience obviously feeling clear as glass.

"No, it's not," I insisted.

"I don't mean you're lying to us, Ezra," he pressed. "I meant you're lying to yourself."

I dragged my hands through my hair and sighed.

"Exactly," he said.

"Exactly, what? I can't be with her," I told him.

Mike and Rosie each took a cup of coffee down the hall toward Milo's room. Bear followed to eavesdrop, no doubt.

"Why not?" Kai asked, swigging a gulp of orange juice.

I turned around and sat on the bench just as Bear came galloping back into the kitchen.

"They kicked me out of that part of the house," he explained. "Threatened to ground me."

I smiled at him. Bear sat down again and became engrossed in a comic book.

"Why. Not," Kai repeated. I grasped both triceps

again and studied the ceiling. "You really are quite the pansy. You know that?"

"Whatever, Kai."

"Whatever, Kai," he mock whined.

"You can be a douche sometimes," I told him.

"Why? 'Cause I point out the obvious and you don't like that? 'Cause I call you out on your weird baby hurt-feelings crap?"

I felt myself losing control of my emotions, something I prided myself in keeping in check. "That's an asshole thing to say. Jessica screwed me up, Kai! Do you know what it's like to be cheated on? I wouldn't wish that shit on my worst enemy," I said, slamming a hand on the table. "I've had compound fractures in both my legs, intense and painful physical therapy for almost a year, and the pain I experienced was *nothing* compared to what it felt like when I walked in on them! *Nothing*. I can't go through that again. I can't risk it."

Kai lazily took a bite of his food, staring at me as if I was talking about the weather and not having an outburst, then swallowed. "All right, dude. Calm down."

I tried to hide the smile that caused. "Why do you have to be such a dillweed?"

"I'm not, actually. You are, though. Listen," he said, wiping his mouth with a napkin, "get your ass up, pack your shit up, and go after Jupiter."

I slid my hands down my face. "How am I going to explain this crap to her?" I asked, entertaining the idea that maybe I could risk myself after all.

The truth of the matter was Jupiter wasn't a game to me. She never was. Kai was right when he said I was lying to myself. I was lying to myself when I watched her every move those two months of our senior year and that just watching her was all I really needed. I was lying to myself when I said yes to her coming to Seattle with me and thought being close to her would be fun while it lasted. I was lying to myself when I watched *Almost Famous* every day after work over the summer so I could watch Penny Lane and somehow feel close to Jupiter. I was lying to myself when I took the bet with Milo and thought it was just to see what she tasted like and that was all. *I'm done lying.*

Kai interrupted my thoughts. "You walk up to her. You say, 'Jupiter, I lok you alawt. I want to have your babies.'"

"Shut up."

"How the hell am I supposed to know, jackass?" he shouted.

"You don't have a single suggestion? You're useless!"

"Please, you hobo."

I sighed. "I've got a long car ride to Seattle. Maybe I'll think of something then."

"Good idea, mold muncher," Kai said.

I packed up all my crap, kissed my aunt goodbye, hugged my uncle, Bear, and stupid Milo, and Kai walked me down to his dad's garage.

"She's going to get there a week earlier than everyone else, and I don't think they'll let her stay at the dorms yet." I looked at my cousin. "I don't really know what I'm doing, Kai."

"You're wrong again," he said.

"Will you stop saying that! It's getting old."

He laughed. "It's true, though. You do know what you're doing. You're just scared of it."

"I really like her, way more than I ever liked Jessica. I-I think I love her a little. It would really suck if she screwed me over, not going to lie."

Kai shoved me with his shoulder. "For someone who digs that girl as much as you do, you sure don't know jack shit about her." I shook my head at him. "Seriously, Jupiter is a fly chick. I mean, she is a little dorky for my taste, but she's perfect for you. She's goofy in that genuinely charming sort of way. Smart. Loyal. Really nice. Plus, she has a killer bod."

"Yes to all of that."

"And I can tell she really likes you too."

"Not as much as I like her, though, right? That's what I'm afraid of. I'm afraid I'll fall deeper in love with her than she will with me because that's my MO and she'll be like, *Peace out, I just realized I dig some other dude.*"

"Damn, you really are some sort of something. Get your crap together, Brandon! Don't let your past affect your future and you'll be all right. Just chill out."

"You're right."

"I know."

We reached Mike's garage and they'd fixed all the damage that'd been done to my car. Mike said he wouldn't tell my mom as long as Rosie was okay with that. I hadn't gotten a telephone call from Mom yelling at me, so I supposed everything was all good.

The key to the trunk was a little tough to turn, but I figured I could oil that out. I stuffed my crap into the back of the car and closed it. I fished a pair of vintage-looking blue-tinted sunglasses, something that reminded me of Penny Lane, out of my pocket. "I found these at a gas station all the way down in Florida and was working up the nerve to give them to her."

"They'd look good on her."

"Yeah, I know. I'm hoping they might open up a line

of communication."

Kai slap-hugged me before I got into my car, starting up the engine.

"She purrs like a kitten," he yelled.

I smiled. "Let's hope she makes good time," I yelled back through an open window. "I've got somewhere I need to be. And soon."

CHAPTER TWENTY-SEVEN

Jupiter

After some serious sweet-talking, I somehow convinced the school to let me into Haggett Hall early. I had to stay in a hotel the first night while they got it ready, which ate up a huge chunk of money, but they gave me a single dorm, which rocked socks! It only took me two hours to unpack my case, since I hadn't really brought much, but I had a feeling it would eventually fill up with stuff as that's how life usually goes.

Although the building was a little dated, it was still infinitely better than back home. I didn't realize what having an average home, well, average for seventy-five hundred other students like myself, would do to my insides but that was the point, wasn't it? University of Washington was a clean slate for me. No one would know about my place back in Florida. No one would have to know anything about me that I didn't want them to. *Do I not want people to know about the people I love, though?*

It was with that sudden thought I realized I was no longer embarrassed by my silly family, nor that I cared what anyone thought about me anymore. Watching Ezra, and sometimes even Kai, showed me that ninety-nine percent of being cool was owning what you loved and not giving a damn what people thought. When you show you don't care, people start to accept what you are. It's crazy to think about, but it's true.

I dug through a drawer at the desk that held the laptop Frankie gave me and found the only album of pictures I'd brought with me, then proceeded to tack random images of my family, my house, and my friends with me and Frankie, all over the board against the desk backing.

I studied a picture of Frankie and me, then one of myself and Mercury, and felt sick to my stomach. I missed them so much. I grabbed a handful of quarters, locked my door, and studied the key on my way down to the pay phones. Having my own place felt so strange. I was going to live alone, in a strange, foreign place, and the only person I knew there shattered my heart in a million pieces in Chicago.

I fought back the tears, refusing to let them fall. I needed to be strong for myself. I wrapped my cardigan tighter around my arms, feeling the nip of fall already and beginning to wonder what the hell I was thinking going to a school in the northwest.

I slipped four quarters into the old, dilapidated-looking pay phone and clicked out my home phone number. It rang and rang and rang but no one answered. I allowed three tears to slip down my cheeks but stopped myself there. I hung up the phone and the machine ate my quarters. Two more tears came, but I refused to allow any more. I stuck another dollar worth of quarters into the slot and dialed Frank.

She picked up on the second ring.

"Frankie's House of Frankfurters!" she greeted.

"*Frank?*" I sobbed into the phone.

"Oh, cheese and crackers! Jupiter! What's wrong, sweetie?"

I mumbled something unintelligible, trying to suck back tears, only they didn't care and came anyway.

"Honey," she interrupted, "I literally don't have a clue what you're saying. Take a deep breath."

I did as I was told. "I don't have a phone."

"I know. You told me."

"Right," I remembered. "I'm in Seattle."

"That was fast. You weren't supposed to be there for a few days."

I began to sob again. Frankie waited for me to collect myself.

"Please deposit fifty cents," I heard over the receiver.

I stuck another dollar and two quarters in the coin slot.

"Ezra is an arsehole."

Frankie paused then harumphed.

"He is!"

"Okay," she said, "how?"

"His cousin bet that he could get me in the sack by the end of our Chicago visit."

"*That* guy is the arsehole."

I hitched a breath. "And Ezra bet that he could seal the deal before his cousin could."

Frankie paused for several long seconds. "That doesn't sound like Ezra, Jupiter."

"Well, believe it. It happened."

Frankie's bed squeaked as if she'd been lying down then leapt up. "Did Ezra try to explain himself?"

"What? No! I wasn't going to stick around there to listen to his sorry excuses!"

Frankie took a deep breath. "Okay, well, I can understand that." But I could tell that wasn't all she wanted to say.

"Spit it out, Frank."

"Well," she hesitantly sang, "I wouldn't go jumping to conclusions just yet." I scoffed. "Listen, listen, listen. I'm just saying boys do a lot of stupid crap and almost none of it they mean to do. They're a lot of talk."

"Frank!"

"Listen, I'm just saying, if he comes around, hear what he has to say. If he doesn't have a plausible excuse, then kick his ass to the curb, babe."

"I don't believe it."

"What?" she asked.

"You!" I said. "Willing to give a boy the benefit of the doubt while he tried to explain himself for something that is pretty skeevy."

"I know. Trust me, I'm the last person I thought who'd be saying this, but I know Ezra Brandon and he's a lot of things, but skeevy boy is not one of them."

I sniffled. "I'm so mad at him, though, that I don't even want to listen to what he has to say."

"I get it. So let him stew in his own guilt for a few days before hearing him out, just promise me you'll hear him out, at least."

I paused, unwilling to concede. Finally, I sighed. "Fine."

"Good. I love you, baby butter billy goat."

"Love you too, wittle woolly wombat."

She snorted. "You're an idiot."

"Please, billy goat? They always look like they've

smoked a bunch of weed!"

"Whatever! At least billy goats are cute!"

I acted offended. "Excuse me? Baby wombats are friggin *adorable!*"

"Fine. Bye. I love you."

"Bye. Love you too."

I hung up the phone and swiped my palms beneath my eyes. I didn't want to cry again for the rest of the day and promised myself I wouldn't. I decided to head back up to my dorm to grab my bag. I needed a few things for the room that I hadn't anticipated. Like, a mop and broom? The room had tile in it and I suspected it'd been swept, but it definitely had not been cleaned. I also wanted to buy a rug because I couldn't imagine putting my feet on cold tile in the dead of winter.

I would have looked up the nearest thrift store on my phone, but that wasn't going to happen for painfully obvious and really inconvenient reasons. Instead, I tried getting directions the old-fashioned way. By talking to a person. Gasp! I know.

I walked around the campus, half familiarizing myself, half enjoying the walk, and stumbled across a man in a blazer with elbow patches. I took a shot in the dark.

"Professor!" I shouted, and he turned around. *Score!*

"Sorry, I'm looking for a thrift store around here. Would you know where I could find one?"

"Sure," he said. "Just head that way down the path. You'll hit Fifteenth. Look for Forty-Third then walk two blocks until you get to University. There should be a thrift-type store there, I think."

"Thanks!" I told him with a smile and set on my way.

There was a thrift store on University named the Nifty Thrifty. It had this old-school sign, probably from the fifties or so, and it was so.freaking.cool.! When I opened the door, it had a recorded chime that rang out, "You go, girl!" and that made me laugh, and then for some reason, also think of Ezra so I started to cry, and then I started to laugh again at my own idiocy.

"Are you okay?" a clerk asked, a witness to my Kathy Bates in *Misery* moment, no doubt.

I cleared my throat and wiped my eyes dry. "Yes, I'm fine, thanks."

I grabbed a shopping cart from the five they had available and started perusing the quirky, narrow aisles barely big enough to fit one cart. Since Ezra hadn't let me pay my part in gas, I had a little bit of money left over in my budget, even after my bus fare and the hotel stay. I felt the tears begin again at the thought of his generosity and cursed myself. Steeling myself yet again, I pushed the cart forward. I had no intention of spending every dollar I had left from the savings, but I did intend to make my dorm as comfortable as possible. I needed it to feel like home or I was never going to last.

There was a large rainbow-colored braided rag rug for seven dollars, and I thought it was great. I rolled it up and put it in my cart, along with an ancient Paramount desk phone circa 1930s because I had no intention of calling people on the pay phone anymore, and my dorm had a phone outlet. I asked the clerk I'd wigged out earlier in front of if I could plug it into theirs to see if it worked and it did. I snatched that up for four bucks along with a framed poster of Kurt Cobain smoking a cigarette that someone had taken a set of watercolors to, to make their own, I guess. It was pretty rad.

I was browsing the framed images when my eye spotted one of a UFO print that made me laugh. It was only three bucks so I threw that in. I got a huge black-and-white medallion tapestry I planned on tacking up in lieu of wallpaper for the wall next to my bed. They even had a mop still in its original box, though a little beat up, but I didn't care, it was still a new mop. They didn't have a broom, but I figured I could get one later.

I scored a big blue velvet curtain for the window with a rod, an industrial copper-esque floor lamp I had the perfect corner for since the light in the room was pretty crappy, and a couple more little tchotchkes. I didn't spend more than a hundred dollars, which I was particularly proud of, but I also didn't think about how I was going to get all my stuff back to Haggett.

Fortunately for me, the store's owner, Aida, did free deliveries. I asked if she'd deliver me too, to which she laughed and told me it was no problem. She was a bad ace. When she dropped my goods and me off at my dorm, I thanked her and dragged everything to my room. I set to work right away to distract myself from how lonely I felt and how empty all the other dorm rooms were. The first thing I did after I mopped the floor was hook the phone up and call Frankie just to get the number that popped up on her phone. Then I called my family again and this time they picked up. Mercury was out, but I talked to both Mom and Dad and tried to act as cheery as possible, finishing by giving them my dorm number. Trying to explain what happened to my cell would have been difficult, so I lied and told them I misplaced it. Eventually I knew I would have to replace it, but I had no idea when or how, really.

I washed the curtain, tapestry, and braid rug in three washers and dryers since no one was around to complain and around five that night, when I was done putting up all my new-to-me stuff, I looked around the room and for the first time since Chicago felt somewhat secure. I knew it was only a matter of time before the dorm really felt like home. I needed to tough it out.

I took a deep breath, lugged my shower stuff to the showers, and proceeded to clean the day off. In the cold, cubed alcove, with the flimsy curtain, and room-temperature water, I felt what happened between Ezra and me bubble up to the surface, but this time I couldn't stop it. It was too powerful to convince so I let myself feel the pain that needed to be felt.

CHAPTER TWENTY-EIGHT

There was this little vented window above my bed behind a slim metal door. I was sure it would have been handy during the day, but at night, when the temperatures dropped to levels I was definitely not accustomed to, the thin sheet and blanket I'd brought from home wouldn't cut it, and the cloth tapestry was pretty but useless. *Kind of like Kai. Aww, Kai.* My eyes burned. *Dang it!*

Other than the blanket issue, I was pretty happy with my little cocoon room. I dragged myself out of my bed and over to my little sink to brush my teeth. To kill time, I got my hair did. I don't know if it really counts when you do the hair yourself, but I thought it did 'cause I was a fly gal. I played around with my makeup a little. I dropped some sick beats on my laptop, jumped and danced around my room a bit, then decided I'd had enough and needed to go to a grocery store for a broom and a few food staples like peanut butter and bottled water. I made a mental note to get one of those grocery carrier things on wheels that little old blue-haired ladies loved so I could shop without regret and dignity.

I wore a pair of cutoff jean shorts, because I was grasping at summer with everything in me, and threw on my boots along with my super worn T-shirt with the phrase **TEA DRINKERS UNITE!** It had a picture of two hands with their pinkies up. I tossed a floor-length sweater on, a scarf around my neck as well as my wide-brim fedora, and opened the door.

"Get busy livin'," I told the hallway.

Over the next few days, I was on my own. All too often I found myself wondering if Ezra was already in town, what he was doing, where his dorm was, if I'd ever run into him on campus. I called home and Frankie every day. I really missed my phone, as did Frankie. We lamented often how inconvenient it was not to be able to text each other any time we wanted to.

Eventually the dorms started to fill up and the noise comforted me as well as gave me anxiety. It was so weird knowing I'd be living with the strangers surrounding me for an entire year. Since I'd been there for so long already, I was familiar with where everything was, which proved useful in making new friends.

A girl named Mickey who lived across the hall and had come all the way from Dallas was immediately homesick, I could tell, so that first night, I invited her over. Over the next few hours, I had pretty much rounded up everyone at Haggett and there was an impromptu partay, what-what, downstairs on the main floor. I met so many people and answered a lot of questions when they found out I'd been there for almost an entire week.

"Wait, what did you say your name was?" a guy named Stephen asked.

"This is Jupiter," Mickey introduced.

"Yeah, yeah, that's it." Stephen turned to another guy a few feet away and shouted, "Hey, Brad! Remember that dude who came up to us in the quad?"

"Yeah, astronomy guy?"

Stephen laughed. "Yeah, that one." He pointed at me. "This is Jupiter!"

"Get the hell out, dude," Brad said, leaving his conversation and sprinting over to us. "Nice to meet you," he said, shaking my hand. "So you're Jupiter?"

"That's me."

"Know a tall guy named Ezra?"

My heart started to race. "Yeah, I know him."

"Dude, he's been looking for you for a few days."

Oh my God.

"Who's Ezra?" Mickey asked.

"Uh, he's this guy I'm sort of seeing, maybe, I don't know. We went to school together back home."

"That explains it then," Stephen commented. "Dude was on some crack about how he was looking for you and that the school couldn't tell him where you were because there's some privacy policy and you didn't have a phone so he couldn't get a hold of you, which we didn't believe. We thought he was mental or something. Who doesn't have a phone?"

I laughed. "Uh, it's true. My phone was jacked by some insane hitchhiker we picked up on the way here."

Both boys started laughing. "That's crazy," Brad said.

"The guy has been looking for you for days apparently," Stephen commented. "He's been asking everyone he sees if they know you."

Brad leaned over and yelled toward a group of boys. "Guys! This is Jupiter!"

They all started cheering, "Jupiter!"

My throat felt hot. "Damn, I wonder where he's staying."

Brad shook his head. "He told us but I don't remember."

"Sorry, didn't think I'd need to remember," Stephen apologized.

"It's cool. I'm sure we'll bump into one another," I said, aiming for casual.

Inside, though, I imagined I was Data with my accordion boxing glove and Ezra was the Fratellis.

"What's your dorm number and I'll give it to him if I see him," Stephen offered.

"That's cool," I said, yanking a pen off a nearby pinboard and writing it on the top of his hand. "If you see him, tell him to call me no matter the time."

"Got it," he said.

I can't wait to hear his excuses, I thought.

Mickey was a sweet girl, so I decided to be her friend. We agreed we'd go to orientation the next day together. At eight a.m. I shuffled out of my room and knocked on her door.

"Hey, Mickey! You're so fine! You're so fine you blow my mind!" I shouted through the door.

I was greeted by a sore-looking Mickey, which made me laugh. "Hardy har har," she bit out.

"Oh, so you've heard that one before?" I snapped my fingers. "Dang, I thought it was so original too."

She sighed but smiled and shut her door, locking it behind her. "So, uh, what do you think we're going to be doing today?" she asked as we walked toward the elevators.

"Ritual sacrifice followed by an informal get-to-know-you, then a quick mandatory facial piercing, and a break for lunch." Mickey's eyes blew wide. I wrapped my arm around her neck. "Oh, Mick, we're gonna be great friends, I can tell."

When we reached the lobby, there was a group of at least twenty-five students getting ready to walk over to Edmundson Pavilion, and they invited us to walk with them. We all meandered through the quad and I tried not to frantically search the grounds for Ezra but failed. *I'm an idiot.* He wasn't there. We hung a left on Spokane toward Edmundson and I began to get to know a few people I'd yet to meet the night before.

When we arrived, we found a huge open section that hadn't filled in yet and filed in, scattering amongst five rows.

"Whoa," Mickey breathed. "There are literally thousands of people here."

"We're ants on the anthill, Mick."

"Yeah, but who's the queen?" she asked, raising a brow.

Just then a literal blonde Barbie sauntered by and all the boys' tongues started to wag. "My guess is her," I said.

Mickey laughed. "It's always the one with legs for miles."

"Always," I agreed. "But I know something Marie Antoinette over there doesn't."

"What's that?" Mickey asked.

"I know how to incite a mean riot."

"Let them eat cake," she teased.

After half an hour of waiting around, a couple of important-looking people graced the court below us and began shuffling card tables full of paper, etc., then set up a podium with a microphone.

"Good morning," an older gentleman announced to a room full of hormonal freshmen.

"Take it off!" someone yelled, making us all laugh. *See?*

"Okay, okay," he huffed, "let's all calm down." He took a deep breath like he thought he didn't make enough money to put up with what he put up with. "Welcome to the University of Washington!" he greeted with false cheer, making me snort. "I'm school administrator David Angleberg. We're going to go over a few procedures and a few rules with you this morning," he began before droning on and on about mess hall rules, what our student IDs were good for, yada yada yada.

"I'm a little overwhelmed," Mickey admitted to me.

"We're all overwhelmed. The cool part is we can all be overwhelmed together."

Mickey nodded and smiled.

"Where do you think your Ezra is?" she asked.

My eyes followed row after row of students. "Dude, he could be anywhere." *The bastard.*

"Let's begin with campus behavior," the school administrator droned on when we heard a loud rumbling come from the seats on the other side of the court.

"What's going on?" Mickey asked.

We leaned forward a little to see what was going on.

"There's some guy down there yelling," Mickey observed.

"Where?"

"There," she said, pointing down toward mid-court about ten rows up from the floor.

"Oh shit," I whispered. "That's Ezra."

She leaned forward. "He's yelling something at you."

I studied his mouth and arm movements but couldn't

make out what he was saying. I shrugged my shoulders and lifted my hands. Ezra let his own fall in obvious frustration before turning around and gesturing wildly.

A chorus of "Jupiter!" erupted from the other side of the stands, followed by a "Can! We! Talk!"

"Excuse me, young man," the school administrator admonished over the speakers, "sit down!"

My chest began to pant. "What do I do?" I asked Mickey.

"Answer him!" she urged.

I turned toward my section of the stadium and shouted, "Yes!"

They followed suit and yelled my answer back to Ezra.

"Everyone, sit down this instant!" a red-faced David Angleberg insisted.

"I! Can't! Find! Your! Room!" Ezra's side of the stadium shouted.

"Haggett! Six-oh-three!" I told my section, which they relayed back just as security went bounding toward Ezra.

They chased him through several rows and he dodged them with ease before he bolted up the stairs toward the exits but not before he relayed a last message.

"Jupiter!" the crowd shouted as Ezra crested the top of the stairs, turned around, stared at me, and placed his hand over his heart. "I missed you!"

CHAPTER TWENTY-NINE

I rushed out of the orientation, Mickey promising to tell me if I missed anything important, and sprinted toward Haggett Hall. When I reached my room there was something on the floor at the foot of the door.

I crouched down. Wrapped in brown paper was Ezra's reversible velvet-and-sherpa blanket. My hand went to my mouth. On top was a pair of blue-tinted sunglasses, almost identical to the one's Penny Lane wore in *Almost Famous*. In between the blanket and the glasses was a note.

I picked it up, sat down with my back against the flat of the door, and read its contents.

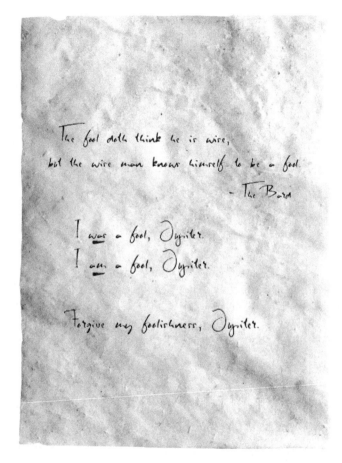

The fool doth think he is wise, but the wise man knows himself to be a fool.
- *The Bard*

I <u>was</u> a fool, Jupiter.

I am a fool, Jupiter.

Forgive my foolishness, Jupiter.

"I never expected you to find out," I heard down the hall.

I looked up to see Ezra strolling toward me, both of his hands in his pockets, looking sheepish and adorable at the same time.

"How comforting," I told him, not ready to forgive him so readily.

He stopped in front of me. "It's not what you think."

"So you didn't bet Milo that you could sleep with me before he could?"

His face tinged pink. "In a way."

I stood and picked up the blanket and card, the glasses sliding to the floor, and shoved them into his chest. "Take your bribe and leave then."

"No," he said with conviction.

"Go!" I told him, pushing him a little, but he didn't budge.

"No," he said again, softer. "Not until you hear what I have to say."

I thought about Frankie and cursed her to the moon and back. "What happened?"

He looked surprised but didn't argue. He set everything at our feet again and insecurely folded his hands around his triceps. "I'm embarrassed, but the truth is I just said it because I didn't want Milo to get anywhere near you. The idea of Milo even laying a finger on you sent me into a jealous rage. I decided to match the bet so he wouldn't succeed, but I never intended to sleep with you, I swear. I swear it, Jupiter. I just didn't want him to take something from you that didn't belong to him, and I planned on letting you down gently when we were on the road."

I felt my eyes gloss over. "You never intended to stay with me?" I asked in disbelief. I stuck out the heel of my boot and watched the tip of my foot swing back and forth as if from very far away.

"No, I didn't."

Tears spilled down my cheeks. "All that stuff you said? The kissing? The conversations? They were a front to your plot? They were just distractions so I wouldn't notice your cousin? What about what happened in that stadium back there?" I asked, throwing a hand the direction of Edmundson.

He ran his hands through his hair. The top flopped across his temple. He let his arms fall helplessly at his sides. "No," he said with feeling. "The only lies I told were told to myself. I didn't want to want you, Jupiter, because needing you like I do means a hard fall when you decide to leave. And you will leave. Girls leave me. They just do," he admitted with utter vulnerability, making my heart sink for him.

"I thought if I could spend a little time with you," he continued, "that I'd discover you are an illusion. But I was wrong. Then I thought if I could touch you, you wouldn't feel like heaven. But I was wrong. Then I thought if I could kiss you, whatever I imagined you tasted like would prove false. But I was wrong. Then I thought if I could just keep you close but never fully entrenched in myself that I could fall in love with you without getting hurt. But I was wrong."

"Are you in love with me?" I asked him.

"I think so," he said truthfully, making my heart race.

"I'm falling quickly." He looked straight at me, a pained expression on his face. "I tend to do that," he explained with a slow shrug.

I studied his right hand before pressing my palm to his. I decided I would wait and let him thread his fingers with mine. We sat for a long time, never making eye contact, but eventually he did.

"Can you forgive me?" he asked.

I nodded at his feet then my eyes met his. "You know, no matter what ends up happening between us," I promised, "betrayal would never be a move I'd play."

"I know," he said, taking my keys from my hand and opening my door. He sat the blanket inside on my bed, made a comment about how my room rocked his socks, and dragged the sunglasses he bought me with him as he shut and locked the door again.

He stood looking at me briefly with that Ezra grin that made my skin tingle before slipping the glasses over my face.

"Come on, Jupiter Corey," he said, dragging me toward the elevator.

"Are we going somewhere?" I asked him.

"Yes," he said as we stepped into the metal box, pressing the floor for the lobby. He brushed the back of his fingers across my cheeks as the doors shut.

"Where did you get the paper for that note?" I teased him.

He smiled at me. "What? Not up to Jupiter par, is it? You'll have to excuse its state. It seems it got drenched when someone sprayed a water hose into my car."

I pursed my lips. "Hmm, I bet that person had good reason, though."

"Maybe," he said with a sly grin, wrapping his hand

around mine.

The doors opened and he led me out of Haggett Hall toward the housing parking lots. When I saw his GTO, I almost cried.

"She looks so good," I said, dropping his hand when he opened the passenger side for me.

"She cleans up well," he agreed.

Before sitting down, I asked, "Where are we going?"

"Get in the car, Jupiter."

"Yeah, I will, but first where are we going?"

"To get you another phone." He laughed. "I'm not shouting across stadiums every time I need to speak to you. Now get in the car, Jupiter."

I smiled. "It was awfully romantic, though."

"I think security is still looking for me," he teased. "Get in the car."

"Ezra?"

"Yes, Jupiter?"

"Before I get in the car—"

"Yes?"

"I missed you too."

EPILOGUE

"You look nice, Kai," I said as he straightened his tie.

"Please, woman, I am impeccable," he teased. He smiled down at me. "You excited?"

"Uh, duh."

"Eloquent as always, I see," he prodded.

"Shut up, Kai."

"Another one for the history books."

"Go," I ordered. "Now. Over there. With your wife. This instant before I tell her that I caught you pinching Mrs. Eisenberg's tush."

"She's a hundred years old!" Kai complained.

"I know! Who knew you had such a geriatric fetish? You're such a creep, Kai!"

Kai acted mock offended. "You're no fun," he whined. "Gaw, Jupiter."

I watched Kai walk away and turned to find Ezra. I spotted him at the entrance of Fountainhead, the name of our new geriatric and pediatric day center. It was our launch day, our maiden voyage. He looked nervous.

"Dr. Brandon?" I called out.

Ezra turned toward me and smiled, holding his hand

out for me. "Are you ready?" he asked.

"It's been thirteen years of hard work, late nights, failures, successes, heartaches, and joys, so, yes, I'd say I'm ready."

"What a ride," he admitted.

"Indeed."

"I have a surprise for you," he told me, dragging me toward the automatic doors.

"We have a press conference in less than ten minutes," I said.

"It won't take long," he said.

"Words every girl longs to hear."

He burst out laughing. "Please, you know I'd treat you better than that, Brandon."

"That's right," I said, slapping him on the rear.

"Jupiter!" he complained, looking around.

"What?" I asked, playing innocent.

"Here," he said, shoving me through his office door.

On his desk was a bottle of champagne and two flutes. He took the bottle in his hand and began unwrapping the cork.

"Before things get crazy, before we get too busy, before we're both pulled a million directions, I need you to take a glass," he said, popping the cork and pouring champagne into a flute.

He handed it to me and I took it, then he poured himself a glass.

"To you," he said.

"No, to us."

We clinked our glasses together and toasted to our incredible life. I drank then set my glass down and glanced at the corner of his office piled with moving boxes and bags.

"Oh my gato," I said, picking up a bag and holding it up. "It's your suitcase from our road trip."

Ezra stepped closer and examined it. "So it is," he said, nodding his head.

I stared at it, a few tears in my eyes. "So many memories ago, but it still feels like it was yesterday." Something dawned on me then. "Remember outside that motel, when we were covered in burnt grass and black soot?"

"Yeah," Ezra answered absently, moving around the room, looking for something.

"And remember when I tried to dig into your bag for something but you shot me down with a quickness?"

Ezra's hands froze. "Uh, yeah," he answered, but there was a hitch in his voice. *Got him.*

"What was in the bag, Ezra?"

Ezra stood and turned toward me, the biggest grin on his face. "I suppose ten years of marriage and three kids has guaranteed me a permanent fixture in your life."

"Ah, you-a would-a be-a correct-a!"

"Every day after work the summer before college, I would watch *Almost Famous* just to watch Penny Lane and be reminded of you. I brought the movie with me. I knew if you saw it, you'd be onto me, and I couldn't have that."

I snorted. "Okay, but that's not so bad. Why even bother?"

"Because I knew if you picked up the case, there would be a chance you'd open it and I definitely couldn't risk that."

I laughed. "I feel like this is déjà vu, but what was in that case, Ezra?"

"Your yearbook picture, cut out and taped on the

inside cover."

I belly laughed, like a real gut laugh. "You're such a psycho!"

"Hey!" he said, punching me playfully on the shoulder and trying not to laugh. "Be nice, man. I was dark and moody and worked hard to keep up the persona. Your finding that film *and* the picture inside would have shot my chances to hell with you."

"Uh, no, I was riding high on an Ezra cloud. I probably would have walked around with 'Raindrops Keep Falling on my Head' on repeat while skipping around with a dreamy-eyed expression on my face."

Ezra laughed. "You're an idiot."

"Takes one to know one."

"Bite me."

I looked mock offended. "You're a doctor, do you know that?"

He rolled his eyes but couldn't fight his smile. He came around his desk and leaned against the edge. "I loved you, you know."

"What do you mean? When?"

"When we were on that trip. I loved you, I just didn't know it."

"No way, babe."

"Way, Jupiter," he mocked with a smile. He wrapped his arms around my triceps. "Were you in Simpson's class? I can't remember."

"No."

"In that class, I learned about Plato's The Symposium. Familiar?"

I scrunched my nose in thought. "Vaguely."

"Okay, so according to Greek mythology, we were each born with four arms, four legs, and a head with two faces. Zeus, fearing what powers we might possess, split us in half and scattered us across the earth, doomed to search for our other halves. He says that love is simply a pursuit of our whole self."

"The idea of that is romantic," I admitted.

"Indeed," he agreed, pulling me toward him and wedging me between his knees. "I count my lucky stars you needed that ride to school, Jupiter. I feel like I stumbled upon my other half on that trip. It was strange, and fated, and imminent.

"When was the last time I told you I loved you?"

"Stop." I giggled, pushing at his chest.

Ezra caught my chin and forced my gaze to his. "Jupiter," he said, "I don't say it nearly enough. It would have to be a repetitive utterance on my tongue for it to be said tolerably, and there aren't enough moments in the waking day to accommodate me."

I smiled at him, placing my hand on either side of his neck. I felt his pulse quicken beneath my fingertips.

"I love you, Jupiter. I love you, Jupiter. I-I *love* you, Jupiter."

"As I love you, Ezra." I kissed his mouth softly. "Did you know a kiss is worth a thousand *I love yous*?"

"You see, I didn't know that," he told me, wrapping his arms around my back and settling a hand on the nape of my neck.

I nodded to confirm it. He ran his bottom lip across mine several times.

"These poor lips," he promised with a devilish smile.

ACKNOWLEDGMENTS

Thank you to my fabulous editor and lovely friend, Hollie Westring. I'd be nothing without you, love.

Thank you to Matt and all my tiny rugrats, my forever crew. I love you all to the moon and back.

Short and sweet this time, y'all!

READ MORE FISHER AMELIE

Interested in reading more from Fisher Amelie?

www.fisheramelie.com